TINPLATE

TINPLATE

NEVILLE STEED

m
c.1

St. Martin's Press
New York

Library of Congress Cataloging in Publication Data

Steed, Neville.
  Tinplate.

  I. Title.
PR6069.T387T5   1987   823'.914   86-26177
ISBN 0-312-00196-7

First published in Great Britain by George Weidenfeld & Nicolson Limited.

First U.S. Edition

10 9 8 7 6 5 4 3 2 1

To Kate, with love

TINPLATE

One

I shouted 'Stop' at the top of my voice time and again, but the car seemed not to heed me at all, and careered on towards an unthinking group of soldiers who stood directly in its path. Out of the corner of my eye, I saw my cat jump out of the way in a characteristically elegant leap. And the next second, the unyielding metal of the bumper and sloping grill of the car struck the first soldier. He fell helplessly forward against his colleagues, who in turn tumbled like ninepins under the relentless forward thrust of the gleaming maroon projectile. I got to my feet to see the car at long last come to a stop with its front wheels jammed against the legs of a drummer of the Coldstream Guards. For the life of me I couldn't understand why any of this should have happened. After all, I had had the car in pieces on the carpet only ten minutes before.

I went across to Bing, who had retreated to the settee and was washing himself in a very serious and adult manner to show his disdain for my childlike cavorting.

'You don't reckon me as a mechanic, do you Bing?'

His eyes didn't move from his fur grooming. And that was enough of an answer for me. But when I stretched out my hand, Bing rolled over onto his back and played easy to get. Yet I knew he hadn't really changed his inscrutable Siamese mind.

It took me another hour to get the shutter on that little pre-war Schuco toy car working properly so that it would depress when you said 'Stop' breathily enough at it through the grille on the roof. Then the shutter dutifully tripped and stopped the clockwork motor. Breathe 'Start' heavily enough, and the shutter depressed again and restarted the car. Devilish in their cunning were those twenties and thirties German toymakers, the most inventive the child's world had ever seen – and never equalled since, except in a few products of the post-war Japanese toy

1

manufacturers, who had kept the tinplate tradition going longer than most.

I picked up the soldiers and put them back in their original Britains Ltd box. 'No. 37 Coldstream Guards, Full Band of . . .' as the makers' catalogue had described them in 1940. I was lucky to get them. You don't get full mint condition sets offered to you every day of the week. And they would be a definite attraction in the window of my little shop. I just hoped the old man who had brought them in would never discover what I would be asking for them. He'd die of shock – after he'd killed me first, that is. The Schuco car, Kommando Anno 2000, I decided to keep myself as the maroon paintwork was very nearly mint and none of the tyres was cracked or perished. All in all, it was a fraction better than the otherwise identical one I had owned for some years, which could now join the soldiers in the window and bring me in a much needed fifty or sixty pounds.

Just as I was about to work out whether I had enough energy to begin thinking about lunch, the phone rang. It had to be either Deborah with another of her tales of woe or Gregory Chalmers, confirming the money for my trip abroad. I very much doubted it was a man from Littlewoods with the answer to all – well, almost all – my needs. I breathed a sigh of relief: it wasn't Deborah.

Chalmers was charming, as usual. Unlike most ardent collectors of anything, his fanaticism did not infect every word and sentence – quite the opposite, in fact. He was so laid back it was hard to realize he was phoning to inform me he had arranged for £22,000 in French francs to be deposited in a bank in Nice to await my arrival; 22,000 smackeroos for just eleven pieces of folded and printed tin that had been intended for an eight- or nine-year-old's amusement in the early decades of this century, but had now become a rich man's nostalgic indulgence, a delicate and haunting reminder of an innocence that had gone forever.

'Don't hand any money over unless they're as good as he claims, will you?' was Chalmers' only note of anxiety in the whole conversation.

'No, of course not. You say he states they are all mint, so mint they must be,' I replied, knowing, as he did, that 'mint condition' is a slightly elastic term when applied to a plaything of that venerable age. I just prayed my piece of elastic had the same rebound as his. 'But they all looked pretty good from those Pol-

2

aroids he sent you,' I added, trying to shift some of the onus of responsibility back onto his wealthy shoulders.

'Would you marry a girl from a Polaroid photograph?' Chalmers enquired nonchalantly.

'I think I once did,' I replied, but neither of us laughed.

'And if some are mint and some are not, he won't split them, you say?'

'No, he insists on selling them as a collection. So you hand over the £22,000 or nothing. If it's the latter, don't feel too badly, I don't get the toys but you still had a free trip to St Paul de Vence, and the sun, and £500 for a rainy day back here.'

Put that way the deal did not sound too bad. But real life rarely works out so simply; real life has hiccups in it. In this case, if I didn't bring back the toys, the giant reverberating hiccup would be of the frustration of a fanatical collector, a frustration that would probably vent itself in front of other important collectors, no doubt – and to my cost. My living depended on my reputation with these strangely varied individuals. I was beginning to regret that I had agreed to act for him.

'Look, if you're worried that I'll make the wrong decision . . .' I offered, but he cut me short instantly.

'My dear fellow, I chose you because I know you won't make the wrong decision. And anyway, you know why I can't go personally. I don't want any publicity surrounding the purchase, and right now I'm in the throes of fighting off that Consolidated take-over bid. I couldn't go even if I wanted to, you know that.'

'I know that,' I repeated dutifully.

So that was that. He wished me bon voyage and said how he envied me. I laughed. I had to, it was so absurd: A multi-millionaire businessman envying a divorced ex-advertising man whose only means of support nowadays was his hobby. I promised to ring him from the south of France when I had some news.

'I'll be waiting all day with my fingers crossed,' he said with all seriousness. And he probably would be, and the sight of those fingers would puzzle Consolidated out of their minds, and maybe out of their bid. I chuckled at the thought as I put the phone down.

But a second later I wasn't chuckling at all as the realization that the trip was now definitely on hit me. It had all been a pleasant fantasy up to now – a springtime run down to the Mediterranean at someone else's expense: two nights at a small hotel

3

that Chalmers had praised to the skies; an hour or two looking at fabulous old toys I couldn't possibly afford in a month of Sundays, and all the other days to kingdom come; then a few hours off, perhaps at Cannes, assessing the topless on the Croisette in between brushing sand from my face. Then cruising back up the *autoroute* with not a care in the world and the toys parked on the back seat of my Beetle. And suddenly, I didn't like old toys any more, for it all rested on what I thought of that collection. If the decision was marginal one way or the other, then Chalmers might raise the roof – either because I had bought them, or because I hadn't bought them. Only if they turned out to be absolutely mint was I sunny side up. I prayed Monsieur Vincent was not a joker, or a dab Gallic hand at retouching Polaroids.

I suddenly felt like a beer. So I locked up shop and strolled across the road and down the lane towards the sea. I hoped the balmy spring day had not enticed Gus Tribble out in his leaky boat.

'Shouldn't make promises. Never. You can always get by with a "maybe".'

Gus poured me another half from a fresh six-pack of beer. 'Always get off the hook, you can, with a "maybe", because you're never on the hook to start with.' He grinned at me and pulled the tab on a Heineken, his huge work-hewn hands dwarfing the can, their network of veins like blue worms burrowing under the skin.

'But I didn't say "maybe", and I *am* on the hook,' I said weakly.

'Then see you don't get eaten, that's all.' Gus unfolded his giant frame, weathered by some sixty-five summers and an untold number of winters, rose from his chair and bent his head to go into the kitchen. 'And if you do get eaten, see it happens back here and not in France. They'll put garlic on you.' His laughter seemed to make the beams sing.

I had lunch at Gus's and before long, I began to feel a good deal better. And it wasn't because we had punished the second six-pack, but it helped.

'Do you trust him?' Gus asked out of the blue.

'Who?'

'The fellow who's sending you. What's his name?'

'Oh, Chalmers.' I thought for a minute. 'You know it's funny but I don't really know.'

4

He looked at me in surprise, but said nothing. I went on, 'I suppose I haven't thought about it, because it shouldn't matter. The money is waiting in cash in a bank in Nice. I only pay it out if the collection is at least next door to being superb. He's paid me in advance for my expenses, including the hotel, so all I've got to do is bring the toys back.'

'Oh,' was all I got from Gus. And I knew what he was thinking. Anyone who has clawed his way up to a mountain of money must have knocked out a few stones on the way and never looked down to see where they landed.

'Anyway, it will charge the battery in the Beetle,' I joked. Gus changed the subject.

'Going to the meeting tonight, or too busy packing?'

'Of course I'll go. Packing for one isn't exactly a drama.'

'Good. Didn't want to lose your vote all because of a load of old toys.' He took a long draught from his glass, then went on. 'I wonder what it will look like when they find it. Used to see them all the time over the bay during the early part of the war.'

'It will be lots of sad little pieces, I expect. All the others they've excavated have been – all except for the engines, that is. They seem to survive anything.'

'Wasn't called a Merlin for nothing then,' Gus smiled. 'Magic, I mean,' he added in case I hadn't got his joke.

'You're right. Magic.'

I looked at Gus, sitting back in his old leather chair, the horse-hair stuffing coming up for air at the ends of each armrest. Despite his age, he looked solid as a rock. He knew who he was, and where he was heading – which was nowhere but where he was right now. And 'maybes' let him live his life the way he wanted every second of the day. Owed nothing to anybody, never asked for thanks. I envied him.

'Do you think we'll win the vote?' I asked after a while.

'Depends,' he murmured.

'You mean on how many of our side turn up?'

'No,' he smiled. 'On how many of their side turn up.' And he handed me another beer.

I always hated leaving Gus's cottage. Its thick walls and sturdy mullioned windows were as reassuring as its owner, though some two centuries older. Not that my place was particularly flimsy or Johnny-come-lately. It was just different. And don't get me wrong: I'm very fond of it. Always was when my great aunt lived in it. I used to visit her when I was a boy and it never ceased to amaze me that anyone could have such incredible good fortune as to live over a toy shop, let alone a toy *and* sweet shop all in one. And own the lot! It sort of amazes me still. And now it's I who live in it and own it. My aunt left it to me in her will. It's not a sweet shop any more, and it's not really a toy shop either, not a regular one. It's a toy collector's corner. And it's not open all that much because I'm often away chasing something to trade in or stock it with. So I open mainly by appointment. That usually frightens off time-wasters who otherwise would have me demonstrating every trick of every old toy without any intention of ever buying anything. There are millions of those in the old toy game.

The house is Victorian; red brick, with a curious tiny tower and a little lead-covered steeple signifying nothing. It stands on a corner bang in the middle of what I call Studland High Street, but which isn't a High Street at all: it's just the road that leads through the village *en route* for the ferry to Bournemouth and Sandbanks to the east, and Swanage and Corfe to the west. A narrow road that's wonderfully empty October to April, up to the brim May to September. But curiously, Studland, for me, survives on even the hottest of Bank Holidays; maybe because it was where I spent loads of my childhood vacations, and the place was always humming with people even then. And, anyway, nothing can change that breathtakingly English view of the sea that opens up as you descend the steep, tree-shadowed lane to the beach. It's like a poem. Only better, because it doesn't have to obey any rules. And it doesn't have to come to an end; unless the off-shore oil prospectors eventually get their wishes, and we go the way of Aberdeen. I think Gus and I would personally rather murder every known oil executive in the world than let that happen. Or, at least, begin drilling for oil in their very sitting-rooms.

I returned home and fed Bing, then put the Schuco car in the shop window. I decided I would get a much higher price for the Britains Coldstream Guards at a Christie's auction in the summer and so I hid them under the fibreglass insulation in the attic, away from thieving eyes. I collected up my travellers' cheques, Townsend Thorensen ferry tickets, passport and Green Card Insurance for the Beetle and shoved them in an old

6

'Venice Advertising Film Festival' document zip-case left over from my advertising days. I packed the bare essentials, plus a pair of trousers and a pair of trunks, in my only decent suitcase and then went out to what passed as my garage. It is actually more like a lean-to, only it's not supposed to lean at all. It's got nothing to lean on. To say the wooden frame has rotted is an understatement, and it's really only held together by large unhealthy sheets of asbestos that are its only in-filling. However, it keeps seventy per cent of the rain off the top of my Beetle convertible, which keeps another twenty per cent out of its interior. I've got another car, but it's not running at the moment – except with condensation. It's the love of my life, and I'm restoring it gradually, but the trouble is, it's rotting at a faster rate. It's a 1966 Daimler v8 – the one with the Jaguar style but the sweet Daimler motor. I'll finish it, one day, one way or another. I keep it at Gus Tribble's.

Apart from being a bit dirty (country roads have cow pats, and mud even when it hasn't rained for ages), the Beetle was in great shape. I had had it serviced only the week before by the local Porsche agents. My Beetle is a wolf in sheep's clothing : it's got a Porsche engine and wider wheels, though not absurdly so, to absorb the power. Otherwise it looks absolutely bog standard. I sometimes like to surprise.

I checked the tyre pressures, remembering the spare, and the oil level. Then I painted some yellow gunge on the headlights so that I wouldn't get lynched in some back street in France for showing the whites of my lights, and put a spare set of sparking plugs in the glove locker and a footpump in the front boot. I locked the garage door again carefully, and only had to replace one of the door panels this time.

By the time I had made some tea, taken Bing for a walk on his lead and watched the early evening television news, it was time to get into Swanage for the great meeting. Gus took me in his old, upright Ford Popular of 1950 vintage – a taste for which I've never acquired, as Gus, to my knowledge, has turned it over three times, twice on one day. At least tonight he didn't have a piano on the roof.

The Church Hall was crowded. By the time we had parked, there was only room for us right at the back, which was not so bad for Gus as he was taller then most. I mainly saw heads, and only really knew when the platform speakers had arrived by the lessening of the cacophony. But at least we got seats.

The Vicar of St Sebastian's opened the meeting, as was his due for the land under discussion was Church property. He is a bit younger than I am, around thirty-six or so (I'm just forty, but feel thirty-nine), with an untidy red beard that goes with his Leftish views. He received a slightly self-conscious ripple of applause when he announced he would be brief. And, good for him, brief he was. He raced through the facts of the local controversy, whether or not the Historical Aviation Society should be allowed to commence a dig to recover the wreckage of a Vickers-Supermarine Spitfire of 152 Squadron stationed at Warmwell, which had been shot down on 16 August 1940 by a flight of ME 109s. The pilot, PO Travers Redfern, was not seen to leave the aircraft, and, therefore, it must be assumed the proposed dig would disturb his mortal remains. The Vicar took pains to point out that because the field in which the Spitfire had crashed was owned by the Church, it did not make it hallowed ground. Gus and I nodded our agreement.

The Vicar went on to say that from everything he had heard, or read in the local papers, the community seemed to be grievously split between those in favour of the recovery of the aircraft, and those who did not wish to disturb the last resting place of PO Redfern. He felt the controversy had gone on long enough. Therefore, tonight everyone was invited to air his or her views for or against for a period of two hours. Then, at nine-thirty precisely, there would be a vote taken through a show of hands. He wisely ignored a single shout of 'Rubbish' and the debate began.

'You going to speak?' Gus whispered to me, in a loud voice.

'Don't know. See how it's going.' I replied, holding my finger up to my lips.

The first two speakers were inevitably the head of the Historical Aviation Society, another earnest beard, and the self-appointed leader of the 'leave well alone brigade', a rotund bank manager from Wareham with an embarrassing stutter. I decided I was glad I banked what little I have miles from his clutches. I tried to judge the mood of the meeting by the length and decibels of the applause for each speaker, but on my clapometer they measured about the same. Not a great sign for our side.

I had better tell you what side we're on. We want the dig to go ahead and religion, one way or the other, doesn't come into our thinking. Warmwell aerodrome was right in the front line during

8

the Battle of Britain and that aircraft is a bit of local history. Gus and I, and quite a few others, would like to set up a small local museum commemorating Warmwell's part in defeating the Luftwaffe. England has got precious little now to be proud of so let's at least be proud of our past. Over the years, lots of crash sites have been excavated in other parts of the country and local museums have benefited from the parts that were recovered. And when mortal remains were found, they were decently reburied in hallowed ground by their families with a proud stone to mark their passing. So you see, it isn't just old toys that obsess me; it's all of it, really – all those whispers from long ago. I sometimes feel I was born in the wrong age. Gus's motives are different. His father was killed in a raid on Weymouth, and he identifies with every Spitfire and Hurricane that ever performed a victory roll. That's why he wants it recovered.

The debate droned on, and was not really as heated as I was expecting. I looked across at Gus. He was asleep, but I could tell his sixth sense was still tracking. It comes from his forty-odd years being a fisherman, when it's more than your life, or catch, is worth to be a hundred per cent gone.

After a while I, too, began feeling my eyelids take on considerable extra ballast when I suddenly heard a familiar voice. I looked up sharply, and peered through the sea of heads to pick out the speaker. He was a large man around fifty-five or so, with one of those hairy suits with a big brown check pattern, often worn by preparatory school headmasters in rural districts to pretend they're more important than they are. He had a rather puffy face and those purple cheeks that, as a child, I used to think came about if you ate too much school beetroot. I didn't know him from Adam, and I had missed his introduction. But that voice was unmistakable, and I could not for the life of me remember where I had heard it. It was like an English public school version of Orson Welles, with more timbre in it than the whole of the New Forest. He wasn't half a speaker, and to my horror, he was vehemently in the 'No' brigade.

His objections were paraded with clear precision, and conveyed with oratorical flair. 'We, as a nation,' he declared, 'should not always find refuge in the past, but plan for the future. The money and energy expended on the dig would be better spent in draining more of Dorset's heathland.' For this he was interrupted by a round of applause. I didn't like the sound of it. He went on to detail the scars that would be left in this 'beautiful pasture' by the movement of heavy diggers, and the hordes of spectators any such excavation was bound to attract. Another round of applause. He exploded with indignation and horror at the thought of disturbing the grave of this intrepid pilot just to satisfy the obsession of a few to get their hands on a twisted wing spar or a bent joy stick, to which 'a fragment of thumb might still be adhering'. He continued like an old time actor-manager, to play on our emotions by reading an extract from a letter PO Redfern wrote to his mother, just before his death, in which he said, 'I love my aircraft, Mother, as I love flying. I feel whole when I'm in its cockpit, as if we had always been destined for each other. I know it will protect me . . . .'

The speaker had now reached a tremendous climax. 'Should we now act God, and separate this magnificent hero of the past from the chariot of fire he so adored? Whether we believe in God or no, surely this man has been at peace now for forty-five years and more – still, no doubt, flying his beloved Spitfire in a sky that knows no horizons. We must not, *shall* not, pick at his bones like hyenas now . . . .'

A surge of applause drowned his last words, and I now knew nothing anybody could say would make any difference to the outcome. And I was made the more depressed by my not being able to place his unique voice. I looked across at Gus. His eyes were still firmly shut, but he felt my movement.

'We've lost,' he muttered.

'I know,' I sighed.

'You want to know who he is, don't you?' he went on, without stirring.

'Wouldn't mind.'

'One of the richest men around these parts. Surprised you haven't heard of him. Lives over Lulworth way, in that huge Victorian thing . . . .'

Then suddenly it dawned on me. He was Treasure. Randolph Treasure. He had phoned me a couple of times enquiring about whether I ever had any Marklin toys and had joked about my name also being Marklin, but I'd never seen him – just heard about him, and nothing I'd heard had exactly endeared him to me.

And now I could add an image to his voice, I could understand his reputation, for around these parts, he was known as a bit of a bully; the kind of rich landowner who, I guess, would have gone down a treat at the court of King John. And living in a Victorian folly, bristling with little steeples at each corner like a demon king's Disneyish castle, didn't exactly sweeten his image, either.

I raised my bottom off my seat to get a further glimpse of him, but all I could see now was the back of his head. It was nodding with satisfaction at the next speaker's every word, for the next speaker was yet another who wasn't one of us and as you've probably already guessed, at nine-thirty-two, when the vote was taken, the 'Nos' had it by a mile. So much for our little dream for a Warmwell air museum to make up for the old aerodrome site now being totally disfigured by a gravel pit. Appropriately it was raining as we left. I wondered what Pilot Officer Redfern would have thought of it all, particularly of Treasure's performance. He'd probably be reminded, like me, of another forceful orator who persuaded quite a bunch of people to make the wrong decisions, only he, at least, did the decent thing of shooting himself in his bunker.

Two

'Monsieur Vincent?'

I spoke slowly so that I could practise my rusty French accent. He looked up from his Pernod.

'Mr Peter Marklin?' he replied, in almost impeccable English.

'Yes,' I said, with great relief that I would not have to beg, borrow and steal from my memory bank to speak French to him.

'Come and sit down.' He indicated the padded stone bench next to him. 'You must be tired after your journey. Let me buy you a drink.'

'Yes, thank you. I could do with one.' I sat down in the tiny bar in the reception area.

He turned to me. 'What will you have?'

'A Campari – Campari and soda.'

He did not need to order it as the bar was so small, the barman was already pouring it.

'Well, cheers, as you say.' He held his glass to mine, and I looked at him properly for the first time. And I liked what I saw. He was in his late sixties, tall, thin and tanned. His hands had such little flesh on them, they almost looked like webbed bones. He smiled. 'You could not have chosen a more pleasant place to stay than the Colombe D'Or.'

I chuckled. 'I didn't really choose it. Mr Chalmers did. He often stays here, he tells me.'

'A man of taste.'

'Yes, certainly.' Everything connected with Chalmers always oozed taste, and the Colombe D'Or was no exception. It had knocked me out when I had checked in, because it's not really like a hotel at all. It's a large old French farmhouse with lots of little extensions carried out over the years. Its small, terraced grounds are walled and paved, and ravishingly attractive. White doves strut and coo in the main courtyard, where I could see people already sitting down for lunch under the big umbrellas.

12

On the other side of the house is an intimate swimming pool surrounded by cypresses, its water looking like blue-black Quink, because its sides and bottom are painted that colour instead of the usual downtown Hollywood turquoise. But what really blows your mind is what you find on every wall in every room and corridor in the whole place: pictures. Not your Holiday Inn sunset prints from Plastic Arts, but altogether something else. Just the greatest, most nonchalantly arranged collection of genuine Modern Art I have ever seen – that is, under private ownership, and not in some gallery or other. I'll name just a few artists, and leave your imagination to fill in the rest: Picasso; Dufy; Calder; Modigliani; Matisse ... Getting the picture? But not just in ones: in twos and threes and fours. Not just pictures either: sculpture, busts, figures and mobiles. And nothing is wired or padlocked or nailed down. The Colombe D'Or presumably feels it does not attract that kind of acquisitive guest.

'You had a good journey, I trust?' Monsieur Vincent sat back against the wall and looked at me. His eyes were very piercing.

'Yes. I stopped at a little place I know, near Macon, for the night.'

'Off the *autoroute*, of course?'

'Yes, of course.'

'Tell me, Mr Marklin, are you a toy collector yourself?' His interest seemed genuine, so I opened up a little.

'Yes. I began just over ten years ago. I should have started much earlier. There's so much I can never get now.'

He patted my hand on the table, but there was nothing nasty about the gesture.

'That's the cry of every avid toy collector. They wish they had never lost the toys of their childhoods.' He thoughtfully sipped his Pernod. 'Do you just collect or do you trade in them as well? So many do nowadays.'

I could tell his disapproval, but it couldn't be helped.

'Both, I'm afraid. You see, I used to be in the rat-race, but I retired from it after I got divorced. And I need money to live, so ....'

'So you found refuge and reward in your hobby, so to speak?' He smiled gently.

I nodded.

'Don't worry. I only disapprove when grown men trade in playthings purely for greed.'

13

I began to like him a lot.

'Tell me, Mr Marklin, are you related at all to the founders of the great German Marklin toy company?'

'Everyone asks me that. And I'm afraid I'm not – just an admirer of their wonderful products. I wish I could afford more.'

He finished his Pernod and declined my invitation for another.

'We must adjourn in a moment for you to see what you have come all this way for. It would not be wise to evaluate them through the veil of alcohol.'

I could not disagree, although the drive, even with the soft top down, had dried me up considerably. He rose to leave.

'Do we have to go far? We can take my car,' I offered, but he laughed and took my arm.

'The answer is no to the first question, and we don't need to, thanks, to the second.' He led me through the door, into the courtyard, and out through the main entrance.

His bony fingers pointed up to the walled village that lay above, to the left.

'I live up there. It will only take a minute to walk.'

His house, nestling in a curving stone terrace, was a jewel made even more exquisite by the jungle of geraniums that wallpapered the soft, weathered stone with green and flaming red. Indeed, the whole of St Paul de Vence was magical – a kind of medieval dream world of tumbling stone houses, crowding each other like lovers, with slanted alley ways dipping and climbing between them.

Monsieur Vincent led me up the thousand creaks of a staircase, to an upper room that had a quite breathtaking view of the valley below the village.

'I won't be too long, Mr Marklin. I will fetch them down for you.' And he glided silently back out of the room.

I was still a bit dazed by it all; the journey down, by the Colombe D'Or, and Monsieur Vincent and his habitat. I needed to take breath, but in a moment the toys would be spread before me and Mr Chalmers' shadow would be cast across my decision. I took stock. The room was like a piece of the twenties frozen in time. There was no hint that the last sixty-five years had ever happened. I looked around for my Tardis.

Three giant hat boxes, with legs, suddenly came into sight.

'I'm sorry, Mr Marklin, I will have to bring them in twos and threes.' He put down the boxes, and went to get the rest. We ended up with eleven spread on the floor in front of us.

I felt a strange, unnerving sense of excitement. And I wanted to prolong it a little before the revelation.

'Tell me, Monsieur Vincent,' I said, 'why didn't you arrange for me to meet you here? Why at the hotel?'

He sat down in the chair opposite, and his eyes almost gave me the answer.

'I wanted to see you first, Mr Marklin, to look at you – if you aren't offended, get the feel of you.'

'Oh,' I replied weakly. 'And I passed?'

'Otherwise you wouldn't be here.'

'But . . .'

He held up his hand. 'I know what you are going to say. I have toys for sale, so why does it matter to whom I sell them?' He leaned forward. 'I know Mr Chalmers vaguely. I've talked to him at the Colombe D'Or. Had he come to see the toys, I would have met him here, because I know his love for them is genuine, you see.'

'So if you hadn't liked me . . .'

'I would have asked Mr Chalmers to come down himself, at a later date.'

I was silent for a minute, then plucked up courage.

'You love these particular toys more then just old toys in general, don't you?'

'Yes,' he answered, almost in a whisper.

'May I ask why?'

'Most of them belonged to my brother who died of meningitis in 1932. They thought it was 'flu. I loved him. Six of them have never been played with. You see, he died on Christmas Eve and they were never given to him. My mother, then I, have kept them ever since in these old hat boxes.'

'Why are you selling them now, after all this time?'

'I need the money, Mr Marklin. I have a wasting disease that prevents me from working and my savings are fast running out. I have no dependents now. My son was killed in the war; my wife died soon after.'

His voice tailed away, and I knew it was time to look at the toys.

With the opening of the first old hat box, I knew all my worries

15

were over; and my sense of excitement fully justified. Inside was a Delage tinplate car, by CR, in amazingly perfect condition down to the working headlights, complete with chauffeur and passengers. It measured, I guessed, about forty centimetres. The next box contained a black and blue Citroën taxi with canework sides, also mint, made in the twenties by the Citroën factory itself. The next, a stunning P2 Alfa Romeo race car, made by CIJ of Paris. While I had seen a few of these before, I had never seen one in such pristine condition. There wasn't even the hint of a crack in the tyres.

Revelation followed revelation: a mint Rolls-Royce Phantom by JEP of Paris, circa 1928; a kind of curious, yet stunning Renault with a Berline or Sedanca de ville style body, and beautiful brass trimming, maker unknown to me; another mint JEP, this time an Hispano Suiza dual cowl touring car. A steam lorry by Tipp & Co of Germany, made specially to promote the British company Sentinel. And so it went on. It was like a kind of multiple orgasm for a connoisseur of vintage toys. Their frail beauty exhausted me. And true to Monsieur Vincent's Polaroids, every one was mint, or as near mint as made very little difference.

There was only one rub, really. I didn't quite see how they all added up to £22,000-worth, sensational though they were, until I opened the last, much larger box. Now I'm not into boats the way I am into toy cars and aircraft, but even so what was inside blew my mind. It was a huge tinplate Marklin battleship, over a hundred centimetres long, still with its original box, white and red, every flag, every item of the rigging preserved as new, yet it was at least eighty years old. And in a separate small box were twelve sailors in differing postures, to man the great vessel. I now knew Mr Chalmers would be walking away with something of a bargain.

'You are not disappointed, Mr Marklin?' he asked anxiously.

I laughed. 'How could I be, Monsieur Vincent? They are quite wonderful – unbelievable, really. But tell me, whose was the battleship?'

'It was given to my father as a boy, by a rich uncle. It was my grandmother who put it away for when he was older, and it got forgotten.' He rose and went over to the window. 'My mother insisted on keeping my brother's toys as a memory. We kept almost everything here just as it was the night he died.' He turned and looked directly at me. 'So these are not just toys, you see; they are my brother, my family. Ask Mr Chalmers to remember, won't you?'

'I will,' I replied quietly. It seemed indecent to raise the question of money now, but he sensed my unease and brought the subject up himself.

'I gather Mr Chalmers has arranged for cash from a Nice bank?'

'Yes. It's waiting for us. £22,000 in francs.'

'In the morning, Mr Marklin, in the morning. I'm tired now. I'll drive down with you at ten o'clock from the Colombe D'Or. What is your car? I'll park near it.'

'A Beetle – I mean, the old model Volkswagen convertible.'

'Ah, I know. It's funny how old models are often more desirable, isn't it? Except when they're human beings, that is. Au revoir, Mr Marklin.'

The rest of my stay was plain sailing and hugely enjoyable. No doubt, you can detect a slight hesitation in that comment, and that hesitation was Monsieur Vincent. I hated to take his brother from him. And it wasn't just his brother I was plundering – but his mother, his wife, his son, a load of his memories, a load of his past. As if his future was not bleak enough. And what was worse, I had grown to like him enormously.

The Colombe D'Or food lived up to its art collection, and I never got to the topless on the Croisette at Cannes, even though they were only twenty minutes away. Except for a quick trip to the bank in Nice, I stayed in St Paul de Vence, where the sight of toasted breasts seemed to be relegated to its proper ranking in the list of the world's most pressing priorities. Not that the Quink in the Colombe D'Or pool did not attract a few beautiful nymphs. There were five while I was there. Four were aged about sixteen or seventeen years, but their German parents never let them out of their sight. One formal father never went anywhere without his binoculars, and made a Prussian general look like a CND supporter. It was the fifth who fascinated me: tall, tanned and leggy, blonde streaks in her hair, and a look in her eye, the kind of girl the Beach Boys used to sing about. Only she wasn't from California, as I heard her speak Roedean English to the waiter. And she seemed to be alone, which, somehow, seemed insane in this world.

I don't want to lead you on. I didn't get anywhere with her.

17

The Colombe D'Or isn't the kind of place where you saunter up to a girl and say, 'Gee, honey, you look swell. How about a . . . ?' I tried to get a sunbed next to hers, but they were always taken. When she dived into the pool, by the time I had gingerly lowered myself in, she was getting out. And we were sat at least three Picassos, a Modigliani and a Matisse away from each other at dinner. C'est la vie, sod it. And the rotten thing is, I know she had her eyes on me. Nothing else, unfortunately but, definitely, her gorgeous eyes.

I got up at five-thirty the second morning so that I could make an early start home. I aimed to get back without stopping anywhere for the night. I was getting worried about the responsibility of those irreplaceable items, now carefully packed into two separate boxes that would fit in my Beetle, one smaller one, for under the bonnet, the other to fit in the back behind the front seats. Stopping somewhere for the night seemed asking for trouble.

Autoroutes are tedious, but magically fast. In no time at all, I was at the Marseilles junction, where my road swung north towards Paris. I was just thinking of breaking for a coffee at a petrol station, when I saw a red Ferrari in my rear-view mirror. Now it wasn't the car that grabbed my attention – red Ferraris are a sou a dozen along the Côte D'Azur – it was the shape behind the wheel. Or rather, its head. It looked uncannily like my Quink girl. At first it didn't bother me one way or the other. After all, it might not be her. Secondly, if it was her, why shouldn't she be motoring back the same day I was anyway? Even the French don't have a law against that.

So I fantasized my way to the next Fina station and filled up the tank. I spotted the attendant noting the wider wheels. Maybe he had recognized the Porsche sound as I drew up. Certainly he cleaned my windscreen better than most. I pulled over to the coffee shop, and downed a cup and a croissant among the squabbling Gallic families.

When I came back to the Beetle, I was surprised to see the Ferrari – or what I took to be the same car – hidden behind the souvenir shop. And she didn't look the souvenir type, unless it had diamonds in it. I checked the packages were still there, and went on my way, now a little more conscious of what I might see in my rear-view mirror.

For ten miles or so I saw nothing – that is, millions of Peugeots,

Citroëns, even a 'Maigret' type Light Fifteen, but no Ferraris. Then as I crested a long incline, I saw it about a dozen cars behind me. It was beginning to bug me, so over the rise I slowed right down and a cluster of cars went by. I could see the Ferrari had too much acceleration on its side to slow in time and as it, too, went past, I saw for certain it was my south of France super-dream at the wheel. She didn't throw me a glance, clever girl.

And she was clever too for the next fifty miles or so, for I saw neither gorgeous hide nor blonde hair of her. But around Beaune she was back behind me, after, no doubt, a judiciously timed pit-stop to let me go by. I was beginning to wish now that I was taking the toys back in an armoured car. It's amazing how vulnerable you can feel on a motorway, for I had the modesty to figure it might not be my virile body and slightly less virile mind she was after. And I had a strong feeling she might have friends somewhere up ahead – the kind that feel kinky enough about ladies' stockings to wear them over their heads.

I tried to keep in a bunch of traffic as much as I could, and never get left alone. It's curious how difficult that is mile after mile. There's always someone who doesn't twig what's going on, and breaks up the pack. And that red menace was never far behind. I began wondering what Clint Eastwood would do in a predicament like this. Then I realized I didn't have a stand-in, and would be a nervous wreck by Calais.

As we approached Paris, I began to feel a little easier. Surely no one would try to hijack my cargo with so many autos around? I started to think clearly again, and realized that young Quinky could be just playing a game with me – you know, man-and-woman type game, and I'd been too uptight to see what she was really getting at. Just as I was kicking myself for not taking her up on what could well be a most rewarding form of steering wheel seduction, I saw her peel off (in her car, I mean) down the Orly Airport exit, and disappear. And that was that. For you don't U-turn on a French motorway, unless you've always had a hankering for the Foreign Legion. So Peter Marklin had done it again – panicked his way out of a proposition.

The rest of the trip to Calais was uneventful. I grabbed a hamburger at another service station so as not to waste time. And though I kept a wary eye out, Quinky was nowhere to be seen. I was lucky at the ferry terminal: there was a boat in fifteen minutes. I bought some booze for Gus to thank him for looking after

19

my shop and feeding Bing, then drove the Beetle on board. Though there seemed to be only eight cars and two container trucks on the ferry, a spotty seaman, enjoying his only power, made me park within a gnat's whisker of the truck-like bumpers of a Volvo estate. Behind me, he invited a Chevrolet to go up my exhaust pipe. I took down their numbers just in case. Before I got out to join the brown ale brigade I could already hear making for the bar, I threw a travelling rug over the large package laying across the rear seat and footwells and locked the car. At least no one could see the other one in the boot under the bonnet. Mind you, the rug hardly looked natural, but there was little else I could do to disguise the package. A Beetle is hardly a pantechnicon. I decided to drop down to the car deck every now and again to check things out, then went up to the passenger level. I hoped the crossing would be fairly smooth, as water is not actually one of my favourite things. I tend to take Qwells to have a bath.

I was back sitting in my car ten minutes before we arrived at Dover. The tartan shrouded mountain was still behind my seat, and the package secure in the front boot. And besides the ferry food, I had experienced no reason to feel queasy. My only delay now would be at Customs, where they would no doubt go into a huddle as to what duty, if any, I would have to pay on a load of old toys. I had a receipt from Monsieur Vincent for £850 in full payment for eleven items. He was loath to sign a lie, but realized the need for it in the end. I hated making him do it, but knew Chalmers would hate me more if I didn't. After all, £22,000 needs the extra import duty like a hole in the head.

It seemed to take ages before they would let us off, and contrary to their manufacturer's advertising, the Volvo ahead of me would not start; so Spotty and his mates had to push it off to one side before I could leave. My headlights picked their way to the Customs building, where I pulled up in the fourth lane down the line.

'Anything to declare, sir? Drink, cigarettes, perfume . . . ?'

'These two bottles of wine,' I replied, holding up a clinking carrier bag that had been lying in the front passenger footwell. 'And a few old toys and things I picked up in France.' I indicated the tartan mountain behind me.

'Ah, I see, sir,' came the measured reply. 'Would you mind stepping out so that I can take a look at them?'

20

I got out and the rather seedy-looking Customs officer, who looked as if he hadn't smiled since the last car had fallen into the dock, got in and knelt on my seat. He pulled the rug off. 'Do you mind if I undo the string, or would you like the honour sir?' I nodded that he could go ahead. 'Toys, you say, sir? Old toys.' The string fell away, and he slowly and deliberately opened the lid.

'Please be careful. They're all individually wrapped up. Easily damaged . . .' I stopped and smiled at him, in case my concern led him to believe they were more valuable than my receipt said they were.

I heard his hands disturbing and rustling paper, and then there was a curious silence, and he backed off out of the car.

'This one of them, sir?' He held up a cheap plastic model of a 1980 Camaro.

Three

'You look terrible. You should go back to bed again.' I looked at
Gus, who did not, quite, ooze the sympathy I had been counting
on.

'How can anyone sleep when the whole world is falling apart
around him?' I complained bitterly.

'Churchill did during the war. Cat-napped his way to victory.'
Gus got up and pulled himself another can of beer. 'Worrying's
no good. Never solved nothing, worrying.'

I exploded. 'It's all very well for you, Gus. It's not you who
owes £22,000 to an irate and frustrated multi-millionaire, who
can ruin your chances of ever making an honest bob out of toys
again.'

'You can always fall back on advertising,' he said quietly.

'Advertising's not exactly a thing to fall back on. It's more
likely to fall back on you. Anyway, I gave all that up over
two years ago, with Deborah and all her neurotic hangers-
on.'

He took a long, slow draught of his beer. 'Well then, we'll have
to find the toys, won't we?'

I breathed a sigh of relief, and Gus smiled. I knew then what
he was doing, and he was right. I was just too tired to think
straight. So would you be if you had, one, had the shock of finding a fabulous collection of unique vintage toys replaced by
eleven plastic Camaros made in Macao. Two, an hour-long fight
with Customs officials and officers from the ferry to energize a
search of the ship. Three, searched the ship with them for over
an hour, knowing damn well the toys had probably been taken
off before I had even reached Customs myself. And, four, all the
time been not quite certain that the packages had not been interfered with either just before leaving St Paul de Vence or on a

coffee or hamburger break on the long journey. The real toys might never had embarked on the ferry at all. And the whole dreadful disaster came on top of being knackered from a hard nine-hundred-mile drive. Meanwhile, Gus had been minding the store and feeding the cat. I could be calm with such onerous responsibilites.

'What did his voice sound like?'

'Whose voice?' I asked irritably.

'Chalmers – on the phone.'

'Cross. What did you expect?'

'I didn't mean that. Did he sound genuine?'

I suddenly twigged what he meant. I thought for a minute. 'I *think* he did, but I don't often hear cross multi-millionaires. But I know what you're getting at.'

'Well?' Gus looked at me from under the tangle of his eyebrows.

'I don't think so. I don't think he would steal his own toys. There would be no point.'

'Put you in his power, though, wouldn't it?'

'No point in that either. He knows I don't have £22,000 hanging about.'

'What about your own toy collection?'

'Not worth more than about £10,000, I reckon. And he's seen them, so he would know that.'

'Nothing specially he wants in it?'

'Wouldn't have thought so. He's got most models. Anyway, I don't think he's the sort of man . . . .'

Gus laughed. 'Well, it's got to be a collector of some sort, hasn't it?'

I had another beer while I brewed on it. Gus was right again: it had to be a collector, and one who knew I was going to the south of France, and why I was going there. And I hadn't told anyone except Gus. I tried to tread carefully.

'Gus, there's no question it has to be another collector. But he would have had to have known about my trip, wouldn't he?' I let the thought filter through the Heineken.

'Yeah. He'd have had to have known.'

'And only Chalmers, you and I knew about it.'

Gus thought for a second. 'And that bloke in the south of France you bought them from.'

I had forgotten about Monsieur Vincent. 'Yes, and him.'

23

I realized the oblique approach was getting me nowhere with Gus, so I came out with it.

'Did you mention it to anyone, Gus?'

He didn't seem at all concerned but took a sip of his beer, and made a church with his hands. 'Didn't try to keep it a secret. I might have done.'

My heart sank.

'Think, Gus, think. Whom did you tell?'

'Can't remember. Nobody special.'

'What do you mean – "Nobody special"?'

'Well, nobody in particular. I just mentioned it in the Black Lion, that's all.'

'When, for goodness' sake?'

'The day Chalmers first rang you with the suggestion.'

I groaned and put my head in my hands. 'And you said it was to get vintage toys?'

'Of course. I thought that was the funny bit – old toys being worth all that lot.'

'Who was in there?'

Gus put down his beer. 'I can't remember now. It was quite full that night and I seem to think I drank a fair bit.'

I knew I wouldn't get any more out of him.

'Should have been insured,' Gus grumbled in some sort of self-defence.

'I know. But it would have taken ages to set it all up. Any insurance company would have had to bring in an expert to see them first. Monsieur Vincent would never have stomached that, let alone Chalmers who wanted the whole thing kept as quiet as possible.'

'I'm sorry,' Gus mumbled.

I leaned across and patted his hand, and Bing looked most annoyed as I had disturbed his paw on my lap.

'Don't be,' I said, with the nearest to a smile my face could muster. 'In a funny way, you may have helped a little.'

'Can't see that myself. I shouldn't let drink do the talking.'

'Forget it, Gus. Regrets won't bring the toys back either. What I mean is this: there are about twenty collectors in this country with that kind of determination to get exactly what they want, whatever the price, and I've dealt with most of them. But only a very few, I think, would stoop to stealing. Now, say half of that twenty would. That's a list of ten

24

suspects I know of, though there may be more. That's supposing the culprit is someone from this country and not a foreigner.'

'Don't trust any foreigner,' muttered Gus.

'Shut up a minute, Gus, and listen.'

'Well, I don't see how my blurting out about your trip in the pub has been any help,' he grumbled.

'Well, it might have because it's probably narrowed down our field to this particular area. Of those ten, only three live within a hundred miles of here, so those are the three we should start with. If we don't get anywhere, we'll have to think all over again.'

'Who are they then? If I'm going to help, I'd better know their names.'

'I'll have to double check in my address book. But the three I can think of are Mr Gerald Rankin at Blandford Forum, Chalmers, of course, at his country place near Bridport, and Vivian Stone from Bournemouth.'

'What are you going to do – ring 'em all up and ask them if they've stolen any toys recently?'

I felt like wringing his neck, because he had realized the predicament. I got up and went to the door. 'I'm going to take your advice: I'm going to sleep on it.'

To my surprise, I slept like a top and woke up feeling fairly chipper for a man who had a sudden debt of £22,000 and the sword of Damocles hanging over his means of making any money. For a moment or two I missed Deborah – but only for a moment or two.

I made Bing and myself some breakfast, then went through the post I hadn't had the courage to open when I got back. Besides one of the usual from the Inland Revenue, a water rate final demand and an electricity bill, the rest was about par for that many days away: two letters protesting that the shop was closed too often, three offering 'playworn' Dinky toys that they, no doubt, expected the earth for but which wouldn't fetch a penny from a serious collector, and one from a school teacher in Fyfe, who had been given my name by a cousin of his in Dorchester. He was after any Minics I might have for sale. I only had about three left for sale, as I was a keen collector of the small clockwork cars, buses and lorries myself. I scribbled a reply, and went out to post it.

When I got back, I took a quick glance at the local paper, which had just arrived. This was a big mistake, for amongst the myriad other bits of local news, it carried quite lengthy coverage of the Spitfire debate at St Sebastian's Church Hall, and my chipperness rating plummetted to zero again. I needed reminding of Mr Treasure like Lynmouth needs memories of flood waters. To make matters worse, the phone then rang. It was Chalmers without any charm. Just an ultimatum: find the toys in the next four weeks or come up with the money instead. There was a little extra inducement as well, if I didn't find the toys – something about 'never being able to deal again'. Bing got out of the way smartly as I grabbed my address book, and went out to the car. Old blue eyes knew what he was doing – which was more than I did.

I took the road to Blandford Forum. It's a pretty road, but I didn't see much of the scenery – just the end of the line. Gerald Rankin's house was bigger than I had imagined it, even with a name like Purbeck Hall, and you could have run the British Grand Prix on its driveway. Even when I had pulled the bell handle, I had no idea what I was going to say when someone answered the sepulchral dinging.

A woman I took to be a maid answered the door. I introduced myself as a fellow toy collector, and could I please see Mr Rankin? She went away, and a moment later, led me into a drawing-room, that could have housed the mammoth Howard Hughes flying boat with acres to spare. Mr Rankin was not as I remembered from his visits to my shop. Relaxed in his own home, he seemed twice as nice and ten times more unlikely to have robbed a cross-Channel ferry. And what's more, he had an impressive tan, on which his greying military moustache seemed to sit a little incongruously.

His first words set the seal on my visit. 'You're lucky to find me home, Mr Marklin. My wife and I only flew in last night from South Africa. Spent two months there with my daughter and her family. Ever been?'

I smiled and said 'No', anxious now for the abortive visit to end as soon as politely possible. But Mr Rankin had other

26

thoughts in mind, like showing me the family photographs from Cape Town, taking me round the house, giving me the rare privilege of seeing his antique toy collection (which was magnificent – over five thousand pieces, nearly all mint – but I wasn't in the mood) and entertaining me to coffee and biscuits. He was the very essence of the perfect host, and I felt the very essence of the worst form of rat for refusing a walk round the grounds, and not hiding my impatience to leave. He seemed genuine enough, and it was pretty unlikely he had organized a toy heist from as far away as the land of Apartheid. But then, that could be the cleverness of it all. A perfect alibi in black and white. I asked him what airline he flew.

'British Airways,' he replied, a little nonplussed by my interest, and I felt a rat once more. But I would have to check, just in case my vibes were letting me down. Then I touched my forelock and left.

I headed south to Bournemouth, where Mr Vivian Stone had his address off Branksome Chine, an exclusive part of the town where even to breathe costs you money. I had been there before, delivering a Marklin Junkers 52 aircraft in mint condition, so I knew what to expect. Even so, the conspicuous opulence was still hard to take. Mr Stone's jewellery business had to be doing rather better than awfully well. Like having at least fifty Liz Taylors as clients, for a start. The electric gate opened at the touch of a button and I drove in.

He answered the gold plated knocker himself. I had refused to repeat what I had done on my previous visit – inadvertently playing selections from *Fiddler on the Roof* in chimes by pushing the doorbell button. Mr Stone was around forty-five, thinnish, with silver-grey hair, and the short-sighted look that comes from always counting money. He didn't waste any time (I guess because time *was* money) and soon whisked me through the house and outside again to his swimming pool, beside which lay someone a little younger but a good deal more developed, nay, overdeveloped, dressed in flesh and bikini bottoms. She was lucky – it was the first really warm day of the year. He ignored her. She ignored him – and me. I guess that made her his wife.

'You were lucky to . . .'

I laughed and interrupted, 'I know, I know. I'm lucky to find you in.'

27

He looked puzzled, then went on, 'Never mind. I've just come back for some lunch and a swim. Then I have to be off again. Can I get you a drink?'

'That would be nice. A Campari and soda, please.'

He mixed one from a gilt trolley loaded with all sorts of booze, then poured himself some orange juice.

'Never drink when I'm working,' he said. 'Got something that would interest me, Mr Marklin? Is that why you called?'

Mrs Stone turned over to toast the other side – the top side – and, besides other things, I saw where some of his money had gone. And every finger was aglitter from podgy knuckle to fleshy first joint. The bikini top still lay by her paperback, which, surprisingly, was *Barchester Towers* by Anthony Trollope. I decided to go in the deep end.

'I've got the chance of a very fine collection from the south of France.' I watched his eyes carefully. But nothing seemed to be registering. I went on, 'Eleven tinplate toys, which I'm told are mint. Mainly from the twenties.'

'Go on, Mr Marklin, but they sound pricey to me,' he said, sipping his orange juice. Nothing yet.

'Yes, they are. But they're quite unique: JEPS; a Marklin battleship, turn of the century, an original Citroën taxi cab with basketweave sides....'

The lady began pouring oil on what once were assets, and I took a large gulp of my Campari.

'Now I *know* they're too pricey, Mr Marklin. Pity, but I can't be in the market right now. I'm just opening another store in Geneva and all my money is tied up. Great shame, isn't it, Mrs Stone?' He was one of those men who addresses his wife as if they were merely acquaintances. Maybe these two were. She nodded, and plucked a lip salve out of thin air, and began a life preserving exercise on her mouth. I couldn't stand much more of this, yet I had really learned almost nothing. Either he was telling the truth, or he was an accomplished liar. And his wife gave nothing away. She probably never did.

I finished my Campari, and made my farewells. Vivian Stone asked me if I could find my own way out as he was going to take a dip. I gave the whole jaded Hollywood scene a last scan with my Cinemascope eye and, frustrated as hell, walked back to the Beetle. I saw a Panther de Ville displaying its Bugatti-like rear out of his threesome garage, and snuggling beside it what looked like a Ferrari. But his electric gates had shut behind me by the time I could be certain of its colour. It was, surprise, surprise, red. But then most Ferraris are, damn it.

I went via Sandbanks and took the ferry route home. Even though it only clanked and jangled its four-minute way on its huge chains across the inlet to Poole Harbour within sight of Brownsea Island, it always gave me a sense of adventure, a lingering left-over from my childhood days of wonder. But today even that feeling was muted as I stood by the rail under the shadow of what could be in store for me unless . . . This morning had taught me next to nothing. So now I only had twenty-seven mornings left.

I got back in the car and drove off the ramp and along the slim road between the dunes. The first holiday-makers were already busying themselves trying to find lots of things not to do : mainly young people enjoying that sexual springtime before they start having kids. I envied them. Not that I have any kids, but the fact they didn't know, or probably care yet about, what lay ahead. I pulled the Beetle off the road, into the entrance of one of the car-parks that seemed the least occupied. I needed time to think.

Gerald Rankin I felt I probably had to discount, but I would ring British Airways just to check. He certainly did not come across as enough of a fanatic to act in such an ungentlemanly fashion as to stoop to robbery, nor enough of a sadist as to stoop to the trick of substituting plastic Camaros.

But then I didn't think Vivian Stone would either – substitute Camaros, I mean. Maybe he was up to the robbery and he just might be fanatical enough, but it took a touch of class to bother to buy eleven Macao-made Camaros and drop them into the boxes instead. And Mr Vivian Stone had everything except class. What's more, I bet he would think it a wicked waste of money to shell out for plastic substitutes when he could get away with leaving nothing. But I could be wrong. He might be cleverer than I thought and be pulling a double bluff – and he did have a red Ferrari in his garage. I kicked myself at having been so obsessed with the girl on the *autoroute* that I never checked her car's number plates. I somehow don't think Roger Moore will ever play me in a movie.

The more I sat there in the dunes, the more depressed I became, despite the May sun through the open top of the Beetle. Even if I was pretty certain someone like Vivian Stone had the toys, I did not see how I was going to prove it, or how I was going to get possession of them. And it could still be Chalmers himself playing a double or treble game, or, indeed, anyone in this whole wide world who had a crush on old clockwork relics. Still, I had to start somewhere, and Rankin and Stone had seemed the most likely lads for investigation in this neck of the woods. I started up the Beetle, U-turned in the almost empty car-park, and went back to the junction with the ferry road.

I waited for a Rolls-Royce Silver Cloud to go by, which I saw was being driven by a rather striking girl with violent-coloured hair. I pulled out and kept behind it. (Men are such dreamers.) As we swept along towards Studland, I noticed the rear of the car was somewhat different from normal Silver Clouds. It had a rear window that lifted up in addition to the boot lid – a kind of millionaire's hatchback. I had seen one some years before at a motor show. It was a conversion by an English coachbuilding firm called Harold Radford, who produced it for the huntin', shootin' and fishin' set. Bloomin' nice, if you could afford it. I decided I couldn't right now (either the car or the girl) and pulled off to park behind my little 'Toy Emporium' – that's the rather twee name dreamt up by my ex-wife who is still in advertising. The Silver Cloud swept on westwards.

Bing would not speak to me when I got in, for one of his passions is riding in the car. I made myself a rather sloppy omelette, but forswore any frozen chips as I had put on quite a few unwanted pounds at the Colombe D'Or. Then I opened up shop, and sat dejectedly behind the little counter without a plan in my head. At least this way I might make a few pounds from local punters while I tried to sort something out.

Small, relatively inexpensive, die-cast toys were the backbone of the old toy business – the kind of things everyone had as a child, however poor: Dinkys, Corgis, Spot-Ons, Lesney Matchbox, and early Yesteryears were a particularly hot line. I had a mass of them, ranging from a pound or two up to around £1,000 for a pre-Dinky ss1 from Hornby. I divided my stock into pre-war and post-war on labelled shelves, so that any customer could identify immediately with his own particular nostalgia rating. Larger and more expensive toys were in glass cabinets, and very rare items were listed in my stock sheets available on demand. These toys I kept secreted in my attic or over at Gus Tribble's. There's no point in making a burglar's life too easy – which, come to think of it, was just what I had done on my trip to the south of France.

The afternoon proved to be not exactly a seller's paradise. As always there were quite a few time-wasters who just wanted to touch and stare. However, I did sell a mint boxed fifties Dinky De Soto for £18, an unboxed, rather chipped 39 series Buick for £12, (both to one forty-five-year-old customer) and a Dinky aeroplane, a Republic Thunderbolt fighter made until the company's demise in 1979, for £14 – a reasonable appreciation rate over its original price of £1.95 in 1979. It's a funny old business. I worked out that this left only £21,956 to find.

My suicide was forestalled by the phone. I prayed it wouldn't be Deborah after money again. It wasn't. It was Gus with a drop of good news to plop into the maelstrom of my mind, though unfortunately, not about the lost toys. It was more of the Spitfire saga. Apparently, he had heard from a friend of his in Swanage, who was a good boy and went to church, that the Vicar of St Sebastian's had just received a letter from the aged mother of PO Redfern, who lived in what I still call Rhodesia. In it, she stated that she had just heard about the controversy over the proposed dig for the Spitfire and wished it to go ahead so that her son could have a proper burial in hallowed ground.

I said to Gus, didn't that now settle the matter our way? He replied that he thought the Vicar was terrified of Mr Randolph Treasure, and that he would only sanction the dig if the rich landowner agreed to drop his objections. I said that was ridiculous. Gus said that was life. I said we can't put up with that. Gus said he thought he had an answer. I said what, and he said I should go and see Treasure, try to persuade him to drop his objections and threaten to call another public meeting if he didn't. I said I'd got enough on my plate at the moment. Gus said how selfish could anyone get, and how he'd always reckoned I was a kind of regular guy and would always fight for what I believed in, and never let go. I said I

31

wasn't going to be talked to like that. So he said what was I going to do about it? So I said I would go and see Treasure. And that's what I did, because I'd suddenly remembered something else.

Four

Next morning that 'old Victorian thing near Lulworth', as Gus had described it, turned out to be quite an assembly of stones. Victorian folly it may have been, but it was still quite impressive with pointed steeples at every turn and abbey-like windows with sharp tops. And it was a hell of a size with, as I discovered later, around twelve bedrooms, four bathrooms, five reception rooms, an indoor swimming pool and a jacuzzi big enough for a regiment. And then there was the nine-hole golf course and a drive almost as big as Mr Rankin's. I parked my yellow Beetle, and was admitted to the house by a sour-faced woman who said she was the housekeeper. I just hoped Mr Treasure would not say I was lucky to find him in.

He didn't. He just asked me how the toy business was, and had I had any more Marklins recently. I said I hadn't, and had he? He said unfortunately, no, they were a bit thin on the ground. I agreed and he offered me a drink. For some reason, I declined. There was something about Mr Treasure that made me think twice about accepting anything from him. He would have been a star turn in the time of the Borgias, and within his own stone walls he came over, somehow, as even more frightening than in your average church hall. He poured himself a large straight Scotch, and sat down opposite me.

'If it's not toys you've come about, Mr Marklin, what can I do for you?' He leaned forward, his hairy hands clasping his glass as if I was about to filch it from him. This man was certainly not the type to let go.

'It's about the Spitfire, and Pilot Officer Redfern.'

He suddenly sat back in his chintz armchair and guffawed as only a certain inbred and expensively educated type of Englishman can.

'Oh, that! Mr Marklin, all that controversy is dead and buried. We had the vote at St Sebastian's. . . .'

'There's been a resurrection, Mr Treasure. Redfern's mother is still alive in Rhodesia, and she has written to ask for the dig to go ahead, and for her son to be properly buried.'

Treasure sat up straight again, and took a measured sip of his Famous Grouse. I could detect his mind working overtime.

'I'm sure the Vicar would not want the whole issue raised all over again, Mr Marklin. The affair has caused enough local trouble as it is.'

I looked at those hairy hands again, and decided the Vicar would be putty in them.

'But his mother is his next of kin, Mr Treasure. And she wants him to have a decent burial in hallowed ground. The Vicar's duty, if I may say so, is to her and not to the public meeting that did not realize she was still alive.'

Treasure, I could see, was not a man whose judgements were usually questioned. His grip on his glass tightened and I was pretty certain he was pretending it was me he was throttling. He looked me directly in the eyes.

'What's your interest in it all, Mr Marklin? Hoping to filch some poor bits off the Spitfire to sell to some aviation nut?'

I didn't rise to his taunt.

'Mr Treasure, some friends and I would like, as you must be aware, to start a small museum to commemorate the part Warmwell played in the defence of the country. Every part of the Spitfire recovered would go into that museum, which would be run in conjunction with the South Western Historical Aviation Society. The museum would be non profit-making. That is my interest in it all, as you put it.'

He got up and began pacing around the chairs and settees as if waiting for feeding time.

'I can't quite believe you, Mr Marklin. It's too altruistic to be true. And what's more, if PO Redfern's mother had written to the Vicar, he would have been in touch with me.'

I couldn't resist it. 'Why? Does he owe you something?'

Treasure stopped in his tracks, and carefully put his glass down on a sidetable. It saved him crushing it to smithereens.

'I think, Mr Marklin, you have now outstayed your welcome. I'll get Mrs Fitzpayne to see you out.' He made for the door.

'Don't be so hasty, Mr Treasure. I answered your question about what was in it for me if the dig went ahead. Now I want to know what's in it for you if it doesn't.'

34

For a split second his eyes wavered. 'After all,' I continued, 'you pleaded on Pilot Officer Redfern's personal behalf in the church hall. Now surely, he would want to obey his own mother's wishes rather than yours.'

I knew I would get no verbal response, but his eyes had been enough. He bellowed for Mrs Fitzpayne, and I heard footsteps outside the door. But is was no sour-faced harridan who made her entrance. It was the girl with the violent hair from the Harold Radford Rolls-Royce. It wasn't just me she took by surprise.

'What are you doing back, Arabella?' he muttered, quietly.

She swaggered into the room. 'I felt like it, that's all. It's not warm enough on the beach.' She came across to me, I was glad to see. 'And who's this rather interesting new face?' She held out her red-tipped hand. I took it – it was no hardship.

'Marklin – Peter Marklin.' I looked her in the long-lashed eyes. She winked the left one.

'I'm Arabella, as you'll have gathered. Full title – Arabella Donna Trench. My enemies call be Belladonna. My friends call me often.'

I liked this girl; she was as corny as I was, only prettier.

Treasure liked me even less now, which was mutual.

'I was just seeing Mr Marklin to the door. He's a busy man. Sells toys for a living, would you believe.'

She turned to him. 'Don't knock it, Randolph. You collect toys – you're crazy about them. You just don't like anyone knowing how infatuated . . .'

He almost ran to her and grasped her wrist. 'That's enough.' His voice made it quite plain he meant what he said. 'Mr Marklin is going right now, aren't you Mr Marklin?'

I wondered what she saw in him, beyond a vast house, a Rolls and all the money you could throw around.

'I'm going, Mr Treasure, aren't I, Mr Treasure?' I mimicked him, and Arabella smiled. She was definitely growing on me. 'But I think I'll be back, Mr Treasure. And I won't just be talking about Spitfires. I just may throw in a battleship or two.'

I looked for his reaction, but Arabella was in the way. Soon Mrs Fitzpayne had me down the steps and into the drive. As I left I caught a glimpse of a Silver Cloud in a thatched barn. It had the Harold Radford conversion, and, beside it, was what I took to be Arabella's own little car, a silver Golf convertible. I had a feeling it would be useful if our two Volkswagens could get together, and we could let our tops down.

I did not go straight home. It was not very often I came Lulworth way, so I dropped down to the Cove to grab a coffee and a think. The day was on the grey side, so the horse-shoe shaped pebble beach was not crowded. In fact, there were only about ten or so people around, and half of those looked like locals. I could hear the Army booming away on the hills, pretending the Russians had landed. It annoys me that the military choose places of natural beauty for their unnatural games. I was the only person in the tiny café having coffee, and the proprietress looked very annoyed when I left and did not buy as much as a shell or a picture postcard.

I strolled amongst the pebbles and tried to take stock. In no time at all, I was kicking myself for having put Treasure's back up so early. If I had been a little more diplomatic, I might have led him on to the odd indiscretion or two. But then, as my ex-wife would tell you, diplomacy isn't exactly my strongest card. And patience isn't either. I went on to kick Arabella for interrupting us, and then I withdrew the kicking as I worked out that she could be my way into Treasure if I played my other cards right. After all, she seemed vaguely interested in me, I thought. But maybe she was interested in anything that looked more or less like a man. Don't get me wrong, I'm not actually too bad looking. On a dark night and with the right cigar, I am told I look a little like Clint Eastwood. Mind you, I was only told it once, and she did have what looked suspiciously like spectacles made with glass pebbles.

I sat down on a grassy tuft, and looked out over the bay. It was one of those still grey days, when the flat sea seems to merge with the flat sky, a perfect day for playing ducks and drakes when one was a kid. But I was grown up now. And anyway, the water was too far away.

I wondered what Treasure's motive could be for not excavating the Spitfire, for it was now pretty obvious that PO Redfern's wishes didn't come into it. Was the Vicar doing a shady deal with him, on selling or developing that bit of Church land? But he would have the Church Commissioners to contend with, and they could not all be corrupt too. Or could they? Or was Treasure a man who never liked to be beaten – a case of a grossly oversize ego? That certainly fitted his character, in which case I would have to find a way of giving him a graceful 'out', if that Spitfire was ever to see the light of day.

I was also kicking myself for not having included Treasure on my original list of suspects for the toy theft, when I saw a familiar outline chugging into the bay. I waited until it almost reached the tiny jetty, then got up and strolled over. He didn't see me at first, busy as he was tying up the boat.

'Hello, Gus. What contraband are you dealing in now?'

He looked up immediately, then relaxed as he saw who it was.

'Oh, it's you,' he said with relief.

'Who did you think it was? Her Majesty's Customs?'

He didn't laugh. Old Gus had made the odd clandestine trip across the Channel before now. In fact, I never enquired too deeply into where Gus's sudden flushes of money came from. He didn't probe into my private affairs, except by invitation; I didn't into his. However, this time he did let me into what he was doing.

'Old Mrs Blunt next door asked if I could pick up a settee and two chairs she bought last week from a lady who died. Got 'em cheap, she did. They're too big to go on my Popular, so I brought the boat round. Care to give me a hand?'

I was somewhat amazed he had not at least tried to get them on the roof of his car, as he had reckoned it strong enough for a piano, but kept my mouth shut and went off with him up the little road to a cottage with the 'For Sale' notice in the garden. It took us three-quarters of an hour to lug the stuff, piece by piece, down to his boat and stow it on board. How Gus had intended to do it on his own, I had no idea. But Gus is a great optimist at heart; he always reckons something will turn up – and I did.

When we had done, Gus sat on one of the faded uncut moquette armchairs with the tell-tale loose threads from a cat perpetually sharpening its claws (Bing did the same, despite having his own bit of wood precisely for that purpose), brought out a hip flask from his pocket and offered it to me. I took a swig, and then looked around for my breath. God knows where Gus gets whisky like that. The Devil, most likely. I relaxed back in the other chair, and we must have looked a prize pair of idiots in our floating sitting-room.

'What you been doing then? Seen Treasure?' Gus asked, taking another swig with no apparent after-effect.

'Yes.'

'Win him over our way, did you?'

'No.'

'Waste of petrol, then?'

'No, not really. I may have learnt one or two little things about Mr Treasure. He's still dead against digging up the Spitfire, but I can't yet fathom the reason. It's certainly not to let Redfern rest peacefully in his aeroplane.'

'Strange man,' was Gus's only comment.

'Secondly, Gus, a girlfriend of his let slip that he is a fanatical toy collector, which I hadn't realized. I had known him before from the occasional phone call enquiring about Marklins, but I didn't suspect how deep his interest really is.'

'So he's a suspect now, is he?'

I nodded.

'Don't want too many suspects, do you? Never get through them all.' He chuckled to himself.

Really, Gus could be very irritating at times.

'Gus,' I enquired, ignoring his last remark, 'what do you know about Treasure? What's his background? After all, you've lived here all your life, and I haven't.'

Gus took another swig. 'Don't know much really. He has lived round about for donkey's years. Moved into that Victorian thing about ten years ago, when it was restored. Used to live over Wareham way before that.'

He made himself more comfortable in his chair. A holiday-maker on the jetty pointed us both out to his girlfriend. They sniggered and turned away. I don't blame them.

'Don't know much about him, otherwise. He inherited a lot of money from his father, I believe, then made a bit more himself, buying and selling houses and land and the like. Clever bugger. Not so clever with women though, I hear. Had a wife much younger than himself once. She ran off with one of her lovers to Switzerland, I think, or some place like that. That was not so long ago. But he's always got women around him, so they say. Not too difficult is it, when you live in a dirty great house and ride in a Rolls?'

He laughed and the boat rocked.

'How long ago? The wife running off, I mean?'

'Three, four years, I reckon. Something like that.'

I wondered if Gus had got it wrong, for I could not see a man like Treasure putting up with any wife of his having lovers. But then, maybe he didn't know until afterwards. That's often the case.

'Didn't he try to get her back?'

'How would I know? Might have, might not. Anyway, I can't sit around like this all day doing nothing, and nor can you, I'd have thought, my old dear.'

He got up and made it plain he was off. As he began fiddling with the old engine under the hatch, he mumbled, 'I'm not being much help, am I? What would you like me to do? All you've got to do is say.'

'I will. Thanks. When the time comes.'

He got the engine reluctantly to start.

'Got any ideas, have you?' He had an uncanny way of reading my mind.

'Maybe, I'll let you know.'

I got off the boat onto the jetty.

'Thanks for lugging those old things.' He waved his hand.

'Pleasure.' I watched him until he disappeared from sight around the curve of the cove, then went back to my Beetle in the car-park. Somehow, I felt a good deal better for my little visit to Lulworth.

I grabbed some lunch in a pub in Wareham, then went home, fed Bing, and opened up shop. After all, I still had a living to make when and if this whole calamitous affair came to an end. I sat behind the counter for a bit, and then made a phone call to a mate of mine from my advertising days, who worked on the *Western Gazette*, to see if he had any more gen on Treasure. He said he could not look it out right then, but would ring me back the next day. I said I wanted to know everything there was to know. He said he knew what I meant, but newspapers weren't MI5, and he would do his best. So that was that.

Then I dialled Heathrow, and eventually got through to a Welsh lady at British Airways, who put me on to a man with a Scottish accent, who put me on to a dim-witted girl who made Goldie Hawn seem like Einstein. After five minutes chatting to her, I'd almost forgotten why I'd rung in the first place. In the end, she asked me to try another number. I replied I loved her too, and tried it. Eventually a man with an Indian accent ferreted out the information I was after. I was kind of relieved to learn

39

that Mr and Mrs Gerald Rankin had indeed not returned from South Africa until last weekend. They had been away two months. Now, unless Rankin had spies permanently in the Black Lion waiting for Gus to blurt out my every move and intention, it looked as if I would have to, as they say, eliminate him from my enquiries – at least at this stage of the game.

The afternoon turned out to be like the curate's egg. The good bit centred round my shop, the bad bit round my ex-wife. I sold a mint Dinky Toy Shetland flying boat of 1949, in its original box, for my asking price of £350 with no haggling at all. A rather scruffy guy in a raincoat peeled off £285 in oncers for a pre-war Dinky Horlicks van. And a sixties Schuco BMW Formula Two went for £15 to an eighteen-year-old. But the big news was not what I was selling, but what I bought. An old lady tottered in and shakily unwrapped some old newspapers to reveal a superb Wells thirties Rolls-Royce in blue and cream tinplate, and a Distler twenties tinplate racing car. Found them in her attic and did I want them? I pretended I wasn't very interested and got them for £15 each, knowing I could sell the Rolls for £300 or more, and the Distler for maybe £450 – £500. Aren't I a rat? Not really. I forgot to tell you, the old lady came in a chauffeur-driven Daimler.

Now for the bad bit. Dear Deborah rang soon after I put the phone down on the *Western Gazette*. Sounded a bit upset (but then she normally does) and said could I see her because she needed someone to talk to about a problem she had, and that I had always been a good listener and given sound advice, if nothing else. I explained I had loads to do and huge problems of my own, but then she began crying and I began weakening, and her problems flooded mine out.

She came over at seven, but at least had the decency to bring a bottle of Graves. We had been apart now four years, and divorced two, but each time I saw her again rekindled the old original flame a little – not enough to cause first degree burns, but a singe nevertheless.

She entered the house as usual, as if we'd never been apart, and flopped into a chair as if she'd just been out shopping for an hour or two. I opened the Graves and filled a couple of glasses.

'Bottoms up,' I said, and she smiled, remembering the old joke we used to play whenever I said that in the old days. The memory excited me for a split second, and I looked across at her. She was still a pretty attractive woman; dark hair framing high cheek bones and a very generous mouth – generous in every sense. Perhaps the eyes had less hope in them now. Comes from having crows-feet move in next door, and too many temporary lovers. But it's what she walks with that have always been nothing short of sensational. And they reach to her armpits. She crossed them deliberately in front of me. I crossed my own in self-defence.

After a bit of banter about how well we were all looking, and how was Bing (she had always hated him and did he know it) and was she still enjoying advertising (yes, she was – a full Account Executive now) and how was her Bournemouth flat (very light and airy) and did I still have that weird old car (I didn't ask whether she meant the Beetle or the derelict old Daimler), we gradually got around to the point of her visit. By then she was three drinks into the game.

'Peter, I hate to ask you, but could you give me a loan?' She leaned forward, very intimately, in her chair and was taken aback when I burst into laughter.

'My dear Deborah, you've chosen just about the worst time in the world to try that on me.'

She looked very hurt, until I explained my little dilemma, which I did, leaving out all the detail, locations and names of dramatis personae in case her knowing too many of the facts got me into even deeper trouble. Her mouth is generous with words too, and often loud (one of the nails in our marriage's coffin), and I didn't want all the details going round the whole locality like wildfire. Wouldn't be good for business.

'. . . so there you are, my love. It's more a case of "could you lend me twenty thousand quid?"'

She looked heartbroken. I think more for herself than for me, but I gave her the benefit of the doubt.

'Oh Peter, I'm terribly sorry.' She leaned over and took my hand. My heart skipped a beat, but got back on tempo. I got up, ostensibly to open another bottle of Graves, which I just happened to have.

'Anyway, Deborah, how the hell are you in financial trouble? You're doing well in that Bournemouth agency. You've got your own flat, your own car. You don't live extravagantly, unless you've changed recently. You've no dependents to support. So

41

. . . ?' I looked at her, and then suddenly realized what the answer must be. She was like that.

She didn't reply for a minute, then it all came out in a flood, with appropriate tears. '. . . he said it was to set up this printing and design operation which would soon be in profit. I believed him, and took out a second mortgage on the flat, and sold that sapphire pendant you gave me, and some shares that Father had left. And I loved him so, Peter, and he seemed so wonderful. I wanted him to have everything. . . .'

Well, she succeeded in her wish. He'd taken everything. And I felt very, very sorry for her. Deborah has not had the greatest luck with men. There is a childlike naïvety about her, which will always land her in trouble. Yet it is that same naïvety that makes her devilishly attractive at times. God knows why she likes advertising so much. It is hardly a sentimental business, and the childlike do not usually survive for long. Or wish to. And it was my growing dislike for, and her growing like for, advertising, that had split our marriage further apart. I took her in my arms and realized I had been without something soft for far too long.

We stopped short of the whole hog – just. Neither of us really desired that. We just wanted to prove we could still raise it if we wanted to. And the warmth helped us both. And the wine, of course, played a not inconsiderable role.

After that, she cooked me an amalgam of bits and pieces she found in the fridge, and we had choc-ices from the freezer for afters. Graves is the connoisseur's recommendation for choc-ices. It goes down a treat.

Then we got round to comfy chit-chat, both sitting on the sofa. I began to feel very sleepy, and began nodding off as she rambled nicely on. But then, out of the blue, she said something that got through to me, and I had to get her to repeat it.

'. . . all I said was that Derek is luckier with his boyfriends then I am with mine.'

I sat bolt upright. 'No, not that bit. Before that.'

'Oh, you mean when I said this rich guy took him out to all the best places. No expense spared.'

'You said something else.'

'Oh, it was only a joke, Peter. Derek said his boyfriend was a real treasure because that was his name. Was that the bit?'

'Yes, that was the bit. I take it he meant he's a Mr Treasure?'

'Yes. Why are you so interested all of a sudden? Going queer in your old age?'

I couldn't tell her. But I suddenly saw Treasure in an entirely new light. 'No, it's just that someone was talking of a Mr Treasure the other day. Lives in a Victorian extravagance near Lulworth. Gathered he liked lots of girls.'

'So he does, so Derek says. And he doesn't mind as long as old Treasure doesn't go out with any other boys. Derek's a strictly one man Art Director, faithful as they come, silly idiot.'

I remembered Derek of old – talented at the lay-out pad, but pretty sad otherwise. It didn't take much to know which one of the two lovers was the dominant partner. I thought for a moment. Then decided it was worth taking the risk.

'Listen, Deborah. There's a little something you might be able to do for me . . . .'

Five

I went down to the beach early next morning, immediately the post had arrived. Bing came with me, on a lead of course. There wasn't a soul about, which suited me. Suited us, I should say, as Bing did not like crowds either. And Bing hadn't read the post.

Both the letters were depressing, one in particular. The first, from Chalmers, was to be expected. Just a repeat in writing of the terms he had stated on the phone – like, get back the toys or return his money, all in just over three weeks from now. But it was the second one that disturbed me most. It was from France, from Monsieur Vincent. In astonishingly neat handwriting, he just said he hoped I had got back all right, and that Mr Chalmers liked the toys. I suddenly realized that with all my preoccupation with a possible huge financial debt, I had completely forgotten that the toys weren't just tinplate objects, but a living, breathing part of Monsieur Vincent's soul. I had, in fact, lost his brother, his mother, his past . . . I wasn't very proud of myself, so I was hoping the sea air would blow some of my guilt away.

Bing and I walked one complete length of Studland beach, from the rock pools to the nudist end. Well, that's not quite true. I walked it all. Bing only walked two thirds of it and then I had to carry him. I could understand it: his legs are a tiny bit shorter than mine, though he does have two more. We finished up with the crabs and shrimps by the rock pools, with the old wrecked World War II gun emplacement grinning at us in the background. I sat on a rock and pondered, while Bing watched the tiny crabs, who were wondering where all the big blue sea had gone. I knew how they felt.

I soon realized it wasn't just the letters that were depressing me. For when I analysed my situation, it was clear I had no real leads at all to the lost toys, not a shred of real evidence against anybody. Rankin seemed to be as pure as the driven snow, or was he ? Vivian Stone, crooked though he no doubt was, did not really seem the type to get involved in a toy heist that, if discovered, could lead to the collapse of every one of his jewellery stores from Bournemouth to Tel-Aviv. Yet he obviously was acquisitive, and he did have a red Ferrari. But his wife was certainly not Quinky from St Paul de Vence.

If Monsieur Vincent was the thief, then I knew as much about people as I did about nuclear physics. Nevertheless, every good whodunnit I had ever read ended up with the one you least expect being the baddie. So Monsieur Vincent had to remain on my list, as a Riviera con-man with a beautiful mistress with a taste for fast cars.

And then there was the man I had come to love to hate from just seeing him twice. No, that's not true : I disliked him the first instant I saw him in the church hall. Randolph Treasure. Rich, spoilt, arrogant, overbearing, clever, emotional and ambidextrous. I tried, unsuccessfully, to separate out my envy and my anger. He could have done it, certainly, and his girlfriend had said he was fanatical about toys. And yet he was not on my list of great and avid toy collectors. I knew of him only as an occasional purchaser, so it did not seem all that likely that, fanatical by nature or not, he would have gone hellbent after the Vincent collection. Or would he ? I was getting very confused. And that's without bothering about Treasure's attitude to recovering the Spitfire, which I could not fathom at all. I looked over and saw Bing had flipped a tiny crab out of a pool and onto its back with his paw. I had a feeling Treasure might do that to me one day, unless I could get something on him first.

I was about to get up and go when I saw a figure back over where the little road drops down to the steps onto the beach. A girl figure. She stopped near the water's edge and quickly doffed her dress, revealing a dramatically shaped body in a whisper of a bikini. The next moment she was in the water and swimming powerfully. I admired her courage at this time of year. I'd seen enough to know who she was, and that she was even more attractive than I had at first thought. I was about to pick up Bing and move over to where she had left her dress and sandals, when I changed my mind. Somehow I felt I needed to know a little more about Mr Treasure from other sources before I began drilling Arabella's little well. But I had the feeling she had come bathing on this particular beach for a reason, otherwise Lul-

45

worth Cove would have been her obvious choice for an early-morning swim. One day soon I would probably know the reason, but not quite yet. I gathered up Bing and crept quietly off the beach and back up the hill while her delectable body was still being kissed by the waves. Hell, I had will-power.

My old mate at the *Western Gazette* came through just before eleven, while I was sitting in my shop waiting for something to turn up – anything. I took down what he had to say on an old advertising agency pad. This is what I wrote:

> Randolph Louis (!) T. Born Ilminster, Som. 1930. Street Court School, Barrington, then Trenton. Oxford. Christ Church. Law. No recorded Nat. Service. Married once. '75. Veronica Charlotte Telling. Left '81. Rumour – to lover. Lausanne. Three farms. 1700 acres. Lloyds underwriter. Clubs: Reform. RAC. President of S. Dorset Soc. of Marksmen, (?) and Historic Homes Trust. Interests. Antiques. And Sex.

I'd better point out that the *Western Gazette* didn't add the last two words. I did.

In between selling two mediocre Dinkies to a taxi-driver, and a rather nice Tootsietoy La Salle coupe to a hotel owner from Swanage (£135 – not bad), I read and re-read my notes. I decided I would like to meet Mrs Veronica Charlotte Treasure. She, of all people, would know Treasure backwards, and in all sorts of directions. But if she was still in Lausanne the prospect was extremely remote. I did not have the time or the money to go hunting for her.

So I did not seem to be really any further forward. And if Treasure was really my sworn enemy, then I did not like the sound of the S. Dorset Society of Marksmen. I'd rather he had been nutty about wild flowers. And I was annoyed that Treasure had been to Oxford, of all places, and to a better and richer college than mine. (I spent three delirious years at Exeter College, physically only half a mile away from Christ Church but a million miles away socially.) I had only just about heard of Trenton – it was one of those minor, yet expensive public schools where you only go if your father went too. His prep school I'd never heard of. So much for all that.

I now had only Deborah to rely on, and I was just beginning to think I missed a trick not doing a *From Here to Eternity* with dear Arabella on the beach when, would you believe, Mr Rankin came into the shop. His tan still glowed, lucky man.

'Just passing,' he extended his hand, 'a reciprocal visit, you might say, from a confirmed old toy buff.'

I asked after his wife. She was fine, apparently, but missing the heat of South Africa. I couldn't tell him that, right now, I found England quite hot enough for me. Soon he came around to 'the real point of my visit, Mr Marklin.' He fingered his pepper-and-salt colonel's moustache.

'Toys?' I smiled.

'Battleships,' he replied. And my smile disappeared, for Mr Rankin's extensive toy collection had embraced cars, buses, lorries, aircraft, tractors, you name it – everything except ships. Why the interest all of a sudden? My mind went immediately to the prize item in the missing Vincent collection.

'I didn't know you were interested in ships, Mr Rankin,' I said in as nonchalant a voice as possible.

'I haven't been up to now,' he replied, strolling around my shop, gazing at my stock, almost like a professional valuer earning his crust. (It's funny with collectors. Even if they've got the very same toys as another collector they'll often be just as interested in looking at them as different toys they haven't yet acquired. And certainly Rankin had almost everything I'd got in my shop.)

I came out from behind the counter. 'What's tempting you to change?' I probed gently.

He chuckled. 'Oh, when you've got as many toys as I have, Mr Marklin, it's hard to add any more decent pieces to round out the collection. So I thought I'd get into boats. Only tinplate, of course.'

'Of course,' I agreed, as if one would be struck dead for buying a ship in any other material.

'Bought a new Sutcliffe Valiant battleship yesterday. Found it still in stock in a toy shop in Bournemouth,' he beamed. 'It's a start; and a friend of mine is selling me a Hornby *Curlew*, green and cream.'

'But that's not what you would really like, is it?' I probed further.

'Of course not, Mr Marklin. It's those magnificent boats the

47

Germans made from the turn of the century I want to get eventually. You know, by Bing, Carette, and so on ...' He gave a little snort as if he were taking snuff. '... and especially by your namesake, sir, Marklin.'

If I'd been sitting down, I'd have sat bolt upright. Marklin's battleships were steaming into my life a little too often.

'I'm sorry. Boats are very hard to come by.' I explained the obvious – that clockwork boats were used in water, and rusted like mad, especially if it were sea water, so few had survived over the years compared with other old toys. And all the while, I watched his eyes.

'I don't mind the cost, Mr Marklin. Just thought I'd pop in and tip you off that I was now in the market.' His eyes gave nothing away.

'Thanks, I'll keep a look out. But I haven't got anything like that at the moment, more's the pity.'

'Great shame so few survived, isn't it? My telephone number's in the book, so give me a ring if you hear of anything.'

I nodded, and he buttoned up his dark blue blazer and made for the door. 'I'd give anything for one of those classic ships in mint condition.' He pulled at his moustache and was gone.

I leant back against the counter and wondered whether he would *do* anything to get one ... Had he been probing, or just making an innocent enquiry? And if it was the former, what was he probing to find out? How far I had got with my enquiries? Curses. Why had he come in and further muddled my already murky sleuthing mind just when I thought I was narrowing things down a bit? Bing jumped on the counter and rubbed himself against my back. I turned to him.

'You know, Bing, it could turn out to be like Agatha Christie's *Murder on the Orient Express*. They're all in it together – a massive conspiracy to make me look a fool.'

But all I got from Bing was a purr, which was as indecipherable to me as KGB code. I was about to give him a bowl of Whiskas, when I heard the unmistakable shriek of Gus Tribble's Ford's brakes outside. I turned the notice on my door to say 'Closed' and waited for him. I suffered a mild shock as, for once, he had the next best thing to a smile on his face.

He wouldn't say a dicky bird until he had a Heineken in his hand, though I could tell he was dying to. Bing jumped up on his lap, and began sniffing his sweater, trying to find traces of all the fish Gus had caught over the last forty years. I began to lose patience.

'Come on, Gus, or I'll tell Bing "go kill".' He chuckled and put down his can.

'Well, old dear, I've suddenly become quite a convert to the ways of the church, I have . . . .'

'Come on. Don't stretch it out,' I snapped irritably.

'I'm not,' he replied quietly. 'I've been having a long chat to the Vicar of St Sebastian's.'

I saw at last what he was getting at. 'And?' I asked.

'And he's given in, that's all.'

'You mean to our lot or Treasure's lot?'

'Don't be thicker than you are. To us, of course.'

I got up excitedly, and frightened Bing off his lap. 'You mean, he's agreed to the dig?'

'Yes. As long as we clear up nicely afterwards. "So as not to leave scars on God's land" as he put it, the pompous twit.'

I couldn't quite absorb the news. It had now all happened so suddenly, after long tedious months of controversy.

'How did you do it, Gus? Tell me?'

I sat down again and took a long gulp of beer.

'Just rang him up. I knew you'd got nowhere with Treasure, so I thought it was time I did something for a change.'

'You reminded him of Redfern's mother's wishes, and all that?'

'Yes,' was all he said. But I knew there was more.

'Come on, Gus. I'm your friend. It wasn't just that, was it?'

He really did smile this time. 'Nope.'

'Okay,' I said, and went and got him another beer. 'There you are. Now tell me.'

'Well, I had a little something on him. Not enough to work if the pilot's mum hadn't written as well. But when you put the two together . . . .'

'What was it?'

He relaxed back in his chair.

'You know old Mrs Blunt next door? Her we picked up the old chairs for yesterday? Well, when I delivered them she brought out a bottle of sherry, and we got to drinking and talking and all that. I told her about the old Spitfire and how we wanted to dig it up and put it in a museum. Her boy was lost in a Lancaster a month before war ended so she knew what I meant. And she asked what the trouble was. And I said, mainly the Vicar and old Treasure. And she said she didn't know about Treasure, but she certainly knew about the Vicar. And I said what did she mean? And she said about three years ago there was a bit of trouble after choir practice one night. It was her grandson. He was in the choir. About twelve he was, she said. And the Vicar is supposed to have made advances, you know, or so her grandson said, and she claimed he was never given to telling lies – ever. Never got out – the story, I mean. The boy's dad went to see the Vicar, and he denied it, saying he was a happily married man and all that, so nobody knew who to believe, and the whole thing was dropped. But Mrs Blunt said she was sure. Can tell by a man's eyes, she said.'

I suddenly realized what Treasure might have had on the cleric all this time. I kept quiet and let Gus finish.

'So I made up my mind to take a little gamble. I said if he didn't agree to old Mrs Redfern's wishes, which was right and proper, I would have to raise a little matter of choirboys and things that weren't quite right and proper.'

'And he agreed right away?'

'Well, he said my vicious threat had nothing to do with his decision. He had already made up his mind the dig should go ahead, seeing as how the pilot's mum wanted it that way. And he said he was telling the local papers today. So we won, my old love, we won.'

I went over and clasped him by the hand. 'Congratulations. I'll ring the Historical Aviation boys this afternoon. They can have a digger here by the weekend.'

And in my excitement over the aircraft, I forgot all about that £22,000 thundercloud still hanging over my head.

After Gus had gone, and I had cleared away our lunch things, the rest of the afternoon was a hell of an anti-climax. Okay, we had won on the Spitfire and that was marvellous, but in a way it had shut one of my doors into Treasure, for I now had no excuse to go and talk to him, which the controversy over the excavation had given me. He was still on my list of suspects for the toys but I certainly couldn't go straight in and ask if I could have my toys back, please. So my secondary sources of information would have to suffice, and I could see I would have to manufacture an excuse for seeing Arabella sooner than I thought.

So that still left Vivian Stone, and now Rankin again and all the rest of them, and they bugged me so much, that after seeing the TV news, which wasn't exactly a pick-me-up (another plane hijack, another strike in the public sector, another landslip in Peru, another hike in the oil price, and another mediocre weather forecast), I bundled myself and Bing into the Beetle and made for Bournemouth. And just to make me feel even better, the heavens opened before I had even reached the ferry; in marked contrast to the morning. But that's Britain for you.

Now Bournemouth in the wet doesn't look quite right somehow. Not that it's Los Angeles or anything, but rain, as my old English tutor used to say, 'doesn't sit well' on the south coast spa. It was certainly coming down today, sheets of it, wall-to-wall, and swishing down the Chines to the sea.

Stone's white and gold, flat roofed, thirties mansion looked a trifle absurd against the dark backcloth of thunderclouds, and I had to park the car in the road, as the electric eye controlling the drive gates did not seem to respond. I cursed my luck, told Bing to bark if anyone tried to steal the car, and throwing my tartan travel rug over my head, as I had neglected to bring a raincoat, ventured out into the elements.

I opened the little side gate and went up the drive. But long before I reached the Spanish-style, over-decorated front door with the great gold knocker, my travel rug had become a real embarrassment. First of all, it was so full of water, it now weighed more than I did, and secondly, I could tell from my hands that the colours (which were many and varied) had started to run. However, the male animal being what he is, I stuck with it and knocked the knocker.

Five minutes later, I had not only knocked the knocker senseless, but had instigated many a fine medley of tunes from *Fiddler on the Roof*. Neither the bangs nor the chimes produced a response. I stealthily moved across a flowerbed full of early geraniums, and looked in the nearest window. It was quite a shock. Vivian Stone had either completely changed his ideas on furnishings, or he had gone. The room was as the builder sold it. Empty. Completely empty. Not a curtain, not a rug, not a chair, not a picture.

I stepped back on a geranium, and looked up at all the other windows I could see; not a curtain in sight, no lights, nothing. I quickly ran around the outside of the house, peering in every window on the ground floor. A big fat zero. Mr Stone had left Branksome Chine behind him. And goodness knows where he had gone, and, what's more important, what he had taken with him. Like Monsieur Vincent's toys, for instance. And maybe my future.

Round the back of the house, the surface of the pool skipped and jumped with the huge raindrops, and it was hard to imagine the scene of only a few days before. I wondered if Mrs Stone had taken off with him, complete with her Trollope. I made my soggy way over to the garages, but they were locked as I had expected. I tried to look in the window at the side, but it was too high. I gathered together a heap of large stones from the nearby rockery, and stood on those and peered in. It was then I felt the firm hand on my shoulder. I jumped.

'Just hold it there, sir or madam. Step down slowly and don't try anything.'

I did and I didn't. My heart was going five hundred to the dozen as I slowly lifted the sodden rug aside to see who my captor was. To my relief, it was a policeman.

'Look officer, I wasn't doing anything. I just called on Mr Stone, and was amazed to find he'd gone, that's all.'

He quickly frisked me, to see if I was bristling with firearms.

'That may be, sir. But I think you had better come down to the station with me, just in case.'

He began leading me back up the drive towards a flashing blue lamp I could now see parked ahead of my Beetle.

'Look,' I protested, 'that's my car behind yours. It's got my cat in it. Would I bring my cat along with me if I was a burglar?'

He looked at me through the sheets of rain and smiled. 'I suppose you might, sir, if you were a cat burglar.'

He sniggered, and I should have seen it coming. None of my protests made any difference. I sat beside him in the nice white Ford with the flashing light all the way to the station. But he did have the decency to radio for one of his colleagues to come and pick up the Beetle. Poor old Bing. He would begin to feel he was mixing with the wrong kind of company, and he would probably be right.

It took me an hour and a half to convince the po-faced lot of the Bournemouth division that I was not the man at whose door they could lay every burglary carried out in Bournemouth in the last twenty years. If you've ever been in a police station you will know it takes you half an hour to explain who you really are, rather than anything else, let alone refute accusations about every job they want sewn up. And, by that time, I was beginning to feel I would soon be dying of pneumonia if I did not get into some dry clothes pretty sharply. They finally agreed to let me go, and it was, at that point, that I felt it safe to begin asking them some questions of my own. Like where Vivian Stone had gone, for instance.

'We don't know for sure, Mr Marklin. All we can ascertain is that he left Heathrow on a Swissair flight to Geneva. Whether he's still there, we have no idea.'

I remembered Stone saying he was opening a new store there. Or, at least, claiming he was.

'You have an interest in him, then?' I asked innocently.

'I don't think I should answer that, Mr Marklin. That's police business.'

'It's my business too. He may have some property of mine, and I want to get it back.'

'Oh.' The constable seemed decidedly interested. 'And what property might that be, Mr Marklin?'

'Toys. Old toys,' I replied, and knew it was the wrong answer immediately. His interest evaporated.

'Well, if we hear anything about ... er ... your toys, Mr Marklin, we'll let you know.'

I played the only card I had left.

'They are worth £22,000.'

My card turned out trumps, and five minutes later I was ushered into a much more civilized room at the station with a large desk at one end.

'Come in, Mr Marklin. Let's hear about these playthings of yours.'

And it was then that I met Detective Inspector Trevor Blake, known as 'Sexton' to the criminal fraternity.

He was around forty-five and a big man. Not fat. It was all bone and gristle – the burly stuff of a million scrums. But his face did not quite fit the rest for it was the face of an academic, finely chiselled, as they say, and with eyes that didn't just see, but probed and penetrated. I was quite impressed.

I took him through my tale of woe, but left out some of the names, like Chalmers and Vincent, saying I had to preserve my clients' anonymity. (I felt like Philip Marlowe for a minute.) Of course, I didn't mention any other of my suspects – especially someone as locally important as Treasure. I didn't want trouble. Blake sat impassively and listened, and didn't even castigate me at the end for not having told the police before.

'Tell me, Mr Marklin, do you really think Stone took them? I'm a great believer in instinct – greatest weapon in a policeman's armoury is instinct.'

'I don't know,' I replied, 'but his sudden flight is rather strange, don't you think?'

He didn't move a muscle. 'Like you, I don't know, Mr Marklin.'

'Tell me,' I said, 'you're pretty interested in Stone, aren't you? For other reasons?'

'I would be a fool to deny it, Mr Marklin.'

'May I ask why?'

'You may. Mr Stone traded heavily in diamonds. Now that's quite natural, you might think, in the jewellery business. But recently there has been a series of robberies carried out in the Hatton Garden area of London. We were just beginning to get some leads onto, not the actual thieves maybe, but the fences, shall we say. And then Mr Stone decided to leave us.'

He smiled, and I knew I would not get any more out of him than that. All I was interested in was getting out of my wet clothes.

'And you'll interview him in Geneva?' I tried.

'Maybe. If we can find him.'

I looked at the rain outside.

'Still,' I said lightheartedly, 'a trip to Geneva will make a change for you, instead of sitting here in Bournemouth every day.'

He smiled again. 'I don't sit here every day, Mr Marklin, not normally.'

He could see from my expression that I didn't quite follow him.

'It's all very simple. I'm from Scotland Yard.'

Just as I was recovering from this surprise, he tossed another googly.

'And by the way, Mr Marklin, you don't, by any chance, have in your stock a Schuco Kommando Anno 2000, do you? I've been after one for years.'

Six

By the next day I felt considerably relieved that the police were now informed of my little tragedy, as I realized I had had twangs of conscience before about their non-involvement. What's more, there was no way now that I could keep track of Vivian Stone without their help. And there was another thing: I kind of liked Trevor Blake. I just hoped he didn't scuttle back to London before I had resolved my personal dilemma – or *we* had resolved it maybe.

I had another pretty good bit of news too. The agreement to the Spitfire's excavation was all over the local papers, and even got on television, I was glad to see, though the sight of the Vicar hamming it up was a bit sick-making – especially if old Mrs Blunt was right in her suspicions. I got a phone call from the Historical Aviation boys saying that they would be moving in on the site with their digger the next morning. We all agreed that the swifter the action now, the less chance there would be of any other local objections.

So the fact that my deadline from Chalmers was ticking inexorably nearer became temporarily veiled by other events, and for at least one night I began sleeping again. Lonely, but sleeping.

Gus and I were on site early the next day, and I insisted on taking him to Swanage in my car this time. He complained of the softness of the ride the whole way, which I could understand as his own Ford Popular rode the road like a board.

The digger and crew were already there, and the likely area marked out with tape and wooden pegs. I said 'Hello' to ninety-four year old Joshua Phipps, who was the tenant farmer of the land at the time of the Spitfire's crash, and had identified the exact location with stunning certainly. 'About ten yards out from the big oak, it were.'

Luckily the big oak was still there, only even bigger I suppose. I just hoped Farmer Phipps's memory was as strong, otherwise we would all look a bit silly and feel more than a little frustrated.

By the time the digger actually started operating, quite a crowd had collected, as had been prophesied by the proponents of doom and gloom. The Vicar, by then, was in the centre of things, with a gaggle of pressmen crowding him. About ten minutes into the dig, I saw the ominous shape of the Silver Cloud parking about fifty yards up by the side of the hedge. At first my heart sank, but it bobbed up again as I realized it gave me the natural chance of further conversation with Treasure.

As always in digs of this kind, progress was slow and, to most outsiders, boring. The remains of crashed fighters of World War II are often found fifteen feet or more below ground due to the massive weight of the engine, and every inch of earth has to be examined stage by stage to discover smaller, lighter items of the aircraft, which had been ripped apart on the way down. The gruesome bits would probably be quite a distance underground, still, maybe attached to what remained of the seat or cockpit area. We knew we would be recovering only small, fractured pieces of the Spitfire, not whole sections of the airframe, for the impact always shattered everything to smithereens, with the usual exception of the solid mass of the Merlin engine, and, sometimes, the propeller.

There was a round of applause as we found the first evidence that Farmer Phipps's memory had not failed him : a small rectangle of twisted metal, which one of the team identified immediately as the rear-view mirror from atop the Spitfire's windscreen. Then for a further hour we found nothing – except soggy earth that is. As we clustered round the widening and deepening hole, we thanked God it wasn't still raining and, from the forecast, wouldn't until nightfall. Then we came upon a spate of small, severely damaged items : the remains of a fuel gauge, a rev counter, a trim wheel and the base of the Spitfire's radio mast. A quarter of an hour later we found slightly larger pieces : the throttle quadrant, firing button, a bit of wing rib and undercarriage warning horn. Each was carefully washed with a hose and put in large cardboard boxes the Historical guys had brought along for the purpose.

I spotted Treasure standing right by the oak tree but there was no sign of Arabella. He didn't look too pleased and avoided eye-to-eye contact with me. When we broke for lunch half an hour later, I saw him stride up the field and make for his Silver Cloud.

He came back with a small hamper basket that shouted Fortnum and Mason if ever I heard one.

Gus and I fetched our sandwiches and Heineken from the Beetle. We were feeling pretty pleased with things. It was quite moving to see the relics meet the light of day for the first time since that momentous August in 1940. But I knew the afternoon might be a little disturbing as we dug deeper and wider, and the remains were not all made by Vickers-Supermarine. We downed a six-pack between us and polished off the sandwiches as if they had just been invented, for the May air was still a little nippy and we had worked up an appetite. I looked at my Seiko (a present from one of my old advertising clients), and saw there was still another quarter of an hour before the dig was due to resume. I decided to spend a bit of it with a shooting stick and a Fortnum's hamper.

He didn't even look up from his glass of champagne when I arrived. That really annoyed me.

'Trying to read the bubbles, Mr Treasure?'

He could not avoid looking at me now.

'What's that, Marklin?' His timbreful voice was a shade too loud, as always.

'Reading the bubbles, I thought, might be a wealthy man's version of reading tea leaves.'

'Why?' he asked. 'What did you see in your tea leaves for today?'

'I saw a Spitfire being delivered to its rightful home – a Warmwell museum – and a gallant pilot being delivered into the arms of his God, Mr Treasure. What did you see?'

'I saw you, Mr Marklin, unfortunately, making a nuisance of yourself as usual.'

I moved round out of the light to his other side. I wanted to be able to see him properly.

'Mr Treasure, you know I'm not a mischief-maker. I just want to see people's rights and desires are not trodden all over. And that pilot's mother has the right to know her son is going to have a proper burial.'

He did not respond, unless pouring himself another glass of champagne was as good as an answer. I changed tack.

'Mr Treasure, as you are a fellow toy enthusiast, I would love to see your collection some time. I hear you've got some really rare little items.'

He looked up for a split second, but his eyes betrayed nothing beyond what seemed to be boredom. I persevered, on my old mother's maxim of 'nothing ventured, nothing gained'. (My mother, by the way, is still alive and well in Charmouth. She is more full of clichés than a politician is of wind.)

'A little bird told me that you had recently acquired quite a few more. A mint JEP Rolls-Royce, for instance.'

Nothing registered – even his hand didn't shake the bubbles. I ploughed on. 'A CIJ Alfa Romeo, and a Tipp steam lorry, a Citroën taxi cab. Eleven pieces in all. Everyone of them mint. Oh, and the *pièce de résistance* was a Marklin battleship, I'm told.'

He smiled 'By your little birdie again?' he asked. I nodded. 'What's the name of your little birdie, Mr Marklin?'

'Why are you interested, Mr Treasure?'

'I'm not, Mr Marklin. I just feel that if there are liars and misinformants about, I should know who they are, that's all. So that I can avoid them myself.' His voice had taken on a sarcastic tone, which I did not find particularly endearing. He continued, 'I only wish I had discovered some of those items you ramble on about – at a reasonable price, that is. People are asking far too much for old toys these days. It's all those international auctions that do it, in London and Paris and Geneva and New York.' He turned away and put his glass back in the hamper.

By this time, I knew I had ventured but gained nothing from our encounter. I was no nearer divining whether he was the guilty party than I was with Vivian Stone or Rankin. But I did note that I seemed to be hearing an awful lot about that lake-side resort in Switzerland in the last few days.

I left him, and went back to Gus, just as I heard the digger start up again. It wouldn't be long now before we would know more of the fate of Pilot Officer Redfern.

Gradually, the cardboard boxes began filling again. First a turning indicator, and some small instruction plates, then our biggest find to date, a wheel, complete with its tyre. (When washed, the latter looked almost as good as new.) Soon after, the digger unearthed an elevator trim tab, and about an eighteen-inch section of camouflaged airframe. Then some amunition from the .303 Brownings, which the men from the Air Ministry promptly took away, quite rightly.

Then, very suddenly, the flow of relics ceased and it was soon

59

clear there were no more in that particular section. So the digger moved some ten feet or so back towards the oak tree, and started afresh, and with renewed success.

I won't bore you with everything we found, but this second dig made it all very worth-while from our proposed museum's point of view, for it was here we found our biggest remains: the Merlin engine, more or less intact, which we had to winch out, the three-bladed propeller, horribly bent but not totally fractured, the armoured windscreen, amazingly still in one piece, with a bit of its frame.

But we were surprised to find that when we uncovered the main part of the seat, complete with some of its cushion and Sutton harness, there was no sign that a pilot had been in it at the time of impact. There were no bodily remains, no fragments of any clothing or flying helmet or goggles, and no parachute. Nearly all previously excavated crash sites where the pilot was thought to have been on board had revealed some traces of the pilot. I didn't dare look at Treasure. And I didn't like to reflect on the disappointment old Mrs Redfern would feel when she heard.

Once there was nothing gruesome to gawp at or photograph, the press drifted away, no doubt to various hostelries, which were on the point of opening for the evening. Gus and I tried to persuade the Historical boys to have one last go a little further out from the tree than the original hole, just in case, somehow, the pilot's body had been thrown clear of the aircraft during its crushing journey into the bowels of the earth. After a lot of muttering, they agreed to put in an extra hour. The digger moved round and started up once more.

This time, we did not have to wait long. Only some two feet or so under the turf, we came across the first bones. I shouted for the digger to stop, and we all grabbed spades and began carefully lifting the soil off the rest of the pilot's remains. Within the hour we had found an almost complete skeleton, but, seemingly, not the top part of the skull. He seemed to be lying almost as if he had died peacefully, and not rammed into the unyielding earth at over 400 miles an hour. Indeed, nearly all his bones were intact, which made us believe he must have been either partly or totally out of his aircraft at the moment of impact. And, although the comparative shallowness of his resting place lent weight to that theory, somehow or other, I felt uneasy.

The Vicar, tended by the Air Ministry representatives and the police, supervised the collection of what was left of the Battle of Britain hero, and conducted a short service, as a coffin was brought to transport his mortal remains to St Sebastian's, whence they would be taken to a forensic laboratory for the usual examination to determine the exact cause of death – as if we didn't know.

I felt almost sick with the emotion of the day, and declined to go into Swanage for a few drinks with our friends from the Historical Aviation Society. So did Gus and we drove home together in silence. Then the rain started again as if the skies were sad too. Just as Gus got out of the car at his front gate, he said, in almost an offhand manner, 'Funny, I hadn't thought of it before. But we didn't find any bits of his clothing, did we? Nothing. Can't have flown it naked, can he?' And once again, he uncannily read my own thoughts.

So it was Pilot Officer Redfern, and not Chalmers this time, that caused me to lose my beauty sleep yet again.

The next day was Sunday, but not a day of rest. For many vintage toy people, collectors as well as dealers, Sunday is a day for attending one or other of the countless toy swapmeets, that are held regularly all over this country and Europe. And today I had fixed, months before, to go to the Bristol event, where I had booked a table. These enthusiasts' meets are held in large exhibition or conference halls, and each dealer can book as many tables, more or less, as he likes, on which he spreads his wares, rather like a village jumble sale, really. In the main, no real gems are ever traded this way. (As I've already intimated, they pass from collector to collector often via word of mouth, otherwise through a Phillip's or Christie's auction or similar.) But there is a lot there for the average punter with, say, up to £100 in his pocket. There's not much tinplate; it's nearly all die-cast – old Dinkies, Corgis, Matchbox, and, increasingly now, new merchandise. The last mentioned annoys me greatly. You shouldn't be allowed to mix the old and the new, in my humble opinion. Instant classics aren't my number.

However, so be it. I had to go to earn a crust, and attempt to sell off some of my lower priced and more common items that you often have to buy as well, to get the goodie you're after. So I packed the Beetle up to its shell with the die-casts, and took the winding roads up to the M4 and along to Bristol and its conference centre by the now rather attractive dockside.

I noted two other Bournemouth old toy dealers there – the resort has sprouted quite a few – and I passed the time of day with them as I was setting up my table. (Before the public is allowed in, the dealers sniff at each other's stock, just in case there's a little profit in incestuous trading, one with another.) At eleven, the main doors were opened and, as always, the first ten minutes were like the Second World War, with the keenest collectors willing to commit murder to get to the toy or toys they had their beady eyes on. After a while things settle down, and the scene relaxes into gentle pandemonium, which goes on the rest of the day until about four o'clock, when we all pack up and take our unsold stock home.

During the hours there, I tried to concentrate my mind on all my dizzy problems, Stone and Rankin, Treasure and Monsieur Vincent, and last but not least, what was worrying me about PO Redfern, but I quickly found it impossible. And it wasn't the noise or the bustle that stopped me. Nor my rate of sales (I only ended up £185 better off, representing a real profit of under £70. And it's a long way there and back for only £70) but the ever present problem of pilferage. So I was truly thankful when four o'clock chimed, and I could pack up and get out to the Beetle in the car-park opposite.

The journey back was very easy and uneventful, and with Gershwin's *Rhapsody in Blue* on the tape deck, I began to unwind enough to think. Gradually, I came to realize that the problem of the stolen toys was virtually impossible for me to solve. Even Interpol, I reckoned, would find it daunting. I could tell from my conversations with Detective Inspector Trevor Blake that even he thought so too. He certainly didn't offer up much hope. Still, he was after Stone, and he had tracked him to Geneva, so I decided I had to leave Stone to him. I certainly did not have the time or the resources to hang about in Switzerland myself. Nor, really, could I go down and see Monsieur Vincent again, and a telephone call would be worse than useless, as, were he the guilty party, it would put him on his guard instantly.

So that left me with Rankin and Treasure, and I would have to get to know the Detective Inspector a good deal better before I raised suspicions about the latter. It was clear Treasure wielded quite a bit of power round about in Dorset, and as I still intended living there long after this ugly affair was over, I didn't dare go much further than I had done already. What I could do further about Rankin, I had no idea. He had an alibi for himself and his wife, and his interest in battleships could be quite innocent and coincidental. It was very much how the collecting mania worked; you started with one main interest, say cars, and then began embracing almost every other kind of toy over the years. And he didn't seem to be a baddy, like Treasure did.

Thinking about Treasure brought me back, of course, to the intrepid pilot and his curious end. Gus was right. We should have found some item of clothing or parachute or something. It was almost as if his bones had been picked clean. And there was something else that bugged me. Even though the digger had disturbed the skeleton before we had taken to our spades, it still looked too neat and tidy somehow. I felt the impact would have collapsed the body more, even though, it was true, the skull was crushed and part of it missing.

On that sombre thought I decided I needed a beer, something to eat and a little of somebody else's company before I turned in for the evening, no doubt to watch some old film on TV that I would never have gone to see in the cinema. But after my previous experience of losing toys from a parked Beetle I went home first, unpacked the unsold die-casts, stroked and fed Bing, and explained to him why I had to go out again, then left for my usual local just up the road.

I was disappointed not to find Gus there, then remembered he had said he had 'a little business in Weymouth to do'. And I knew her name, so he wouldn't be in tonight. I found somebody had left a *Sunday Times* on the seat by the window, so I buried myself behind it, with my Heineken and, a little later on, some sausages and chips. I had read all the news section, and was two thirds the way through the Review bit (absorbing all the details of a new German film that seemed to be about a one-legged dwarf, suffering from Aids, who fell in love with a plumber's mate, who was a girl, and a lesbian to boot, whose activities made the Bader-Meinhof gang seem like a Christian Aid Society), when I heard a slightly familiar voice addressing me. I was quite relieved to look up.

'Can I come and sit next to you?'

I made room for her on the rather stained window seat.

63

'What are you reading?' She picked up the paper.

'Oh, nothing much. Just about a new film that's bound to close yet another cinema. I'm beginning to think that's why they make them. It's all a great conspiracy by the international television moguls to get rid of every cinema in the world.'

She smiled. 'I've forgotten your Christian name. What is it?'

I felt her warmth next to my thigh. Made the other one seem very cold and lonely. I looked at her, and after the kind of day I'd had, she looked the perfect afters to sausages and chips. 'It's Peter. Peter Marklin.'

'Mine's . . .' she began, but I laughingly interrupted. 'I know. Arabella Donna Trench. Your enemies call you Belladonna. Your friends call you often.'

She grinned a very nice grin. Bit lipsticky, but nice.

'You've a good memory.'

'For things I want to remember.'

'And you wanted to remember me?'

What a silly question.

'Miss Trench, once seen, never forgotten. You're not exactly the kind of girl I see every day of the week.'

She took a sip of her drink, which appeared to be a dry Martini. We both suddenly looked up at each other.

'Here alone?' we said in unison.

'Yes,' we said likewise. And had a little chuckle which, accidentally, was accompanied by a brief touching of hands. Not bad going for the first five minutes.

'What brings you here?' I thought I'd ask.

'A Golf convertible,' she replied in all seriousness. I realized I had met my match.

'I've never seen you here before,' I pressed on regardless.

'I've seen you.'

'That why you came again?'

She nodded and took another dry sip.

'That's nice,' I smiled, 'if it's true.'

'What do you mean by that?' she asked rather coldly.

'Oh, I just wondered if Mr Treasure had sent you along.'

'Why should he do that?'

'Find out what I'm doing – what I'm thinking.'

'Mr Treasure's far too busy with the rest of his life to bother about you – or me, for that matter.'

I looked at her, straight in those dark, mysterious wells, outlined with mascara.

'You left him then?' I asked in a more affectionate voice, hoping our hands might meet again.

'I've never really lived with him, so I can't really leave him, can I?'

Put that way, I couldn't really argue.

'Like another drink?' I asked, as my Heineken was now but froth in the bottom of my glass.

'Yes.' I was about to get up when her hand returned, and she added, 'But not here.'

'Where then? There's a very good place over towards Corfe, Gus and I sometimes use. . . .'

'Isn't there an even better one you use all the time?' she tossed in to throw me.

'Can't think of one,' I replied. 'Unless it's my place.'

She got up abruptly, and pulled me to a standing position (so to speak). 'Your place, you must be joking,' she smiled. 'And anyway where is it?'

'Just around the corner. But I haven't got the *Sunday Times.*'

'It wasn't newspapers I was thinking of.'

I smiled. I had to agree with her.

In the somewhat dubious privacy of my own modest home (dubious only because Bing always seemed to watch my every move with any unattached female), Arabella came over as even more striking. She was a healthy five foot eight, and the proportions that go with it, only more so. Her hair I have described before as 'violent'. Tonight, maybe, it was slightly less so in style, but you still couldn't get away from the colour, or more accurately, colours. They seemed to be alternate streaks of Porsche silver and Ford Sunburst Red, with a little Havana Brown having a breather now and again. With her bodywork, it all seemed pretty natural somehow, and I got used to it in no time.

Luckily I had some dry Martini left over from another en-counter, and I moved over to something shorter than beer – Scotch. And, of course, just as I was about to ask her the story of her life, in the hope she wouldn't ask about mine, Bing jumped on her lap and jogged her glass. I got a cloth from the kitchen, and wiped her lap, which proved to be not a huge chore.

'Bing, you really are the end, you know,' I said to the cat, with mock severity.

She looked at me. 'Why do you call him Bing – after that ancient singer my grandmother loves?'

So that was the generation she ranked me with. If I hadn't got other plans for the evening, I could have gone off her right then on a technicality.

'No, thank you very much. It's the other Bing you won't have heard of: a famous German toy company of the twenties and thirties. I've got a Bing Table-Top Railway set of theirs upstairs with some of my own toy collection.'

She looked across at me with an 'I've hardly come here to play trains' look. I agreed with her sentiments. 'Oh,' is all she actually said.

We sat silently for a bit, on the small settee. Bing was watching every move from the floor. I avoided his eye-to-eye contact.

'Why is it recently I've tended to gravitate to men who, in a way, haven't quite grown up?' she asked, quite ravishingly.

'You mean, they like toys?'

'Like them? Dear old Randolph is nutty about them. You ought to read his diary. Well *a* diary?' she laughed. He's got thousands of diaries. He's obsessive about *them* as well,' she added.

'How long has he been keeping a diary?' I asked, becoming rather interested.

'Yonks,' she replied. 'Ever since he was given his first Lett's School-boy's Diary when he was a kid – so he tells me, anyway. He says life is far too precious not to be able to recall every day of your life on demand. I know what he means. I think he regrets computers weren't invented in time for his first forty-five years or so.'

'And what diary did he allow you to read?'

'The current one, that's all. And then only bits of that.'

I poured her another Martini. 'You didn't happen to read, by any chance, if he went across to France sometime around 9 May, did you?'

She thought for a second, and I could see I was trying to push too hard too soon – an old trait of mine.

'No, I didn't need to. I was with him. He hasn't been out of Dorset since Christmas, as far as I know. I tell a lie, he went to London once, for the day, to see his broker.'

So I was back to square one. I changed the subject.

'Where do you come from?'

'Up in Shropshire, where my parents still farm. Place called All Stretton. We live on the high hill above it – on the Mynd, as it's called.' She smiled at me. 'Very blowy on the Mynd. Sometimes can bowl you right over.'

I was beginning to sense what the Mynd felt like.

'I'm too much of a hedonist for such heights, I'm afraid,' she continued. 'Learnt all that in the lowlands of Bristol University. Didn't do a stroke of work, except to get through tutorials. Left without a degree, but with a lot of . . . friends.' She hesitated, and her expression changed completely from beautiful confidence to a look of almost desperation.

She suddenly leant across and kissed me. I let it go on for more than its usual life-span, which irritated Bing no end. After a while, she whispered in my nibbled ear, 'I want to count you amongst my friends, Peter. Can I?'

'Depends,' I replied.

'On what?'

'On how it goes.' After all, how did I know how it would go – wasn't she Treasure's lady friend?

She got up and took me by the hand.

'Oh, it will go all right, don't you worry.'

And you know something? Right then, I just couldn't go on worrying any more.

'Do you want something to eat?' I looked down at her snuggled into my side, her left and wondrous breast nudging my ribcage. Bing was downstairs, thank the Lord.

Arabella opened the only eye I could see, and asked breathily, 'Is that a naughty invitation again?'

I tickled her waist. 'Nope. Not this time. It's a reminder that God has given us stomachs as well as the rest of the equipment, and we might want to fill those now. After all, other people were no doubt eating supper or dinner or whatever while we were writhing about.'

'Poor people,' she muttered. And I tended to agree with her.

She sat up, and did not bother with the sheet. She really did not need the spray-booth hair. She was altogether stunning from the tip of the Sunburst Red to the tiniest little toe, which could not help wriggling every time we made love. And her skin had that elusive hint of olive that made it infinitely more attractive than the bald pinkness most English girls kid themselves is part of the beauty of an English rose. I moved across and nuzzled the down between her breasts and, lower, towards her belly. But this time it was affection, not lust on my lips. She lay back and made a little whimpering noise. I rested my head against her stomach, and looked back up at her, past the firm mounds of her breasts.

'Did it go all right?' I heard her ask, her ribcage moving slightly, in tune with her voice-box.

'I'll let you know the fourth time,' I rejoined, and her knee came up and hit the back of my head. We rolled over together like two kids in the snow, and then both lay staring at the damp stain on my ceiling, which I had been meaning to fix for months. After a while, I asked her, 'What do you see in Treasure?'

She looked at me. 'Probably not what you think.' She rested on her elbow. 'You think it's all the money, don't you?'

I didn't answer.

'Well it isn't, Mr Peter Marklin.'

I didn't say anything. Presently she went on, 'It's partly the power money provides, I suppose. I've always been fascinated with power. I think I understand why Unity Mitford was so dotty over Hitler.'

'Treasure's a bit like Hitler, in a way, in my book too,' I said, with more than a smile.

'Yes, I know you hate his guts. It shows a mile off. And he certainly hates yours. Why, I don't know. He normally ignores everybody but himself, so in consequence, rarely gets very annoyed. But you're an exception with him, for some reason.'

I turned over, and held her naked body very tightly to mine. We kissed and told each other we liked each other, without using words. Then I asked her, 'Don't you mind his being AC/DC? He is, isn't he?'

She sat up abruptly, and looked at me – a little bit daggers. 'Hey, wait a minute. Why should I?'

'Well . . .' I hesitated, 'you know, it's . . . er . . . .'

'It's because you think Randolph and I are lovers. That's right, isn't it?'

I suddenly realized I had possibly made a ghastly error. 'I'm sorry. I just thought . . . .' I stammered, but she cut me short.

'You just didn't think, did you?'

She moved across the bed, and pulled the top sheet around and over her. Neither of us spoke for what seemed light years.

'I'm sorry,' I bleated at last, and my voice seemed to have gone into the high octaves of a choirboy's all of a sudden. The bed shook as she sniggered under the sheet. I could tell we were both waiting for the next move. It came from me. I told you I didn't have any patience worth a damn. I held out a hand. A white sheet in the shape of five fingers extended towards it. In a moment, we confirmed docking.

'Just because I use his Silver Cloud, and am seen a lot in his house doesn't mean what you thought it meant. So, to get back to your question, I don't care that he's bisexual. And, yes, he is, by the way.' Her voice had reverted to bedtime normal. I leant across and kissed the part of the sheet that looked like a nose. She threw the cover back and I saw that my aim had been accurate.

'I'm glad,' I said, then laughed and added, 'That's the understatement of anybody's year.'

'I'm glad you're glad,' she nuzzled my nose in return. 'But I'm now hellish suspicious of your moral rectitude, Mr Marklin.'

I smiled. 'So am I, but what . . . . ?'

'What? Well, you were quite willing to bed a girl whom, one, you thought belonged to someone else, and, two, whom you would obviously regard as a bit of a tramp for hitting the hay with you whilst still having a lover over at Doom Abbey.'

'Doom Abbey?' I asked stupidly, then supplied my own answer. 'Oh, you mean Treasure's Victorian folly?' And I could feel myself blushing, not because of my inept question, but because the rest of what she had said had hit home and hard. As the lovely Eric Morecambe used to say, 'There's no answer to that.' So I didn't try to give one.

She saw my embarrassment, and came and snuggled tight alongside me, like a companion piece in a jigsaw puzzle, only softer.

'Oh, don't feel all guilty now, Peter,' she whispered. 'I wanted to go to bed with you as much, I guess, as you did with me. It's been quite a long stretch, you see, since the last time I felt that way. So feel complimented. I'm a million miles from being anybody's, as you thought. Maybe my slightly crazy hair gives people the wrong impression . . . .'

I stroked the silken colours back from her forehead. 'Sweeney Todd never had it so good,' I whispered back. She smiled, which was more than my remark really merited, and rested her head on her hand.

'You're still wondering what the hell goes on between me and Randolph, aren't you?' she asked.

'Sort of.'

'Well, I suppose I'm his front. You know what I mean? He likes me because I help him portray the image he likes to present in public: a man who can still attract vaguely pretty girls, a normal, fun-loving host, with me as his bright and caring hostess or companion at dinner parties. The AC or is it the DC, part he likes to keep more or less in a closet. Not that he hasn't tried to get me into bed, but I don't like him that way so I never would, and never will. And he accepts that.'

'What do you get out of it? Beyond the Unity Mitford bit, that is.'

'I meet a lot of interesting people. But I also eat and drink well. And get to drive around in a Rolls when I feel like it. You know . . . .' She winked but I knew she was hiding something.

'Treasure has filled a gap, hasn't he?' I guessed, and I could see from her expression I wasn't far from the mark. 'Companionship without commital?'

'Without commital,' she repeated quietly. 'I wasn't ready for anything more than that when I met him . . . .'

Her voice tailed away, and I didn't follow it. When she was good and ready, I guessed she would tell me.

There was a silence for a bit, then I changed the subject. I couldn't think of anything more innocent than, 'Don't you have a job?'

'You mean nine-to-five type of thing?' I nodded.

'Not exactly. I help my cousin at her nursery in Owermoigne most days of the week, sowing and tending plants, pricking them out, spraying them, weeding them, taking them to Weymouth market. The work load is uneven. Some days are very busy, others are not. But I like it. Working with living things is quite rewarding.'

'Is that where you live, with your cousin in Owermoigne?' I asked, hoping the reply would be 'Yes'. I was lucky.

'Yes. Most of the time. The only exceptions are when I've been out very late with Randolph. Then I stay in one of the thousand

70

bedrooms at Doom Abbey, and lock the door, like a frightened fairy-tale maiden.'

'And tonight?' I asked with trepidation.

'I'm locking myself in with you, if you'll have me.'

I didn't say anything, and in a moment she broke from me, and lay on her stomach, her chin resting on her pillow. Suddenly I found the rising wind of the Mynd beginning to affect me all over again. I let it blow.

Seven

She left very early the next morning. And she did something no other girlfriend of mine has ever done at a similar stage of a relationship, without being asked, that is : she fed Bing before she went. Love me, love my cat.

The Toy Emporium seemed very empty without her. For when she came into a room, you knew it. And when she came into a bedroom, you knew it many times over. I missed her with a kind of ache, for what I had intended to be mainly a means of getting at some of Treasure's secrets had rapidly turned into something very different – what, I wasn't quite sure yet.

I took a cold shower (which was, in a way, like shutting the stable door after the horse has bolted), brushed my teeth and shaved, like a good boy. One orange juice and a piece of toast later, I felt even worse for I knew I wanted to see her again, and, this time, it had nothing to do with Mr Randolph Treasure. But I didn't know what her reaction would be a second time. Maybe I was just a toy she would only play with once, the novelty having vanished with the night, although my instincts told me she wasn't like that and that her occasional brittleness was just a form of self-defence.

In the end, I had to force myself to think of something else. The unfortunate thing was all the other things I could think of were worse, like where would I find £22,000 if I couldn't find those tinplates. I would have to sell my entire toy collection (worth maybe £10,000 to buy, goodness knows how little if I needed to sell them – and in a hurry). I worked out that I could raise (if not repay) around £10,000 maximum on the house, via a second mortgage. While dear old Auntie had bequeathed the house to me in her will, I had been forced to mortgage a bit of it to enable me to get sufficient stock to interest the punters. Foolishly, I had voluntarily resigned (genuinely, not one of those tax fiddles) from the advertising agency where I worked, instead of making myself so obstreperous that I had to be fired (like everyone else does in the game) and be given a year's salary as a golden handshake. As Deborah was always fond of pointing out – especially if other people were present – I was as good at looking after my financial affairs as Paul Getty was at recognizing pre- and post-war Dinky Toys. (For the non-cognoscenti, pre-war ones usually have plain hubs to their wheels, and often white tyres, while post-war, of the same type, have ribbed hubs and black tyres. Much more of this, and you will be able to go into business for yourself.)

So, all in all, I reckoned I had better find the toys if there was to be life after Mr Chalmers. I went back over in my mind what I had learned from the unique Arabella – confirmation of Treasure's ambidextrous facility, and rather more to the point, his predilection for diary-keeping. Diaries can be very useful things – and not just to the writer. I decided that I had better acquaint myself with the diaries as soon as possible. The problem was how? Treasure did not even let his lady friends peruse every page, so he would hardly be likely to allow dear old tea-leaf-reading Peter Marklin. So, heinous though it might be, I had to find a way of reading his little jottings behind his back. My mind boggled. Even if I could find a way to do so, would the dear man have noted down his every thought and action? I strongly doubted he would have an entry of this sort: '9 May, trotted down to Dover, don't you know? Took ferry, waited for ridiculous Volkswagen thing at Calais. Persuaded spotty seaman to steal toys on board, replace with plastic Camaros. Hah! Hah! Hah! Took them home in jolly old Silver Cloud thing. Played with them all evening until it was time for beddy-byes. Goodnight Diary, sweet dreams. See you tomorrow.'

I got fed up with thinking, and opened up shop. In two and a half hours, my grand sales total amounted to fifty pence. One chipped Matchbox Mustang (no box, bent axles) to a nine-year-old boy who looked as if he had just invented chicken pox. (I looked at myself, quizzically, in the mirror for days, after that close encounter of the contagious kind.)

But my whole outlook was changed by the next ding of the doorbell. I looked up and saw a nice shiny white car outside, and coming inside, the shiny white face of Detective Inspector Trevor Blake. I had a feeling he had not just come for the Schuco. Bing got off the counter and went back into the kitchen. He had had enough of policemen recently.

After the usual pleasantries, the Inspector made it quite plain the sitting-room would be a better venue for what he had to say, than a public toy shop. So we went through. He declined my offer of coffee, and got straight to the point.

'I had better disappoint you right away, Mr Marklin,' he began. 'I haven't any more word on Stone yet. He apparently left his hotel in Geneva soon after he booked in. A search of his luggage by our Swiss colleagues revealed next to nothing – and certainly not any toys of yours, or rather, of your friend Mr Chalmers.'

'Yes, that is a bit disappointing, to put it mildly,' I grimaced. 'So how else can I be of use to you?'

'I don't know quite yet, Mr Marklin.' He smiled, and began looking a little less like an officer of the law. 'Let me ask you a question or two first.'

I was beginning to get a little nervous. What questions could he possibly want to ask me? He couldn't suspect me of passing, or receiving, stolen diamonds – or could he? The thought made me blush, the first sign, so they say, of a guilty man.

'Fire away,' I said, with more than a slight crackle in my voice.

'Well, it's about your other little enthusiasm, Mr Marklin, your aviation interest. I gather you were one of the main protagonists of the excavation that took place over in Swanage last Saturday.'

'Yes, but what has that got to do with Stone?'

'Nothing, I expect, Mr Marklin. You see it's a different case, but as I knew you slightly, I thought you might have a few comments to make on the dig that might prove useful.'

I tried to imagine what on earth his interest could be in the Spitfire. After all, the police had been there during the whole of the recovery work, and had made no objections to anything we had done.

'Well, try me. I'm a little non-plussed,' I said, understating considerably.

'It may come as a bit of a shock to you, Mr Marklin,' he continued, 'that you may have found your aeroplane, but it doesn't look as if you've discovered your pilot yet.'

'What do you mean? His remains went off for the usual examination to determine the exact cause of death, as if it wasn't quite clear.'

'Yes, I know. And it's as a result of the examination that I have called on you, amongst other people.'

'Why, what's happened?' I stammered.

'Well, your Pilot Officer Redfern has turned out to be a woman of about thirty-five years of age, who died some forty years or so later than the Battle of Britain; of what, we cannot as yet ascertain, due to certain parts of her skull still being missing.'

Suddenly, all my misgivings about the pilot's remains flooded back to me, and somehow softened the shock of the Inspector's startling revelation. Even so, I was speechless.

'Have I disappointed you yet again, Mr Marklin? It seems to be becoming a habit of mine.'

I saw Bing put his head around the door and pop right out again. I envied his freedom.

'I suppose you have, in a way.' I got up and went over to the window. I needed to see something green and growing. 'But you haven't shocked me as much as you may imagine.'

'May I ask why, Mr Marklin?'

'Because Gus and I – Gus is a friend of mine, you understand – had a funny feeling about those bones. Where they were, only two foot or so down. And how they were arranged, too neat and tidy for a crash. And you see, there weren't any clothes or parachute or goggles or anything, like you would have expected.'

'Well, now you know why,' the Inspector said quietly.

'Yes, now I know.' I looked back at him. 'His mother will be terribly disappointed after all.'

'We'll not tell her just yet. We have now initiated an excavation of that whole area around the crash site. He could still be found, you know.'

I didn't answer, because my mind had suddenly thought of something else; something far removed from the Battle of Britain and 1940.

We broke for coffee just about then. I watched him as he drank, very slowly and carefully, almost weighing up each instant grain. Mine had gone before he was half way through.

'Tell me, Mr Marklin,' he said between sips, 'why were you so very much in favour of the dig?'

'I've told you, Inspector. To create a memorial to the gallant few from Warmwell aerodrome.'

He looked up. 'Nothing else?'

'What else could there be?' I was getting a little irritated.

'Oh, I don't know.' He put his cup down. 'Some people fight for things just to annoy other people – not that I'm saying you are that sort of person. I don't think you are.'

'I'm *not*,' I said firmly. 'And I know what you are hinting at. Has he been at you already?'

'Who's that, Mr Marklin?'

'Good old Mr Randolph Treasure, the big rich cheese around these parts.'

'Oh, him.' He smiled. 'You're very perceptive, Mr Marklin. That's really why I came to you. The police force is dominated nowadays by the diarrhoea of bumf flooding into and out of computers. It's the age of science, we're told at Police College. Think scientifically. Make use of every channel of communication. By that, they mean one channel. The computer channel. And the poor cadets are never told anything about using their own computers – the ones in their heads. The tuition should really be about intuition, as you might say. Then add the science.'

I felt more at ease again, after that little sermon – a cry, obviously, from the heart, which at least proved he had one. He wasn't just an academic face on a rugby player's body. And he *was* a toy collector.

'Tell me, before we go any further, why you are on this case as well as Stone's? Shouldn't you be back at Scotland Yard by now?'

'I had no option, Mr Marklin. Bournemouth CID is up to its blue shirtsleeves in petty- and middle-weight crime right now, and I happened to be finishing off all I could do, this end, on the Stone affair when the results of the forensic examination came through. And Inspector Brough called me in. I don't know how long the Yard will allow me to be on it, though.'

I hoped at least as long as it took to get my toys back and, perhaps, to discover a great deal more about the owner of a local Victorian folly. But I kept quiet about all that.

'Now I won't keep you much longer,' he continued. 'It's lunchtime, and I know you'll be busy, but just a couple more questions. Firstly, what have you got against Mr Treasure, if anything? He raised the roof on the phone yesterday with Inspector Brough. Claimed you were persecuting him, and making unfounded insinuations and so forth. Doesn't sound like you, I must say, Mr Marklin.'

76

'Oh, it can do, it can do, Inspector,' I replied. 'I can ruffle when I get ruffled.'

He smiled and waited for me to continue. I didn't know whether I should, but I took the risk.

'Look, Mr Treasure may be a bigwig round here, but that does not make him the nicest guy in the world, by any means. At least I don't think so. He's getting uptight because I've called on him and sort of "insinuated", as he calls it, that he might have certain toys.'

'*Your* certain toys?'

'Yes, if you want to know, my certain toys.'

'Have you any proof of your so called insinuation?'

'None at all. Just hunch – your intuition, I suppose; my computer brain, maybe working overtime, maybe not.'

'Well, tread carefully, Mr Marklin. Add science before you annoy him too much again, won't you, otherwise Mr Treasure might stop contributing to the Police Benevolent Fund. You get my meaning?'

'I get your meaning.'

He rose to leave, and turned back to me as he reached the door. 'Tell me, Mr Marklin, what your computer brain tells you about this unfortunate woman of thirty or so, who has retained only half of her skull? I would be very interested to know.'

So I told him.

He left soon afterwards, and, though still seeming quite friendly, I could tell that, while he might have forgiven my intuition, he might not forgive my acting on it on my own. Aye, there lay the rub. The bloody great rub. For Mr Chalmers' deadline did not care two hoots about the leisurely pace of routine police enquiries. Or about me and my great Auntie's house, and the Abbey National's stake in it.

I gave Bing his lunch, didn't bother about my own, and then walked us both slowly over to Gus's place. It was time.

Gus, of course, turned out to be one jump ahead of me. Or to be more accurate, one ahead, and around a half behind. Let me explain.

He had chugged around to Swanage that morning in his boat to have his ancient engine seen to – it was misfiring on more cylinders than it had, apparently. Whilst on the quayside kicking his supersized heels, he had met an old mate of his who had told

him the dig had restarted on the crash site, and there were
hordes of police around. Gus, who is even more curious by
nature than Bing, got his mate to trundle him to the field in his
old Standard 10. (I've seen this car, and its condition makes
Gus's heap seem as if it's still under guarantee. It's only the windows that are holding it together.) He had stayed the morning
there but had learnt precious little about what the police were
doing. Pursuing enquiries surrounding the discovery of the Spitfire was the official line, which he didn't really swallow. But as
he was leaving, there was a bit of a commotion around the
digger, and he gathered that another body had been found, and
some items of pilot's clothing. He'd found it curious as no Battle
of Britain MK I or II Spitfires had two seats. That trainer version
of the famous fighter came out much later – after the war's end,
in fact. So he had chugged his way back to Studland and, after
downing some tinned tuna fish and baked beans – Gus lives
almost solely out of tins; he won't die like you and me; he'll just
rust away – had awaited my inevitable arrival with more or less
the same tale. But I still had the up on him about the first body
being a woman, if you can call that an up. And I told him, more
or less, what I had told the Inspector.

Gus just sat there and did not say a thing. It wasn't as if we
were drinking at the time, though I could hear the evidence of a
Heineken or two rumbling around in his stomach. Eventually, I
just had to break the comparative silence.

'Tenpence for your thoughts, Gus.'

'Don't get much for that these days, my old dear,' was all I got
in reply.

'Well, give us what you've got, and blow the expense,' I said, a
trifle irritably.

'I agree with you, really. I reckon old Treasure – or maybe one
of the others of the leave well alone brigade – knew what was
buried there and why. Probably never realized it was an old Spitfire crash site, otherwise they'd have buried it somewhere else.'
How long did you say they thought it had been there?'

'Forty years or so less than Pilot Officer Redfern. That makes it
only a few years.'

'But the bones had no flesh on them – looked fairly old.'

'Maybe the police have got it a bit wrong. But they won't be
forty years out, you can be certain.'

Gus looked at me. One of his serious looks.

'Why didn't you tell the Inspector everything you think?' he asked slowly.

'I did.'

'You didn't. You know you didn't.'

Here he went again.

'All right, I didn't.' How *does* this man do it?

'So why didn't you come right out with it all, that you think Treasure killed his wife for having had it away all the time and hid her body in a field – not on his own land, you notice – a field with easy access from the road? Nice big boot that Rolls of his has got. Get a house in there.' He got up and came over to me. 'That's what you reckon, isn't it? And that she never bloody went to Switzerland at all.'

I nodded. 'You know why I didn't. It's bad enough telling the Inspector that he should investigate all those who were against the dig, and that one of them probably either knew, or was related to the poor woman who was killed, without earmarking a man who wields huge power around here, and up whose nostrils I have charged full tilt on too many occasions already.'

Gus sat down again, and as always, a delicate cloud of dust arose from the chair. His lungs must now have more uncut moquette in them than is left on the furniture.

'And, by the way,' I added, 'the Inspector reminded me that no one, as yet, can be certain of the cause of death. It could be natural causes; badgers could have disturbed the bones and carried off part of the skull; Santa Claus eats four billion mince pies, and downs as many glasses of sherry every Christmas night between twelve and two.'

I think he was getting my point.

'Have to keep the two things separate in your mind, you know,' he mumbled.

'What two things?'

'Your stolen toys and that dead woman. One is your problem, the other isn't. Well, that is, unless you're daft enough to get involved.'

I knew what he meant. I had to keep my head clear. I got up abruptly, startling Bing off my lap. I bent to stroke him reassuringly, but he was already making for the door.

'Thanks Gus. I've got one or two things to do now. I'd better get back and do them.'

He rose and came with me to the little front path.

'Sure I can't help?'

'Not this second, Gus, not this second. But thanks.'

Bing and I strode back up to my place. But I had a feeling Gus would be needed pretty soon. I wondered what fishermen knew about skeleton keys.

The next hour or so, I spent a fortune on the phone. The cheapest call was to my friend on the *Western Gazette*. In a quarter of an hour, he found the information I wanted on the departed Mrs Veronica Charlotte Treasure. Apparently, from the newspaper reports of the time, she left for Lausanne on a Geneva flight on 24 March 1981. Randolph Treasure was reported as saying, 'My wife was not one of the most faithful of wives, and I imagine she has gone off to live with one of her lovers. I know she had many Swiss friends. That's all I wish to say. It's all been very distressing . . . .' etc., etc.

A column in the next week's edition reported that Mrs Treasure had actually been seen to board a British Airways flight to Geneva on the day in question, that she had luggage with her and had taken an internal flight to Lausanne. So it looked as if she had escaped from old Treasure's hairy hands, after all, and found love (or, more probably, something a little more basic) in the cleanest, tidiest little country in Europe. God bless her and every cuckoo clock she winds up, but it wasn't much help to me.

So I rang a few of the more sprauncy hotels in Lausanne, just in case, saying I was ringing from Scotland Yard. Futile hope, I knew, but the Telecom bill would not be along for two months or so, by which time I would probably be in debtors' prison anyway. And, naïve idiot that I was, I struck lucky at the seventh call. 'Yes,' said the man at the front desk of the Hotel Magnifique, in fairly good English, 'one moment, please . . . we did 'ave a Mrs Treasure 'ere the night of 24 March. I 'ave 'er signature in front of my 'and . . . No, I do not remember 'er myself. We 'ave so many guests from England . . . Yes, it looks as if she checked out the next day . . . Of course, the bill was paid. Really, Inspector, I must remind you, some things must remain confidential in our business . . . .'

So that was that. Dear Mrs Treasure had gone to Lausanne, but where she was now was anybody's guess. The one thing one could be sure of was that a woman like that, once gone, would never return. It's new pages they always want to turn, not ones they have already well thumbed.

I got a call then – from a real Inspector. Trevor Blake. He just thought that I would like to know that they had discovered what seemed like the remains of Pilot Officer Redfern, and quite a collection of remnants of clothing, parachute and so on. He thought I would be pleased for old Mrs Redfern – and for our proposed museum. I said I was, very, and thanked him for letting me know. And that was that.

I was sitting in the shop, having just sold a Japanese TN brand tinplate jeep with an electric motor that actuated the soldier passenger to answer the vehicle's telephone (really very cute), and was thinking about all those people I would like to see when, lo and behold, Arabella came back into my life. And I thought, screw it, even a bankrupt has got to take some time off. So I let her in, and turned my 'Open' sign to 'Closed'. A moment later I let her out again, because she had invited me out to tea, and a real cream tea at that.

We went in her car, and she drove like the wind, but well. And in no time at all we were in the uniquely attractive village of Corfe, nestling below the dramatic shadow of its guardian castle, a gaunt and craggy ruin atop its grassy hill.

'You're going to take me up to the top to earn your clotted cream and scones, Mr Marklin, sir.' She pointed at the castle. 'I've never been right up. Randolph has always refused to come with me. He says I'm a born tourist at heart. Should wear Bermuda shorts and all that.'

I said she should. She'd look nice in them. She gave me a glance, then dragged me by the hand up to the castle gates, where the ticket collector was more interested in the crazy streaks in her hair than the colour of our money. And so we began the long climb up and I started to feel better. Even the clouds began peeling away to leave the heavens blue and clear, and seemingly infinite from our higher and higher view-point.

'Does Treasure know you're with me?' I asked, rather out of breath from the slope.

'Yes,' she said, without glancing my way. I stopped her and made her look at me.

'What did you say to him?'

'I said I was going to ask if you would take me to see the castle, as he wouldn't. Nothing more dramatic.'

81

'And what did he say?'

'Shrugged his shoulders, and didn't say anything.'

'So you went, like that.'

'I came, like that.' She leaned across and kissed me. 'I came to be with you, and not to talk about Randolph.' And we resumed walking.

When we got to the massive ruins at the top – the result of Cromwell getting rather annoyed with the Royalists – I suddenly wished I was a real fully blown tourist, complete with clicking Cannon slung from my neck. I wanted a picture of her just the way she was – filmy polka-dot dress, bare legs, flat sandals, wind in her hair and freedom in her soul. And I could almost see her female hormones making sure I got the message.

I made her stand by a fractured wall, an archer's slit window just above her head, on the right. And I made as if I was Lord Snowdon, winding and snapping. She laughed and spread herself against the wall like an Egyptian in a frieze from an ancient Pharaoh's tomb. In a moment I joined her and pressed her against the unyielding stones, body to body. We kissed until a party of Germans wanted to get by. They've never had much sense of timing.

We climbed higher up where the hill became quite precipitous to our left and the ruins were more ruined. A kestrel soared up into the air above us. The path was very narrow now, and I had to go ahead. Arabella said she had got a stone in her sandal, and I heard her footsteps behind me cease. I walked on a little way, to wait for her by another archer's window. I stopped and looked out through the slit at the grey stone and slate village far below. It was then I heard a scream, immediately followed by a stunnng pain in my right shoulder, as I could not stop myself collapsing to the ground. I writhed in agony, and began falling down the sharply inclined bank on the other side. I tried to claw at the tufts of grass to stop my descent, but in the end, a bush beat me to it and I thwacked into its branches. I waited to catch my breath, then tried to sit up but my right shoulder was shouting too much with the pain. I leaned on my left arm and looked around. It was then I saw Arabella clambering down towards me. If she was a welcome sight before, she was a hundred times more so now.

'Peter, are you all right?' she asked frantically, kneeling down beside me and giving me her hand. I took it gratefully with my left.

'I'll let you know when I'm back on my feet. Give me a pull up, but gently. My right shoulder's on fire.'

She did so and I managed to get more or less upright, with my left hand supporting a little of the weight on the sloping grass above me.

'Something hit my shoulder. What was it? Did you see?'

'I think it was one of the stones above you. I looked up from doing my shoe and saw something coming down. The next moment you were on the ground and rolling over.'

'Was it you who screamed?' Arabella helped me get up the bank, shaky step by shaky step.

'Yes,' she replied, almost in a whisper.

When we got to the top, we found we had quite an audience. The Germans were there, of course, a couple of Japanese, two pushchairs and assorted parents, grannies and lovers, and a very butch lady with a Ronald Colman moustache.

We anticipated them by saying we were fine, and rather slowly and painfully made our way back down the hill to the gates at the bottom, Arabella's arm firmly round my waist. The ticket collector's hairdresser's eye appraised her once more, as we passed through.

'Do you want to go home?' Arabella asked anxiously. I felt my shoulder saying 'Yes' rather loudly, but my romantic side won.

'Didn't you say something about a cream tea, my ravishing rescuer?'

'I did, my poor wounded hero.'

'Then let's get clotted,' I said.

Before we actually went in to the Castleside Tea Rooms, Arabella insisted on inspecting my shoulder in the privacy of her own Golf. It proved to be bruised, grazed and swelling by the minute, but everything seemed to function, albeit painfully, so we decided a doctor could wait until we saw what cream, strawberry jam and scones could do. My attempts to kiss her in the car tended to give the lie to any very urgent need for hospitalization, although I did claim it was keeping my mind off the agony.

The tea rooms weren't that crowded, for May was early in the season. We sat at an oak table for two, looking out over a back garden that was precociously early with its summer bedding plants, the antirrhinums already being in flower.

What I took to be the proprietress, a chubby lady right out of

Dickens, took our order, and very soon it was laid out in front of us. If you haven't had such a West Country treat as a cream tea recently, you should mend your ways. It certainly went some way to mending my shoulder.

'Do you think it was the wind?' Arabella asked out of the blue. I wondered what on earth she was alluding to.

'What was the wind?' I retorted, reaching for her hand under the table.

'The stone falling on you, you idiot. Do you think it was the wind that toppled it?'

'I have no idea. I didn't see it coming, or really, where it came from – except above me.'

It was about at this time, that I first noticed a thick set young man, seated with a rather fly-blown girl at a table at the back of the room. He was obviously a great 'toucher', for she was continually trying to move his hand off one part or another of her anatomy in order to be able to eat her scones in peace. Luckily, in his rabbit-like persistence, he didn't notice us – or, for that matter, anybody but his companion. I say, 'luckily', because Arabella recognized him, and did not really want to be seen. He was, as she explained to me in a whisper, one of Randolph Treasure's farm-workers, Ken Gates. That on its own would not have been a problem. But Ken was the guy Treasure most relied on to do any of his personal errands. His unsubtle, brutish ways made Arabella dislike him, and she didn't want to have to speak to him, so I moved my chair around so that only my back showed in his direction – a back that was shielding Arabella from him at the same time. We hoped big Kennie had not already seen us – and we ate our last halves of scone in double quick time.

Paying was a nerve-wracking and frustrating experience. It took about ten minutes to get the bill because the proprietress was obviously head cook and bottle-washer as well as waitress and financial wizard.

But afterwards I blessed that dear Dickensian lady from the Castleside Tea Rooms for her over-busy way of life, for I overheard something that fell from Ken Gates's pendulous lips just as Arabella was, at last, handing her a clutch of pound coins. It was the word 'ferry' that did it. Something about a million cream teas could never make *him* sick, not like that bleeding cross-Channel ferry the other day.

Somehow, Mr Treasure's favourite farm-worker didn't exactly

look the very essence of an international gad-about. I wondered if he had an equally attractive spotty male friend and a penchant for plastic cars.

I didn't tell Arabella. I had other plans for the evening, if I could lie on my left side.

Eight

Arabella left about eleven. She wouldn't stay the night; I think I knew why. It wasn't because of Treasure, I was pretty certain. I think it was a demonstration of freedom – her freedom from anybody. At least, that is what I hoped it was, for we had grown very close that evening, and not just physically. We had wanted to talk about ourselves, what we wanted out of life, what we had not done, and why. And what's more important, we had both wanted to listen. I told her a bit about my undistinguished past, but she seemed rather cagey about hers for some reason. She knew that I wasn't exactly the type Unity Mitford would have fallen for and I wondered what she saw in me – besides imminent penury and debt, that is. And the only Roll-Royces I possessed were inches long, rather than feet. Maybe I was the other side of Treasure's coin.

It was after she had gone and I was left with the night that the fear hit me. A quaking, shaking fear, that I should have felt the instant that bit of castle hit me. I think it's called delayed shock; whatever it's called, the name cannot possibly live up to the sensation. My beauty sleep was again asked to wait outside as my mind became a Hitchcockian whirlpool of terrifying images and pretty ghastly guesses. As I have already intimated, I had been by no means sure the rock was an accident. But now I suddenly put a hand to the rock. The hand that pawed the girl that sat in the café that lay near the castle that could have killed me. And I could see another hairy hand pulling the strings. And I could hear a sweet voice enticing me to go and visit the ruins before we settled down to tea. I got up out of bed, dripping with sweat and shaking like the proverbial leaf, and with one shoulder throbbing like hell. In the end I went downstairs, checked all the locks on the doors, the latches on the windows, then swept Bing up from his warm basket in my one good arm, and carried the Siamese saviour up to my own worry-blanket of a bed. I had a feel-

ing there were too many reasons now why I shouldn't wait for
the due processes of the law, and Detective Inspector Trevor
Blake. Only one of them was Mr Chalmers' deadline. So sorry,
Mr Blake. It was just the way it was, so help me God.

The next morning, the post brought its usual medley of bills and
letters of enquiry about what toys I had for sale (I advertised
regularly in the old toy buffs' bible, the *Collectors Gazette*), and
the gentleman from Fife wrote to say he would take the Minics. I
performed my clerical duties for the day, then sat in my shop and
tried to make sense of my thoughts. I was not exactly racing
ahead with plans of action worthy of James Bond, when the
phone unexpectedly came to my aid.

It was Deborah, and this time, bless her, with some news that
wasn't just about herself. I almost kissed the receiver for she had
remembered my little request from her last lachrymose visit.

'Derek says Treasure is going away for three days,' she
announced to my flapping ears.

'When?' I asked.

'From tomorrow.'

'Do you know where he's going?'

'Abroad.'

I liked that. It sounded a nice long way away. Everybody
seemed to be going abroad, or were just back, like Gerald
Rankin.

'Not Geneva, by any chance? Or South Africa?'

'Derek just said abroad, and I didn't want to raise any suspicions by pressing it.' She sounded disappointed because I
wasn't exactly jumping up and down.

'No, Debby, that's marvellous news. Keep it up, and you'll be
awarded the Lady Sleuth of the Year award,' I quickly reassured
her.

'By whom?' she chuckled. 'You?'

'Yes, me, if I'm still here to award it, that is.'

'You're not getting up to anything ... er ...?' I knew she
didn't actually want to say the word 'dangerous', so I cut in.

'Of course not. Don't worry. Just a collector of information,
that's me. A kind of poor man's Michael Caine.'

'Bankrupt, more like,' she added, and she didn't quite realize
how accurate her remark was.

I also learned she had managed to get a loan from her boss (I wondered whether it was a loan, or an advance), and that she was now putting her past behind her (what else can you do with it?), and we rang off, the best of mates.

I sat for a moment after the call, and soon came to the conclusion that the plan forming in my head was easier done on the movies than in real life. I regretted not having joined the SAS straight from kindergarten. However, *nil desperandum*, I had to find those toys and quickly. The clock was not ticking my way. So I went to see Gus. I had a feeling he would know about those things.

I was not disappointed. Gus was getting in his two-door terror when I called. But after hearing the purpose of my visit, he got out again, and gave me an instant demonstration of how easy it was to burgle his house with a piece of wire, and my credit card. I won't go into the exact details here as I like Gus and I don't want anyone to burgle his house except me. I thanked him profusely and, after a fair amount of trouble, got my credit card back again. He did not need to ask me what I might be doing with my new-found knowledge. He just said, 'Be careful', and 'Do you need me to come along too?' I said, 'I will' and 'Not this time, thank you.' I left then, and he nearly knocked me down a minute later as he bounced past in his Popular.

When I got home, my shoulder was hurting in a big way again, but like a Spartan hero I ignored it, gathered up Bing and went out in the Beetle. (Don't get me wrong, I don't mean to imply Spartan heroes had Siamese cats or Volkswagens.) I had decided to try Gus's card trick on Treasure first, then Rankin. I just had to get somewhere before Chalmers pulled the rug.

Within half an hour or so I could see the spires of Doom Abbey over the tops of the hedges, and I just prayed Mr Treasure was not on the battlements watching out with his binoculars for Beetles. I parked the car some way past the house, in the mud of a farm gateway, and made my way back towards the abbey on foot. I wished I was the kind of man who always wore a hat so that I could have pulled it down over my eyes, but every now and again, when I thought I might be seen, I put my hand over my forehead as if shielding my eyes from the glare of the sun. Unfortunately, the effect was rather spoilt by it not being out.

However, the reccy was well worth while for my plans of the morrow. I noted that, from the front anyway, there were only two windows that were low enough to the ground to get through without asking to borrow a ladder. And luckily, both these windows were in the lee of a turret so my activities could not be overlooked by everyone else in the house. (I counted on only the housekeeper being indoors. Outdoors was a matter I would have to consider carefully.)

The huge front door, however, was something else. It bore no resemblance to Gus's in any particular, and looked as if it was built strongly enough to withstand the second coming of Attila the Hun. I couldn't see it falling to a Barclaycard, or even American Express. So I reckoned it would have to be one of those two windows, which, from my one visit, I guessed must open from a little corridor that led off from the huge, manorial-type hall.

I did not feel I should hang about very much longer so, with a last lingering look at the stone fortress I was to attack the next day, I went back to Bing and the Beetle. A moment later, I was on my way home.

The afternoon was uneventful, but financially, rewarding. I sold a mint Meccano Aircraft Constructor set, circa 1937, to a tall bald man with a stoop for £285, and a very nice, but not perfect, Hornby Curlew tinplate boat in green and cream, circa same date, for seventy pounds. It was the evening that brought the bad news: number one, I didn't see hide nor hair of Arabella (and I had grown used to both); number two, Inspector Blake rang through with more on the rolling Stone. They had discovered where he had stored all his furniture, cars and effects – in an old aircraft hangar near Taunton, on which he had taken a lease two years previously. Everything was apparently there, from Ferraris to fireguards, from garden furniture to pots and pans. Even his antique toy collection. But as Trevor Blake put it to me ever so considerately, 'We have checked and double-checked those toys with your very detailed description of those stolen, and we regret to say none of them match up. But I must say, I envy Mr Vivian Stone in this one respect: it is a handsome collection, nevertheless.'

I remarked that it didn't mean to say he had not stolen mine, with which the Inspector had to agree.

'There may be another hangar somewhere, Mr Marklin. After all, we did not find any diamonds either.'

As a postscript, I asked him whether the woman's body had been identified yet. He said they were working on it. I thanked him for trying to cheer me up, rang off, and spent the rest of the evening half watching television, half listening out for Arabella. For, whatever she might or might not have been up to recently, as Mr Lerner wrote, 'I'd grown accustomed to her face.'

Next day eventually dawned, and my bed still bore only one depression, and that was me. But I girded my loins, downed a quick toast and marmalade (I collect the Golly badges for my cousin's little girl in Chester), stroked Bing, and explained why he could not come with me today. I reversed the Beetle out of what was left of my lean-to – the plywood panel fell off as I put the key in – and made for Lulworth, the Porsche engine purring powerfully away.

This time I parked in the village itself, in the pub car-park, and walked up towards the forbidding house, first on the narrow roadway, then across two fields, a route I had sussed out on the previous day. Eventually, I found a gap in the hedge through which I had a clear view of the house and grounds. I was more or less invisible to anyone who hadn't put a homing device in my underpants. On the right, I could see the large barn, in which I had seen Treasure's Silver Cloud and Arabella's Golf. Today it only held an old Land-Rover with a dent in the door. In the centre was the house, and on my left, an impressive array of outbuildings and stables surrounding a courtyard that was neatly paved with stone setts. In fact, everything was neat – washed, brushed and tonsured – the epitome of order, if not necessarily of law.

I moved a little further down the hedge to get a better view of my two candidate windows. And as I did so I heard voices and saw Treasure's housekeeper in coat and hat, standing by the front door with the Corfe 'toucher,' Ken Gates. I couldn't hear what they were saying, but soon Gates disappeared down the main part of the garden, in the direction of a five-barred gate that, I assumed, led onto farmland. The housekeeper also disappeared for a moment, but then rematerialized on an ancient, curly-framed lady's bicycle and pedalled off down the drive. I decided I could not have been donated better timing if it had been rehearsed, so, as they always used to say in my boyhood Biggles stories, 'I made my move'.

I 'Pink-Panthered' my way across to the right hand of my two windows, and crouching down, listened hard. Nothing but silence. I had a screwdriver in my pocket, which I applied to the wooden frame of the window. It would not even go in the crack. Oak is like that when it wants to be. After about three minutes of scratching about, I gave up the more scientific approach, and taking my Barclaycard from my wallet, I held it against the leaded window pane next to where I could see the inside handle. Then I gave the card a blow with my fist (not exactly what Gus had intended for the plastic money, but there you go), the glass shattered and fell inside with a resounding series of tinkles. But saved by the Bank, my fist was okay. Not a scratch on the leather of my glove even. I put my hand through the jagged hole, undid the latch, and was in the house before you could count too many incriminating seconds. And I remembered to pick up my Barclaycard from the parquet flooring.

The house smelt of Mansion polish, like my mother's place in Charmouth. (That was the only similarity.) Suffice it to say that, having listened hard once again to detect if my entry had been noted, I made off round the rest of the house at a rate of knots. I had no desire to stay there a moment longer than I had to. I won't take you on a conducted tour of the castle, it would be very tedious. But basically, I searched everything that could possibly house a toy or a diary. The toys were easier – they were all together. I found them in the third room, a child's room with a vengeance, containing a really remarkable collection of both splendid and more mundane toys, dating from around 1920 up to around 1955. Seemingly almost every Dinky ever made, both here and in France, was stacked neatly in its original box or, the early ones, in glass cabinets lining the walls. (The earliest Dinky cars, unlike their aircraft, did not run to boxes.) There was also a wide and varied collection of American Tootsietoy diecasts, aircraft, cars and ships; Solido by the hundred; Mercury models from Italy. And so on, and so on, and so on. I won't even begin to describe the tinplate. Almost every major German, American, British and Empire, and Japanese manufacturer was represented, as far as I could determine from a quick glance at the parade of shelves. Mr Treasure had certainly kept the real scale of his obsession a darkly veiled secret, and I wondered why. It couldn't just be for fear of burglars or the tax man, or could it? After all, Mr Chalmers was a pretty secretive soul about his own toy transactions.

But look as I might in that toy room, and every other place

in the house, bar the attics, my eleven tinplates were not to be seen.

I did discover a few interesting other bits and pieces about the hairy-handed keeper of the castle. Like toys weren't the only thing he collected. In a wardrobe in the dressing-room, off what was obviously the main bedroom, there was evidence of quite a different kind of hobby. And much more of the Unity Mitford kind. Nazi memorabilia: a full Nazi officer's dress uniform, complete with armbands and cap and highly polished boots; a rack full of short leather riding whips and straps; a large drawer, up to the brim with badges, awards, medals, Iron Crosses. Another was full of black and white photographs taken at various Third Reich rallies, and hundreds of Nazi propaganda cigarette cards. Really, Mr Treasure, what would your friends have thought of you, if they knew? But then, I guessed, one or two might have liked it. Derek, perhaps, for one, kissing the toe of Treasure's jack boot. And then, in some tiny plastic bags, were 'some substances', as they say, that did not smell like face powder.

But, amongst other things, it was the diaries I was after, not his sexual apparatus or sensory stimuli. In every room, I searched any drawer or bureau I could find, for Treasure had to keep them somewhere. And, at least the current one, somewhere accessible. It was the current one I was really interested in, and its entries for the last few weeks. But my labours were in vain. Books there were in plenty, from leather bound classics and first editions, to the current outpourings of the popular fiction writers, but short of taking down and examining every single book in his huge library, I could not find anything that approximated to a diary. I thought that was a very curious phenomenon in the home and castle of an obsessive diary writer and memorabilia maniac. But the curiosity of the phenomenon helped me forward not one jot.

I looked at my Seiko, and I reckoned I'd been an intruder quite long enough for the health of my pension plan. On my way out, the way I came, I noticed a small oil painting of a rather striking woman of about thirty hanging in a dark corner of the hall. I memorized the features of her face, just in case, and checked the portrait for a date. It had one – 1979. I guessed I had just met Mrs Veronica Treasure for the first time.

And then I was gone, and I just hoped Marks and Spencer's best brown leather gloves (medium size) did not leave highly individualistic prints. Or my Marks and Spencer trainers for that matter. But then I was not the only person in the world with a pair of those, was I?

The tension of being an intruder began to loosen as I beetled home, and it let in a huge feeling of disappointment and frustration. I had taken a monumental risk for plug zero, and I was no further informed at all – unless you include snooping on another person's sexual life as a giant leap forward for personkind. Treasure just did not seem to have the stolen toys. Yet somehow I was not entirely convinced. After all, he did not seem to be a fanatical diary keeper, from my little investigation, either. Yet I knew he was. Correction: Arabella told me he was. And why should she lie? Unless, of course, she was totally in league with Treasure, and had been lying all the time. But then, how would concocting a story about diaries help Treasure? I was getting very confused – and that was without including the possibility that Treasure had murdered his free-wheeling wife, the lady of the portrait. And I was depressed, too, at the thought of having to go through the same scary exercise with Rankin's home, if hairy hands proved to be as pure as the driven snow.

By the time I got home, I knew there was only one intelligent response to the whole shebang – I went to the pub. But it was a move that I very soon regretted, for I met Gus. Now I rate Gus very highly in the scheme of things, but it was what he said that worried me to death.

'Surprised to see you back,' was his first remark.

'What do you mean? I wasn't planning to stay there,' I said almost in a whisper as I didn't wish every beer brain in the pub to know of my escapade.

He took my hint and lowered his not inconsiderable voice.

'Thought you might be staying somewhere at Her Majesty's pleasure,' he replied.

'Why? I was very careful. Didn't get in quite the way you showed me, but I got in.' I took a draught of my Heineken. 'But I couldn't find a sausage to pin on him. Not a diary, nor my toys. Nothing.'

'No? I learnt something this morning, that's all. Came over to tell you, but you'd gone.'

'Learnt what?' I said impatiently.

'Doesn't really matter now.'

'Come on, Gus. There you go again. Tell me – it might be important.'

'It was.'

'So?' I gripped his wrist – his Heineken raising wrist. That did it.

'Chatting to an old mate of mine in Weymouth this morning, I was. He's an electrician, very good with wires. I asked him what he knew about Treasure. He said, not a lot. But he knew the house quite well . . . .'

'Come on. Get to the point.'

'That *is* the point. He knew the place well because two year ago, he installed an elaborate burglar alarm system. And it's wired direct to the nearest police station. That's all.'

I almost had an attack of the vapours on the spot. I held onto the bar.

'That's why', he continued, 'I didn't really expect you to be back for a bit. So I came round here to cheer myself up.'

I took his hand and led him over to a window seat. I needed to sit down.

'My God,' I breathed, 'then why didn't the bloody burglar alarms go off?'

I couldn't believe that even a mate of Gus's could be that bad an electrician.

My slough of despond was made a trifle less soggy when I got back by a picture postcard lying on my doormat. It bore a rather luridly coloured picture of steep green hills, and underneath 'The Mynd, above All Stretton'. I turned it over. It was postmarked Owermoigne and dated two days before. Beyond my address, it had nothing written on it bar a signature, 'Often'. I smiled. Crook she might be, but it was her almost criminal sense of humour that got me every time. I put the postcard behind a Victorian dish on my kitchen dresser, where Bing couldn't see it, and made myself some lunch. All the time I was eating, I wondered why she did not call. I'd wear a little Hitler moustache for one of her smiles, that's how far gone I was.

By midway through the afternoon, interrupted by a retired Colonel I knew vaguely who bought a pre-war Frog 'Interceptor' flying model fighter complete with box and winder for seventy pounds, and an acned youth who shelled out twenty-five pounds for a Spot-On Humber Super Snipe, I got my mind back into some kind of shape and had decided on my next plan of action. My intuition seemed to bring me to the firm conclusion that the diaries must exist, and that they could provide the answer, one way or the other, not only to the stolen tinplates, but probably, to the fate of the strikingly good-looking lady hanging in Treasure's manorial hall. Once I'd found them, I could either nail Treasure or count him out of my list of suspects. Vivian Stone I just had to leave to Inspector Blake. Rankin I would have to Barclaycard (I dreaded it), and all the other possibles, like Monsieur Vincent, Chalmers himself, and collectors from other parts of the country, had to await the elimination of Treasure, Stone and Rankin. It was the only way I could see to make any sense of any of it, or any forward progress. After all, Blake had said intuition was the policeman's greatest asset. I was banking on it working for laymen, too.

Just at that moment the telephone rang and, speak of the devil, it was Detective Inspector Trevor Blake. How's that for intuition?

'Any news?' I asked, in the half-hope.

'Not about your toys, Mr Marklin, I'm sorry to say. We haven't caught up with Mr Stone yet. It's more difficult once they get abroad, you know. Got to tread carefully. I really just rang to see if you had any more bright ideas about our little find in the Spitfire excavation.'

'No, why should I?' I remarked suspiciously.

'Oh, don't get me wrong, Mr Marklin. I don't suspect you of anything. I just wondered if you had come up with any more hypotheses.'

There was a pregnant silence, and I knew I would be missing a trick if I didn't forward something. It isn't every day you get Scotland Yard on your side, so I took a deep breath, and jumped in way over my head – taking my old Mum's advice again.

'It's Treasure. At least, I think so. It's his wife who is supposed to have gone to Switzerland. She didn't, or something. He murdered her and buried her under the oak tree, where no one would ever find her. Removed most of the skull so the remains couldn't be identified . . . .' I was beginning to lose my confidence rapidly. 'Could be, couldn't it? I don't know. You asked me so I told you . . . and, then again, who knows? It's got nothing to do with me, anyway. It's those stolen toys I want back. What skeletons you find are your problem, not mine . . . .'

I began rambling, but he interrupted me before I could make an even bigger idiot of myself.

'Very interesting, Mr Marklin. Don't get flustered – I'm not going to tell anyone else of your little hypothesis.'

I didn't say anything more, so he went on in his quiet, authoritative voice. 'Let me feed you some more information, Mr Marklin. You'll read about it sooner or later in the papers, anyway. The woman's bones show traces of acid. Could be to help the dissolving of the flesh, don't you think? Make identification harder should the body have been found earlier, I would imagine. And, by the way, we know Mrs Treasure went to Lausanne. We have a copy of her hotel registration form. Apparently there was a man with her. All fits the rumours of the time – that she went off to meet her lover, Mr Marklin, not remained here to meet her death.'

'Look, as I said, that's your problem, Inspector. Avoiding imminent backruptcy is mine. I'm not loaded, you see, like Lord Peter Wimsey was, and I don't receive a steady old age pension cheque like Miss Marples, and I'm not paid a retainer like Philip Marlowe....'

'I'll remember that in future, Mr Marklin. Don't lose any sleep on my account, please. I'll keep you informed if I hear anything.'

'On the toys?'

'On the toys, Mr Marklin. Goodbye.'

I did not give myself too long to digest his call before I decided to act on my intuition and call Deborah.

'What can I do for you today, Mr Wonderful?' she oozed into the phone, and I guessed she'd had one of those advertising meetings with an ample alcohol content.

'Make a little assignation for me?'

'With whom, lover mine? There's Sally, who's been hot for you ever since you worked here, you know that. And cool little Jennifer, the receptionist, could do with a littie of your magic de-icer....'

'No listen, Deborah, this is serious. Are you sober enough to take it in?' I regretted saying that the second I let it out of my mouth.

'I can take it in any time, big boy. Don't you remember?'

'Oh God, Deborah, pull yourself together.'

'All right, all right, all right. I promise.' She coughed. 'Tell me what you want.'

'Fix a meeting for me with dear Derek, will you?'

'You going bisexual in your old age?' she sniggered.

'For heaven's sake, listen. I want to get some information from him. It's very important. Say I've heard of a great opening for an Art Director in a London agency that might suit him down to the ground – big salary, car, and all that. Lay it on. Like to take him for a drink and tell him all about it. You know.'

'I know. When do you want to do it?'

'Tomorrow lunchtime. I'll come over and pick him up.'

'Okay, I'll ask him, and ring you back. You must tell me what it's all about some time over a ... whatever you would like to have it over, with me.'

I did not rise to her. Just said, 'Thanks' and rang off. She rang back five minutes later. Yes, Derek would love to come. Whilst Treasure was abroad, he was at a loose end. She asked if she could join us. I said, 'No, it would be all boys' talk.' I won't tell you what she said in reply, but it sure didn't sound like girls' talk.

Nine

'Do you miss it at all?' He looked at me with his baby-blue eyes.

'If you mean advertising, not one bit.' I poured him another glass of Sauternes (his choice, not mine).

He fingered the stem of his glass. 'Don't you miss the people though? Must be lonely just seeing other old toy buffs, isn't it?' He tried to make his question sound like a statement.

'I do meet other souls, you know, once in a while. I am allowed.' I grinned at him, but not too much, just in case. 'And,' I continued, 'with you and Deborah as worthy exceptions, it was the people in advertising I could stand least. They are so used to hyping the shallow and ephemeral into something significant that in their private lives they seem to do the reverse.'

'Oh,' he replied, and didn't follow it with: 'I see what you mean.' The vacant look in his baby-blue eyes said it all.

Derek leaned back in his Windsor chair, crossed his long, rather bony legs, and looked around the small wine bar. His non-drinking hand drooped at right angles to his wrist. Must be the boys' equivalent of a Masonic handshake.

'But it's the people I adore,' he said in a poor man's Noël Coward voice. 'I never get lonely in advertising, I really don't.' He looked across at me. I poured myself another glass.

'But your *best* friends aren't in advertising surely? Nobody I've ever known has their best friends in the business,' I said, trying to change the subject in my direction.

'Some are, some aren't,' he said, begging me to continue talking about him. Suited me.

'And are yours, or not?'

He took a deep breath, and his chest seemed to go more concave. I couldn't figure it out.

'Well, that would be telling, wouldn't it.' He looked up coyly. 'My very best friend certainly isn't. He's a bit beyond advertising.'

'Important, you mean?'

He put his glass down, and leaned forward to me. '*And* wealthy, Peter. And I *mean* up to the deliciously manly eyeballs.' He patted my knee. Ah well, all in a day's work. He leaned back again. 'He's away at the moment. Abroad. It's a drag, really.'

I could not but agree with him.

'When is he back?'

'Not long. In a couple of days.' He sighed, then continued, 'In one way he's a bit like you.'

I was glad to hear it was only in one way.

'How so?'

'He likes old toys too. Got a lot of them, but doesn't publicize the fact. I think he's worried about people knowing he's a bit of a softie underneath.'

I was starting to feel queasy, but I persevered.

'I think I know now who you are talking about. He's a perfect treasure, aren't I right?'

Derek blushed to the dark roots of his blond hair.

'I'm not saying, am I?' he replied, fluttering his eyelashes.

I drank some more of my wine, then launched in.

'I know of him through the toy trade. Heard he had quite a big find early this month. Eleven pretty valuable tinplates, from the south of France.'

He looked slightly puzzled.

'He hasn't been abroad this year until now, so I think you must be mistaken.'

'I think he may have procured them in Dover, or had them delivered to him somehow. Doesn't matter really. I drink to him. Not often a collector is so very fortunate.'

Derek relaxed again, and sipped his drink as if it were nectar.

'Come to think of it, my friend seemed to be very excited about something about the time you say. Even more ebullient than he normally is. He's wonderful when he's like that; *incredibly* masterful.'

'You mean, about a week and a half ago?'

'Yes, I guess it would be.'

'And you never found out why?' I could hardly hide my impatience.

'I never really ask him about his business affairs, things like that. I assumed he had made another killing on the Stock Exchange, or had a property deal go well. I never thought it might be toys. Suppose it could have been. All he said was that another of his boats had come in.'

I could have kissed him – well, almost. An hour later I poured him out of the wine bar and back to the Willard, Jenks and Pursar agency, established 1928. I clanked back on the good old ferry to Studland. And while I was standing at the vessel's rail, being nine years old again, the sun came out. And do you know something? For once, it was the same sun.

I only opened for a couple of hours that day, and I would have sold nothing had it not been for Bing. It turned out to be a gawpers and touchers time, so the shop always seemed to have a customer or two inside but no actual sales accruing. Just before five, Bing jumped on the counter and a fat man in a raincoat (it looked as if he slept in it), who had been gawping for nearly quarter of an hour, went over and stroked him. As he did so, his sleeve caught a neat stack of mint, boxed Spot-On diecast cars. The pile collapsed and four went onto the floor. To cover his embarrassment he bought one of them instantly for thirty-two pounds – an xkss Jaguar.

With trying to see that none of the gawpers and touchers half-inched anything as they gawped and touched, I had no real chance to reflect on my fortunes until the evening. And when I did, they seemed a little less rosy than the Sauternes had made them appear with Derek in the wine bar. However, there was progress to report, for Derek had now more or less convinced me that Treasure was behind the disappearance of my toys. And that was sort of satisfying, for two reasons: one, he'd struck me as a baddie the first moment I'd clapped eyes on him, and it's nice to have one's instincts proved correct, and two, he was just the kind of man I'd never had any respect for; born with a silver sledge-hammer in his mouth with which he would beat the rest of the world into obeisance to his slightest whim until his dying day. It was sweeter to think of his being a regular baddie than, say, Monsieur Vincent or Rankin or even the diamond fiddler on the run. And three, it didn't half concentrate my mind to narrow the field down to one. Even if I were eventually proven wrong, I would have enjoyed the extra shots of adrenalin pumping through my otherwise rather confused system. And, merciful heavens, I could now postpone my Barclaycard attempt to search Rankin's property. So I settled down to a quiet evening with Bing. Those toys just had to be somewhere amidst the Victorian steeples of Doom Abbey, for old toy collectors almost never keep their previous reminders of youthful innocence secreted so far away that they cannot enjoy instant access to them whenever they feel like it – or whenever their adult consciences prick.

I awoke to a loud 'miaowowowow', and I was sitting bolt up in my bed, my heart pounding like a piledriver. I saw Bing racing out of the bedroom door, and then I heard it. A banging, rattling noise. I tried to pull myself together, and picked up my watch from the table by my bed. It was a luminous quarter to two, and the banging and rattling continued. I suddenly realized why Bing had come upstairs and jumped on my bed (a thing he never usually does – at night). There was someone at the shop door.

I put on my terry towelling robe with 'Hotel Majestic' embroidered on the breast pocket, and very cautiously went downstairs. I armed myself with the appropriate poker from the sitting-room, and went on tiptoe into the shop. I slowly pulled open the door to the length of the security chain and saw, to my delight and relief, the Queen of the Mynd, the strange, yet irresistible Arabella. I sighed, glad yet knowing there was little chance of sleep again.

It wasn't until the sun was forcing its way through the curtains that we really got down to sensible speech, anxious though I was, ultimately, to do so. All I had gathered was that she had been with Treasure to a vintage toy auction in Geneva – separate rooms, thank God – and he had decided to come back early, after receiving a somewhat mysterious phone call, which he would not discuss with her. They had had a blazing row when they had got back to the abbey, apparently about his unbending attitude towards me, and suspicion about my being the mysterious intruder, and she had left and driven straight over. I showed my gratitude in the customary fashion more than once, and she did likewise. When I looked in her eyes, I could not believe she was a Dorset Mata Hari or Studland Salome. I think it's at times like these, you should be able to tell. Shouldn't you? Anyway, it was wonderful having her back, and I told her so.

'I'm not back really,' she said, sitting naked, cross-legged in front of me on the bed.

'You mean because you've never really been away, or that you will be off again?'

'The latter, I'm afraid.' She took my roving hand and held it to her lips. 'I'm not ready yet to settle.' She continued, 'I wonder sometimes if I ever will be. And yet....'

I took a little heart in that I was probably in that 'and yet' bit. At least I hoped so.

'Tell me something, little Miss Often,' I said after a while, 'have you finished with Treasure?'

'I don't know. Almost, but maybe not quite. I thought I had completely when I stormed out last night.'

'But now you've made love with me, you're not quite sure?' I smiled at her, and she elongated her fabulously elegant and luxurious body alongside my bog standard version. She put her finger across my lips.

'No,' she whispered, 'it's got nothing to do with you, or love, or anything but me, I suppose.'

'Will you promise to tell me when you're over it?' I asked softly.

'I promise, as long as you promise to tell me when you're tired of all this stupidity of mine.'

I nodded, but she cut short anything I might have added by rolling on top of me. We did not speak again for a little bit.

I felt a real swine for I could not really tell her that part of me (the sleuth bit) was glad she had not totally broken her association with Treasure just yet. But that was only part of me. And it wasn't the part that felt the pain, sod it.

She left at eleven, and I was relieved to hear it was to her cousin's that she was going. Apparently, she had a lot of pricking out to do to make up for her Geneva break.

Directly her silver Golf was out of sight along the Swanage road, I locked up the house and walked the short way to the one village phone box. I dialled the right number and put in the right money. I was lucky. He was in.

'Who is it?' The timbre of his voice made the receiver vibrate.

'A friend,' I said, but not in my own voice. I'm not exactly Sir Laurence Olivier, but I am passably good at regional accents. This time I was Liverpudlian, a mixture of John Lennon and a trade union shop steward.

'I know about those toys you nicked.'

102

'What are you talking about? Who *are* you?' I could tell he wanted to ring off, but could not afford to.

'Never mind that,' I Liverpooled, and I was afraid my accent was getting a little too stagey, so I began to tone it down. 'I know you've got those toys. And I know you won't want anyone else to know you've got them, will you?'

'Who the blazes are you?' he boomed again.

'I told you, a friend. A friend who doesn't want you to get into any trouble for pinching 'em, that's all. There are eleven of those little playthings – those are the ones I mean.'

There was no reply.

'So,' I went on, 'as I know both of us would like to keep the whole affair our little secret, I think we should meet.'

There was still no reply, and I was afraid he might have rung off. I pressed on, regardless.

'I suggest the Tilly Whim caves. You know – they're on the coast path, up from Swanage. I'll meet you there in two hours from now. Two, exactly. If you don't come, I'll go straight to the police with what I know.' Then I added what I hoped would be a clincher. 'You're not the only one with friends in Dover, you know.'

I slammed the receiver down, and leant back, with relief, against the side of the phone box. I suddenly realized I was covered in sweat from my careworn head down to my trainers.

The two hours I had given him were ample time for me to get over to Lulworth, park the Beetle and cross the fields to the gap in the hedge, which commanded the view over the front of the house and its outbuildings. I was there in under half the time and, to my relief, the distinguished shape of the Silver Cloud was still in the barn. After a while, I wished I had brought my anorak, as it was one of those late spring days that had not made up its mind as to which season it wanted to be. Right now it felt decidedly like winter, and the wind across the field was quite cutting.

About ten minutes after my arrival, I saw the wildly attractive Mr Ken Gates come out of the outbuilding farthest from me, walk around to a Land-Rover parked in the cobbled yard, start it up, drive down the drive and turn left towards Wool. I counted that as a bit of luck. But I had to wait a further ten minutes before I saw any movement from the house. And when it came, it sent a

103

shiver down what was left of my spine. Treasure had a gun with him – one that looked big enough to blast some new Tilly Whim caves. (Actually, it was a normal 12-bore, but it took me by surprise.) He carried it with a natural ease, and then I remembered with horror, he was president of some marksmen's club or other. He went over to the rear of his Rolls-Royce, fumbled with some keys, and opened up the special Harold Radford tailgate-cum-bootlid. He seemed to bury his head and hands inside the boot for a minute or two, and then reached back for the shotgun, which he had propped up against the rear wing. It, too, disappeared inside, and when Treasure stood up straight again, the beautifully lined interior of the boot seemed empty. He appeared to think for a minute, then closed the lid. I guessed he must have stowed the gun away in the special compartment I knew was a speciality of this huntin' and shootin' conversion.

He reversed smoothly around in an arc, swished off down the gravel of the drive, and turned right onto the road, I guessed, that was leading to Swanage and his appointment at Tilly Whim caves. I reckoned that little expedition should keep him away up to an hour and a half. That left me a safety margin of only an hour for my appointment with his outbuildings. And maybe much less, for I would have to keep a rabbit's ear cocked for the Corfe toucher; other farm-workers I didn't worry about, because there's something delightfully gentlemanly about them. If they found me scouting around, they would probably assume I was from the Min. of Ag., or the NFU, or was some farming adviser old Treasure had called in. After all, wasn't I dressed posh (other than the trainers) and didn't I speak proper? That's what I was counting on them thinking.

Of the three main thatched outbuildings, I chose the largest first, and put on a pair of dark glasses in some sort of hope of disguising my appearance. I sprinted, in a semi-crouched position, down to its side entrance. Not hearing any shouts or any sounds from within, I entered. Had I been after a farm equipment thief, I might have found him here, for that's all the barn contained, apart from an old Home Guard German aircraft recognition chart tacked on the wall.

I exited flat up against the wall, like I'd seen in the movies, then sprinted across to the smallest of the three buildings, which was the one nearest the house. The oak door opened without even a creak, and I saw I was in some sort of dairy. But a dairy with a difference – a dairy set out as it must have looked in the early part of this century, with churns, strainers, vats and butter pats, muslin and all the shining apparatus of cheese and butter making. For a second, I had a little more time for Mr Randolph Treasure, but only for a second. There was a small door at the back of the Edwardian dairy, and it was locked. However, I presented my Barclaycard – it's like they say in the adverts, it can open a lot of doors. Inside there was a circular cast-iron staircase, which I climbed with incredible care lest I kicked up any noise. At the top, another door, also locked, with a mortise. The keyhole could have taken a large Havana cigar with room to spare. I put my eye to it, but there must have been a cover over the other side. I sat down on the top step, and cursed Treasure and all his antecedents, before I finally decided on desperate measures.

Desperate they were too, for I had to creep back to the first outbuilding to get the axe I had noticed hanging, with other tools of the farming trade, on the back wall. Yes, I have to admit my sleuthing lacks a little subtlety and finesse, but there's not much finesse about being owned by a bank or a mortgage company either. Still, it was one better than being in the slammer or hospital, I suppose. And that's where I was going if anybody caught me butchering the door to smithereens.

Luckily, my first three axe blows were more or less deft, and part of the door frame fell away from the latch of the massive Tudor lock. Before I pushed open the door, I listened for any reaction to the crack of the three blows. As yet, there seemed to be none, so I went in. And, my God, instantly I was in another world, and I felt almost guilty for breaking into it. The room was a breathtaking reproduction of a child's room of the thirties. And that child was so obviously a boy, a very, very lucky boy with generous and imaginative parents. I did not have time to dwell on every playtime gem I recognized displayed within those four walls, and carefully placed upon the cubist style Art Deco carpet, for, beyond the Marklin train set laid out on the polished pine floor by the small windows, were the objects of my foolhardy mission: the Citroën taxi, the JEP Hispano Suiza and Rolls-Royce, and the Marklin battleship being the most prominent. This man Treasure certainly had real class. He had arranged all ten (I now noticed one was missing – the P2 Alfa Romeo) as if the young boy was still in the process of opening them, the gift wrapping still clinging to some of the boxes, and ribbon bedecking the floor. Some of the tinplates were only half visible atop their packing – it was as if Treasure wanted to freeze time; and I remembered Monsieur Vincent, and that strangely charming room in the south of France.

I was about to pick up the Citroën, when I suddenly felt I was being watched. I spun round, and, in the corner, seated in a chair, was the childish figure of a boy. I got up off my knee, and was about to stammer something, when I noticed the fingers of his left hand. One was slightly chipped. I slowly approached him and I saw he was, in truth, a wondrously formed plaster dummy dressed in schoolboy uniform: a grey flannel, long-trousered suit, grey shirt and a bright striped tie I didn't recognize. His size seemed to indicate he was supposed to be about thirteen or fourteen, which seemed to me a little old for the toys he was supposed to be playing with. But that was the least of my concerns, as I was startled back to reality by the sound of tyres on gravel. I ran across to the window, kicking a railway carriage off the rails in my rush, and looked out. It was the Land-Rover, and Ken Gates. It was pulling into the courtyard to park right outside, where I had seen it when I first arrived.

I realized I could not escape Ken Gates's loving clutches with eleven (correction, ten) priceless and fragile tinplate toys strung around my person, nor was there time to take them, so reluctantly I left them in the strange room and descended that spiral staircase as fast as I could. At the oak door to the barn, I stopped and listened. I could hear hobnails on the cobbles, but the noise did not seem to be getting louder. I inched the heavy door open and peered outside. There was no sign of lover-boy, only the rear part of the Land-Rover being within my eye-line. I did my spreading myself against the wall act, and crabwised my way out, and along the stone wall towards the back of the building, from where I might be able to sprint back to the hedge without being seen.

The hobnails seemed to be going farther away, so I continued my slow progress along the side of the building. As I did so, I tripped over something in a tuft of grass, and it let out a loud clank. I looked down, and saw it was part of an old wooden plough. Beside it was a pile of rusty chains, which were the noisy culprits. I could no longer hear the hobnails, so I assumed Gates had gone to the house, or into another barn, but I picked up the piece of old plough shaft, just in case, and continued edging my way along. It seemed an eternity before I reached the corner of the building, from where I could see, about a hundred yards away, my little gap in the hedge. At last, plucking up courage, I began my sprint towards it. Instantly, I heard heavy footfalls and, looking to my right, I saw Gates coming at me like a charging bull. Neither of us said a word, and I knew he had recognized me.

Now I'm not a bad runner (about the only thing I won at school, beyond exasperation from the teaching staff, was the annual cross-country), but fresh air and farmwork had obviously given Gates a distinct edge. He got me in a flying tackle some fifteen yards from the hedge. I slammed forward into the ground, and all the breath went out of me, but, surprisingly, my dark glasses stayed on – not a great plus point, as I had a feeling Gates hadn't quite the sensitivity not to hit a chap who wears spectacles. I was right. After he had rolled off, he picked me up by my sweater, and then swung at my jaw with the nobbly concrete of his fist. My glasses left my face and hang-glided towards the hedge. I free-fell to the ground, and my spine hit something bumpy. I suddenly realized what it was, and as he launched himself down on me again, I reached under me, grabbed the plough shaft, and struck him across where I thought his head would be at the time. I heard it make contact, and a shock wave went up my wielding arm. But the worst bit was to follow. His dead weight collapsed across my body, and I felt I had been hit with nothing less substantial than the Empire State Building with bad breath.

It took me about two minutes to pull what was left of myself together, regain my breath, and ease myself free from the mass of muscle on top of me. I had the good grace to check his pulse, before I crawled to the gap in the hedge. It was pumping away as good as new. I pelted as fast as I could Beetle-wards, before it pumped some modicum of sensation back into his brain.

It wasn't really until I got home, sore chin and sore shoulder again (the fall had not done it much good), that I realized what I had achieved that morning. Even Bing seemed to sense my excitement, and kept rubbing himself against my still shaky legs. I had, with one exception, beaten Mr Chalmers' deadline for the recovery of his £22,000-worth of classic toys. True, they weren't actually in my hands yet, but I knew where they were, and who had stolen them. I celebrated with a large Scotch and soda.

But as my larynx grew warmer, I grew worried. It dawned on me that Treasure might move the toys to a new hiding place, and I actually had no proof at all that they had been in the barn. He could claim I had a grudge against him for opposing the excavation of the Spitfire and was throwing unfounded accusations about just to harass him. What's more, he could have me up for breaking and entering – twice.

I wondered whether I ought to inform Inspector Blake, but remembered what he had said about the Police Benevolent Fund. Nevertheless, I gave him a call and was told he was out and not expected back today, so I gave up the idea – for the moment. Also, any publicity about the toys' recovery might be an embarrassemnt to Mr Chalmers, who had stressed secrecy from the first moment he had contacted me about the French collection. And, in a way, there was another factor, quite a telling little factor. I knew I wanted to pursue privately the riddle of Mr Treasure to the very end – and I suspected the toys were only a fraction of his conundrum. He seemed to be over fond of hiding things and maybe Mrs Veronica Treasure had been another toy he had buried away. But how the blazes would we ever know? And it was then, I remembered the diaries.

After lunch, I put Bing on his lead and went round to see Gus. The sun had come out, and in contrast to the chill of the morning, the day had now decided it was summer. About time.

'From now on, would you, for Christ's sake, tell me what you are going to do, before you do it?' Gus grumbled into his large mug of tea. 'I might be able to help you, or at least it would give me more time to get a decent wreath.'

'I'm sorry, Gus, but *I* lost the toys, not you.'

'You'll lose your head, if you're not bloody careful,' he replied. He offered me a bit of seed cake, which I accepted and ate with relish. It always reminded me of boyhood teas on a winter's afternoon, and the spitting of fresh logs on the fire. Sometimes I think our joint passion for seed cake was one of the major things that bonded us together. That and beer.

'Well, come on,' he said impatiently.

'Come on, what?' I replied.

'Come on and tell me what you're going to do next, seeing as how you won't let the police do the job for you, like you should.

After all, you're paying for them, with your rates and taxes. Why not use them?'

'You know why, Gus. I don't think they'll ever get to the truth about Treasure by conventional methods. Blake's hopeless – completely out of touch until tomorrow. The rest of them are worse. After all, *they* didn't find my toys. *I* did.'

'But you haven't got them yet, my lad.' He sipped the last of his tea with a giant slurp. 'And maybe you never will.'

'Maybe, but I think I will. I have a feeling I've got a way of winkling them out of him. It only came to me as we've been sitting here.'

'And you're not going to tell me what it is?' He got up and put his mug to join the mountain of unwashed crockery in the kitchen. (Gus had a blitz on household chores once a week – a lot of china gets smashed, though.)

'I'd better, otherwise you might ask me to move my Daimler v8 from your garage.' I grinned at him, but he just pulled at his sweater, a nervous habit of his.

'I'm going to ring him, in my own voice this time, and say . . . .'

'Say you've seen the toys? Where will that get you?' he interrupted.

'No. I'll say I have some news from his wife, and I would like to come round and discuss it with him. I won't mention the toys at all – not on the phone.'

Gus thought a minute.

'Ah, I think I know what you mean. But you're playing with fire.'

'Maybe.'

'Bugger "maybe"; you bloody are. If he can murder once, he can murder again. And you won't be wearing a nice blue uniform and carrying a truncheon, will you?'

'I'm not going alone.'

He pointed down to Bing who was curled up on the threadbare carpet.

'He's not going to be much help to you.'

I laughed and Bing twitched his ear.

'No, it's not Bing. I'm taking you with me.'

He stretched his long legs out, and crossed them. 'Oh, you are, are you? Well, we'll have to see about that.'

I looked at him with amazement.

109

'Gus, you've been castigating me for not involving you for the last hour, and now I bow to your wishes, you play hard to get.'

He smiled. 'Well, I'm not actually saying I won't go with you. There's just a little something I'd like you to help me with tomorrow afternoon, in return, like, for my agreeing.'

'What's that? If it's not transporting another piano on the roof of your Popular, I might consider it.'

He made a church and steeple with his fingers.

'Well, it's like this. Old Mrs Blunt we moved the furniture for, remember? She told her daughter-in-law about how I shipped it round, and now she's got me to promise I'll pick up a dining table and chairs for her. Got to go from Swanage to Mudeford. Not very far, just across Bournemouth Bay.'

I did not need to think before I accepted.

'Agreed, Gus. Tomorrow afternoon. But keep near the shore, you sod; you know how I hate water.'

'All right,' he said, 'now when do you want to go and see Treasure?'

'As soon as he'll see me.' I got up, and Bing dutifully followed suit. I think he had had enough of feeling the boards through the carpet. 'I'll get back and ring him now. I'll drop down later and let you know. Okay?'

He saw me to the door, and put his hand on my shoulder.

'It's a deal, you know,' he said firmly.

'It's a deal,' I replied, and was truly thankful it was.

Ten

Randolph Treasure seemed to be out every time I phoned, and I did not dare leave my name when Mrs Fitzpayne, the house-keeper, asked for it. However, I followed another of my dear mother's clichéd phrases, tried and tried again, and got through to him at around eight o'clock in the evening. He sounded none too pleased to hear from me, and, from his tone, I think he must have worked out who the guy from Liverpool was, which was not very difficult really. He only had to read the bump on Ken Gates's head.

But my trump card worked and he reluctantly agreed to see me at nine-thirty the next morning, but pointed out this would be the very last time he would allow such a visit. I said we would have to see about that.

After I had rung off, I could not get him out of my mind. And I found, though I tried my damnedest, I could not quite hate him as much as I had. I think it was that room with the child dummy, and the diary. Mr Treasure was turning out to be by no means as shallow and insensitive as I'd thought him. I tried to imagine his hairy hands deftly arranging the details in that room, the clothes on the dummy, the tying of the tie, the setting up of the railway, the hanging of the Tipp, Meccano and Marklin aircraft on the thinnest of thin lines from the beams of the ceiling. The secret soul of Randolph Treasure – a world of innocence perhaps, to atone for his guilt, a world of obsessive attention to detail, of fanatical devotion to objects, beyond anything I'd ever seen in other collectors. I began to pity him, and kicked myself for doing so.

Then I did as I had promised. I went down and told Gus. I said I would pick him up around nine o'clock. He said, did he need to shave. I said no, because I would be leaving him in the Beetle in the driveway. He shrugged his shoulders, and that was that.

I came back home, and tried to resume reading my current

111

book, Woody Allen's *Getting Even*, which I hadn't touched for days, but my tension interfered with his rare talent to amuse. I switched on the box, but soon decided American soap opera could not wash my mind clean tonight. I went into the kitchen and followed Gus's culinary curriculum. I opened four tins. One, Whiskas. Two, button mushrooms. Three, baked beans. Four, corned beef. The last three were for me, although you would never have guessed it, the way Bing pestered me.

I heated what needed heating up, and ate this rare meal on a tray in front of the *News at Ten* on ITN. They had just come to the first commercial break, when Arabella arrived. I immediately saw from her face that something was very wrong.

'What's the trouble?' I asked, once she had settled down in the sitting-room.

'Can't you guess?' she replied quietly.

'What?' It was stupid of me to ask.

She got up abruptly, and began pacing round the smallish room.

'You know what I'm talking about. Smashed windows, smashed doors, bashed farmhands. Who do you think you are – Dirty Harry?'

I got up and tried to calm her, but she shrugged off my arm. That annoyed me a little. 'Look,' I said, 'I found my toys in Treasure's barn, in the attic bit. I had to do all those things to find them.'

'Sod your bloody toys, Peter. Can't you men think of anything else? Oh, I've forgotten, you can think of sex too. What a great combination – toys and sex, toys and sex.'

I took hold of her shoulders, and shook her.

'I have to pay Chandler £22,000 in two and a half weeks' time, and unlike your friend, I don't have that kind of money to spare. The police aren't getting anywhere and there were no grounds for applying for a search warrant. And anyway,' I went on, working myself up, 'this man Treasure you hang around with so often is a dangerous animal. It's far more serious than just my bloody toys, as you put it. He could be a murderer.'

She looked up at me. I went on, 'Yes, a murderer. That skeleton we found when we were digging for the Spitfire could be that of his dear, philandering wife, Veronica. The one who was supposed to have gone off to join her lover in Lausanne. Now are you getting the message?'

She slowly let me lead her back to the settee. I sat down beside her. She did not say anything for a moment, then asked quietly, 'Did you get that from the police?'

'No,' I replied, equally quietly. 'I deduced it myself. But I think the police may be working their way towards the same sort of conclusion.'

I held her close and I could feel her sobs.

'I want you to promise, you won't go back to him,' I said eventually. She did not reply. I suddenly decided that now was the time to ask her. 'You've got to tell me, Arabella, whose side you're on. His or mine. You can't be on both sides at the same time.'

Again she did not reply. I let go of her, and made her sit up. Her eyes were brimful of tears, and some mascara had run.

'Okay. If you won't tell me, I am assuming you are really on his so you'd better get out right now.' I got up and grasped her wrist. She saw I was deadly serious.

'All right. I'll tell you if you'll sit down again.' I did so and she began. 'At first, I was on his side. Of course, I had to be. I didn't know you. He asked me to keep an eye on you so I did. I hung round those places that I thought you might frequent. You know, the pub, the beaches, and I followed you once in my car all the way to Bristol and back. Did you spot me?'

I admitted I hadn't. She was evidently more expert than Quinky. But then, maybe, Quinky had wanted me to see her.

'Why did he ask you to shadow me?' I asked.

'Said you were a trouble-maker, accusing him of having stolen some of your old toys. He said you might even be the thief. He needed to know what you were doing, if you were up to anything. I supposed he needed something to nail you with. Randolph likes nailing people.'

'So you went along.'

'Yes, I went along.'

'And how much did you report back?' I asked, in a rather hard voice.

'Just the bare facts.'

'How bare, my darling? About our little naked rompings between the sheets, about how good or bad I was in bed? Maybe he loves vicarious sexual descriptions. Turns you both on something rotten . . . .'

She slapped my face hard, and in retrospect I thoroughly deserved it. She got up and made for the door.

'If you think that badly of me, you won't want me around you ever again.' She opened the door. 'If you want to know, I've been trying to help you ever since that first night. I haven't ever wanted to have anything to do with Treasure after you, you idiot. I only went back to see if I could be of some use . . . .'

I just managed to stop her before she reached the shop, and pulled her into my arms. That night, what little sleep we had was restless.

We only made love once. And that was just before she left again in the morning. (I had agreed very reluctantly, for her to carry on as normal for a day or two longer.) For almost all the rest of the night was spent talking about the inimitable Treasure and how to proceed if, and when, I got my toys back. She advised not proceeding at all, but just leaving everything to the proper authorities – the police. I said we should go just one stage further, and then go to the police – the stage being after we had clamped our beady eyes on the diary. For Arabella confirmed what she had said before – that he was an avid diarist, and most evenings at ten-thirty, he would shut himself away and write, though where he kept his diary she did not know. I said, the little book might be anywhere – in the attics, in some secret panel or safe, like in detective fiction, or even in the barns. She said she doubted it; he seemed to have fairly easy access to it. He did not seem to go up in the attics at all, to her knowledge. And she had a feeling, from what he had said over the months, that all the diaries must be kept together somewhere. He kind of spoke of them that way. She added, too, that he had often said he didn't believe in safes. 'For every safe, there's a built-in safe-cracker at no extra charge,' was his usual wisecrack about them.

So you can see that part of the night was none too fruitful. Still, she was beautiful to feel, moored alongside me, as we talked.

So she left, having made me promise I would go to the police immediately I had found the diaries, or, without fail, in two days' time if I was unsuccessful. I sealed the agreement with a kiss, and reluctantly let her go. I never realized before how soppy I could get over someone with spray-booth hair.

Not long afterwards, I was getting the Beetle out of the garage, (if it leaned much more, I'd soon be getting the garage out of the

114

Beetle) and beginning my fateful journey towards Lulworth and the giant's eerie hideaway, with my faithful Gus at my side. I had told Arabella not to turn up there until lunchtime, just in case there were some unhealthy fireworks. She went ashen at the thought, but at last I got her to promise.

It was as we pulled into Treasure's driveway, that I noticed a distinct bulge in Gus's sweater. And by the time I stopped outside the huge studded oak and stone entrance, I had more or less worked out what had been causing it. I unclipped my seat belt, leaned over his way, and whispered, 'Don't do anything silly, Gus.' His eyes instinctively flitted down to his waistline. 'Yes, I mean *that*, Gus. Where on earth did you get it, anyway?'

He looked terribly disappointed. 'From one of those soldiers manning the gun emplacement on Studland beach – during the war it was. Gave him a fiver he owed to a bookie.'

I pulled up his sweater, and saw, as they say, 'the cold steel' of an army issue .38 revolver (my father used to have one) tucked into his trouser top.

'Is it loaded?' I asked nervously.

He nodded.

'Well, don't fire it accidentally, while you're sitting there waiting for me, will you? Otherwise, that lady friend in Weymouth will have to go looking for another boy.'

He looked horrified, as I don't think he had thought about where the muzzle was pointing. Gus is full of surprises.

I gave a Churchillian 'V' sign, and he reversed it back to me, as I got out of the car. Pretty soon Mrs Fitzpayne had ushered me into the giant's parlour, and I gave an involuntary shiver, there being no beanstalk hanging about to help me, and this was no fairy tale.

'Sit down, Mr Marklin. I know the sun isn't even near the yard-arm, let alone over it, but can I offer you a drink?' His voice, for once, was treacled with charm. I felt the same unease I had on my first visit so I declined.

'Well then, Mr Marklin, let me say at once how glad I am that, this time, you have gained access to my house by more conventional means. You are not the most subtle of intruders, you know. Broken glass, footprints, broken doors and door frames, axes – dear me, what would Raffles have thought of you?'

I assumed his question was rhetorical so I didn't make a guess. Instead, I asked him a question.

'Tell me, Mr Treasure, why didn't your super-duper burglar alarm go off, when I opened that window? It's been intriguing me.'

Treasure poured himself a neat Scotch, and sat down opposite me.

'I'm so pleased I intrigue you, Mr Marklin. Yes, I'll tell you. It's very simple. It didn't go off, because it wasn't turned on.'

He saw my look of surprise.

'You see, Mr Marklin, I had a feeling you might eventually try to search the house to find your splendid toys so I thought I'd make it easy for you. I saw to it that you would know I was going abroad for a day or two and before I left, I disconnected the alarm system. Simple.'

'So I would discover the cupboard bare, and give up suspecting you.'

'How astute you are, Mr Marklin. I like a man who doesn't need everything spelled out for him.'

'Then I needn't spell out that I'm not leaving until I've got my toys in my car, which is standing in the driveway, with a rather tough friend of mine sitting in it to see fair play.'

'You don't need to tell me, Mr Marklin. I saw you arrive through the window. There are not that many old Volkswagen convertibles in this neck of the woods, and not many people like your friend. I've noticed him quite a few times over the Spitfire affair.'

I stood up. I didn't want this meeting to go on any longer than was necessary, as I was feeling distinctly like a fly to his spider.

'Look, just get me the toys. I haven't come here to pass the time of day.'

He didn't move from his seat, but waved a hairy hand at me, in what he intended to be a calming gesture. 'I have them all packed up ready for you, Mr Marklin.'

'All?' I enquired, and he got my meaning.

'I'm afraid there are only ten of them. You see, I already had a P2 Alfa Romeo, so I sold it to a fellow collector in Geneva on my trip. You must forgive me. I'll let you have your estimation of its value in cash, of course.'

I looked across at him. 'Why did you steal them? You've got all the money in the world.'

He looked genuinely disappointed.

'Mr Marklin, Arabella must have read you wrong. She has told

116

me you are a sensitive, intelligent, romantic sort of fellow. Now if all that is true, you'll know why without asking.'

'Because there are some things money just can't buy.'

'Mr Marklin, I could not have expressed it better myself. Those toys are a unique collection, in unique condition, and Chalmers would never have sold them. I know him a little from the odd business deal. So what option did I have? I nearly always manage to get what I want – eventually.'

He got up and paced around my chair like a caged tiger.

'You see,' he continued huskily, 'for as long as I can remember I have lived life on a high level of expectation. I can't understand people who don't. Their lives must be deplorably and unutterably dull, without any meaning whatsoever. No wonder they need alcohol, drugs, uppers and downers. I am my own "upper", you see. But the down side is that I find it hard to take disappointment, of course – a very deep down side, indeed . . . .' His voice tailed off, and he went back and sat down. For a second, his arrogance had receded. But only for a second.

'Mr Treasure, I want my toys. And I want them now.'

'You will have them, the instant you promise never to harass me again – for any reason you might concoct.'

'Like where your wife is, for instance?' I asked quietly.

'I imagined from your phone call you were starting some other line of vicious rumour-mongering, Mr Marklin. That's why I agreed to see you. You can have your toys, if you stop indulging your fondness for unfounded allegations. And, I mean right now.'

'But my allegations about your stealing my toys weren't unfounded, were they? And, what's more, you have to give me my toys or I will go straight to the police.'

Treasure smiled grimly, and I could see his hand strengthen its grip on his glass.

'You're beautifully naïve, Mr Marklin. The instant you leave here, those toys will disappear forever. Not a trace of them will ever be found – even with the most diligent police search. And I will get you for breaking and entering my premises on two occasions. I do have the evidence for both, my dear fellow.' He drained his Scotch. 'And talking of police, Mr Marklin, they have already interviewed me twice about the whereabouts of my wife since that other skeleton was discovered at the Spitfire site, and, as far as I can tell, I am eliminated from their enquiries. What's more, they told me they doubt if the bones can ever be definitely identified as a great deal of the skull is missing.'

I could feel the ground slipping away from under me, but had the feeling he would not have agreed to see me at all if he were a hundred per cent confident of his position.

'One day someone will discover all about you, Mr Treasure. And I hope it's soon. But meanwhile, I want those toys and I want them now, otherwise I'll attract a great deal of attention to the activities of your henchman, the irresistible Mr Gates.'

'That won't be necessary, Mr Marklin.' Treasure rose and went to the door. 'I had intended to give you the toys as some slight reward, not for yourself, but for Arabella. She is a very persuasive lady, you know.'

'Keep her out of this, Treasure,' I said with some vehemence.

'She's already in it, Mr Marklin, isn't she ? And if you now go to the police, and tell them you recovered the toys from me, she'll be in it even further. And she's had enough trouble in her short life.'

I moved quickly across the room to where he stood by the door. I was tempted to grab him by his hairy tweed suit, but thought better of it. I compromised with, 'What do you mean, you bastard ?'

He smiled. 'Well, no one will know that she wasn't my accomplice all along, will they ? Love my girlfriend, love me, Mr Marklin. It's a fair exchange, don't you agree ?'

He held out a hairy hand, and showed me into the huge hall, where, lined up by the front door, was a neat stack of ten boxes.

Eleven

I wasn't taking any more chances with those toys. Directly I had checked they were all there, bar the P2 Alfa, that is, Gus and I drove at a rate of knots, out of the castle's grounds and took the road that would lead us westwards to Bridport, Chalmers' country seat.

Gus kept muttering about 'We should get back, as otherwise, we might be late to move Mrs Blunt's daughter-in-law's furniture.' I described, rather rudely, what Mrs Blunt's daughter-in-law could do right then with her furniture, and he shut up. That's what friends are for – to shut up sometimes.

Chalmers' house was even bigger than Treasure's, and I began wondering what the hell I was doing wrong, living over an ex-sweet shop. Gus helped me carry in the ten boxes, and I showed all the contents to a dark girl, who I discovered was Chalmers' daughter. She looked too young to be anybody's wife. She said Mr Chalmers was away for a couple of days, and got the house-keeper to get her a proper receipt pad from somewhere in the huge house, and, in a rather flowery hand, signed each description of each toy as I wrote them in front of her. (I wanted belt and braces on this one.) I asked for some notepaper, and jotted down a brief message for Chalmers about the missing P2 Alfa Romeo. I said I could either find one for him, or give him the money. I did not explain how I had found the toys. Chalmers wouldn't care. Collectors are like that: possession is the whole story.

The journey back to Studland was a joy. The sun was celebrating too, and I stopped and put the top down. You'd think Gus had just been and had an elaborate hair-do by the fuss he kicked up about the stream of fresh air. I couldn't think why. (The draughts in his Ford Popular saloon blew you about more than my open convertible. And that's with all its windows closed.)

When we got back, I offered to buy Gus a slap-up bangers and mash at our usual hostelry, and all the Heinekens he could down, and to my surprise he accepted. Usually Gus does not go for anything that smacks of charity. You even have to be careful of thanking him for anything too profusely. Before we went into the pub, I did, however, ask him to get rid of the bump in his sweater. He was most indignant.

'I'm not leaving it in your car. You've had enough stolen from that, just recently.'

I grabbed him by the arm.

'Look, Gus, you can't walk into a pub in England with a .38 down your crotch. It's not done, unless you've got a stocking over your head. And I'm not letting you go home and get one either.'

I made to put my hand down the front of his rather stained trousers, when a pub customer came past and saw us. He was blasé enough only to raise his eyebrows. Other pub customers would have raised the local constabulary.

'Oh all right,' he grumbled, and I managed to get him to put the gun under the passenger seat. 'But you'll owe me a fiver if it gets nicked, mind.'

Dear old Gus. All the time I've known him, he has never ever made any allowance for inflation. (He told me the other day that he would never waste 1/9d. going to no film.)

It was a good lunch. Not a great lunch, but a good one, because I felt more relaxed than I had done for what now seemed an age. We drank to the Abbey National Building Society. We drank to Barclays Bank, Nat West and Lloyds. We offered toasts to every pawnbroker and moneylender in the land, without being too specific about actual names. We saluted debt collectors, the Inland Revenue, and the Royal Mint. And we were just about to raise our glasses to the great world of international insurance, when we got thrown out. That's how good a lunch it was.

I can hardly remember parking the Beetle back in the garage, or going down to Gus's to leave his gun. Nor indeed, our, no doubt, rather meandering walk down to the beach, where Gus kept his old boat. I do, however, vaguely recall the enormous effort it seemed to take to get the wheeled cradle down to the water. And how Gus seemed to disappear under the boat once we got it floating. He didn't do it intentionally, you understand ; he just went on pushing, after the cradle had stopped. It seemed to sober him up a bit, though. And I'll swear it's the first time that grey-blue sweater of his had seen water since the war.

So, dripping though unbowed, we set out for Mudeford, which is Christchurch way, just a bit further eastwards round the bay from Bournemouth. And true to his word, Gus did not take me too far from dry land the whole way across – which was just as well, as there was a bit of a swell running, and that and the beer made me distinctly unseaworthy.

I won't bore you with all the details of how, when we got there, Gus could not find their house (he had written their address on the back of his hand and his sea-walking had washed it off), and how he'd had to ring Mrs Blunt, and she had to ring her daughter-in-law, who had to ring her husband to get him to bring down a handcart on which to drag the table and chairs to the jetty, and so on, and so on. Suffice it to say, we were away from the boat for about two and a half hours, which was far longer than Gus had originally promised the whole round trip would take.

Once the dining-room table and six chairs were stowed on board, we looked a damn sight more ridiculous than we had done with the three piece suite from Lulworth. And, of course, Gus's sodden appearance (in every way) didn't exactly help. I was relieved when Gus got the old diesel throbbing at the usual eightieth go, and we headed back towards Studland and Swanage. At least I could not hear the laughter and ribald comments any more. I sat at the dining table, with Gus at the other end, and we began laughing – what else could you do? We knew we looked absurd.

But we didn't laugh long. About five minutes or so after leaving Mudeford there was a blinding flash and I felt myself being blown back, then sucked up in the air, surrounded by pieces of I know not what. It all seemed to be happening in slow motion somehow, and for a split second I thought I must be dreaming some alcoholic dream. Then I heard the detonation, my ear drums tried to bury themselves in my mouth, and I knew I was screaming and then ... nothing. And for how long there was nothing, I don't know.

Then I remember choking and coughing, and my lungs filling with water, salty and ice-cold. My whole being was ice cold. I was beginning to surface. I looked around. My eyes could just pick out jagged pieces of wood bobbing about by me. Then I remembered what I had been doing, and with whom I had been doing it. I tried to strike out with my arms, but my left one wasn't obeying me. Frantically I tried to keep myself afloat while looking everywhere for any sign at all of Gus. But all I could see was made of wood, hundreds of pieces, big and small. I made for the largest section, which I recognized as part of the prow of Gus's boat and, once there, clung onto it with my right hand. I looked around again, but still I couldn't see Gus, or anything that looked a bit like him. I turned and tried to see the shore line, and then thanked God I was a bad sailor. It was only some two hundred and fifty yards or so away, otherwise I would definitely have been a goner. The furthest I can swim with *two* good arms, is four hundred yards.

I looked around for Gus once more, but there was still no sign. I began paddling my legs, and succeeded in turning the section of prow towards the shore. I just hoped my good arm wouldn't give up the struggle before I felt sand under my feet.

After what must have been about a minute, I came across the top of the dining-room table, amazingly almost intact, with one leg still attached to it, sticking grotesquely into the sky. Then I spotted what looked like a hand holding onto the base of the leg, and I paddled furiously with my legs towards it. The hand was attached to an arm, and it was Gus's. The arm disappeared under the water and I couldn't see if it was still attached to anything. And then, suddenly, a head seemed to rise like Neptune from the deep, and I almost screamed with fear and anguish. The head spluttered water and blood, and the eyes rolled in their sockets.

I reached out with my hand, and the head turned and shouted, 'Don't hold onto me, you idiot. I can hardly keep *myself* afloat.'

I almost lost hold on my life-preserving prow, in my relief at being told off, once again, in the inimitable tones of Gus Tribble Esquire.

I prefer not to dwell on our joint struggle to the shore. Even now, I get goose-pimples just thinking about it. It seemed to take an eternity, and agonize what was left of every muscle in our bodies.

When at last I felt something firm beneath my feet, I let go of the section of the boat, which promptly sank like a stone. The table, however, with its decades of elbow grease and beeswax polish, still floated proudly with its cocked leg; and Gus and I half stumbled, half swam, with its aid the last hundred feet or so onto the beach. There we lay, covered in streaks of oil, blood and now, in Gus's case, vomit.

The first voice we heard through our blitzed ear drums was that of a middle-aged lady asking if we were all right.

'Get us help, for God's sake,' I slurred.

She didn't move, rooted to the spot as the seriousness of what she had witnessed hit her.

Gus pushed a blood-covered arm forward and grabbed her by the foot. She screamed with alarm.

'Look, you stupid old cow, get us help and quick,' he muttered between fits of coughing. 'We've just had a thundering great bomb go off under our arses.'

By now I could see quite a few clusters of feet. Then a man's face hovered over mine.

'This man's bleeding badly,' he said with the right note of urgency. 'They both are. And it looks as if his arm is broken.' His face disappeared, and I heard shouts, and the drumming of running feet on the sand, and then I decided I didn't care any more. I went out like a light.

When I came to again (that is, as distinct from floating in and out of consciousness), it had all been done. I found myself looking into the clear blue eyes of a blonde nurse, who would have done credit (or something) to *Doctor Kildare*. After telling me where I was – Bournemouth General Hospital – she took me on a guided tour of my own body. She showed me the nice white plaster in which they had hidden my left arm (a clean break in two places), the foot-wide bandage over my right thigh (rather nasty gash), and then she helped me count the individual pieces of Band-Aid plaster that were scattered over my anatomy like sticky confetti. ('Twenty-eight, Mr Marklin.' I didn't agree with her. I counted twenty-nine, but perhaps she did not like to draw attention to where the twenty-ninth was.)

My first question was, of course, where was Gus? She immediately pulled back the curtains at the left side of the bed, and there was an Egyptian mummy with little windows that showed little pieces of Gus. But at least the mummy was sitting upright in bed, and eating grapes, which was more than I was doing.

I whispered to the blonde and white distraction, 'How is he?'

She whispered back, 'Fine. Don't take any notice of the bandages. He's just more badly cut than you are, that's all. But no bones broken – just a mass of bruises. You were both lucky, you know, when your engine exploded.'

So that was what they thought, was it? Old boat, old engine, old petrol tank, old owner, another jolly old explosion at sea. I didn't argue, right then. She was the wrong person to argue with. Instead, I asked, 'When can I go?'

She pointed to the other end of the ward. 'Any time. The loo is just up there. You're fit enough to walk.'

I raised my eyebrows. I'd learnt over the years, it doesn't pay to get cross with blondes.

'I didn't mean that, sweetheart. I meant when can I go home?'

'Tomorrow, I expect, after the doctors have seen you.'

'Well, in that case, would you get someone to ring Detective Inspector Trevor Blake – remember that name, I don't want any other boy in blue – and ask him to come over and see me? Oh, and say he doesn't need to bring any grapes. Just an assassination-proof suit, and an Insurance Policy for ten million pounds, made out in favour of my cat.'

Her goo-goo eyes double-took and I could see that she wasn't one of that year's favourites for the *Mastermind* title.

However, within the hour, I was wheeled into a little office off Matron's room. But my nurse had forgotten the bit about the grapes. He had brought some, after all.

'How do you know it was a bomb?' Blake looked me straight in the eyes. 'You don't know really, do you?'

Up to now, he had listened to my story with the utmost attention and seeming sympathy, and in my present condition, I needed his change of tone like a hole in the head.

'Look, Inspector, I've just bloody well had enough of playing patsy for you and the whole damned police force. So fuck you, Inspector. Do your own dirty work.'

I started to get out of the wheel-chair, but then thought better of it. The room had begun to go round.

Blake rose from behind the desk, and pulled a chair up to my aluminium National Health go-kart. 'I'm sorry, Mr Marklin. I did not mean to upset you – especially after your horrifying ordeal. Maybe we should leave this talk until tomorrow . . . .'

'No,' I replied vehemently, 'we've got to have it now. In your

124

clever, insidious way, you've got me to do what you can't authorize your boys to do, without getting into big trouble, haven't you? You've wanted me to uncover the evidence that lets you take the action without risk of opprobrium from any quarter. Well, sod you, Inspector, *I'm* not playing any more. You've done bugger all on your own. You didn't even discover the skeleton. We did. And it was the forensic boys, not you, who discovered it wasn't Pilot Officer Redfern, but some woman. And I found my toys by myself.' I ran out of breath, and began feeling a little faint. It gave time for the Inspector to lean down and pick up a package resting on the floor by the desk. He began unwrapping it.

'You didn't recover *all* of them, I believe, Mr Marklin.' My mind was fuzzy, but not so bad that I didn't remember I'd implied to him that I had found the lot.

'No. How do you know? There was one missing.'

He had finished the unwrapping now, and held up its contents for me to see.

'Is this the one, Mr Marklin?'

He handed me a P2 Alfa Romeo. I didn't need to inspect it very long to know it was the one from Monsieur Vincent, for no P2 I had ever seen matched its mint quality.

'It looks like it. Where did you get it?'

'The Swiss police found it amongst Mr Vivian Stone's effects, when they arrested him a couple of days back in Geneva.'

It suddenly made sense. Treasure had said he had sold it to a fellow collector on his trip to Geneva.

'How did you all trace Stone?'

'Quite simple really. We thought the international toy auction held there would be too much of a temptation for him to miss. And so it proved. The Swiss police identified him at the auction, and followed him back to where he was living, just outside the city. Got him and his wife – and a Swiss girl he was using as a courier.'

I thought of them both by their baby-blue pool. I guessed that was the last tan either of them would be getting for a few years.

He continued, 'He only had one vintage toy with him. This one. And because it seemed to answer the description of one from your lost collection, I asked to have it flown over for identification.' He smiled at me, nicely, not cockily. 'So you see, Mr

Marklin, we do succeed sometimes on our own. Mr Stone is now the subject of extradition proceedings on a charge of illicit trading in diamonds, and being concerned with others in fencing the plunder of various robberies in Hatton Garden.'

I was silent for a bit, and the Inspector picked the P2 Alfa Romeo gently off my lap, and said quietly, 'I'm afraid I shall have to take this back just for a while until further investigations have taken place. You know how it is.'

I didn't argue. I was now feeling a lot less strong-minded than when first I'd been wheeled into the room.

'What are you going to do about Treasure?' I asked eventually.

Blake sighed. 'There's very little we can do at the moment, whatever our, or your, suspicions may be. And don't jump to conclusions. I'm not implying that our suspicions are the same as yours.'

'What about the bones? Anything new there?' I asked, and I knew I'd made a huge mistake. I was getting involved again. Put it down to twenty-nine pieces of Band-Aid, and the effects of being plastered. And, don't let us forget the insidious timing of Sexton Blake.

'Woman about five-feet six. Around thirty. Average build, probably. Buried about three to five years. Jaw parts of skull missing, therefore no dental records. No fractures prior to death. Traces of acid, probably due to immersion, to dissolve the flesh faster. That's about it.'

It didn't take a genius to ask the next question.

'How tall was Mrs Veronica Treasure?'

'Five-feet six and a half. But don't jump to premature conclusions. We have, on our local files, three women that would fit that description, who disappeared about that same time, and have never been seen since: barmaid from Swanage, a vet's assistant from Wool, and a farmer's wife from Blandford Forum. That's why private eyes can never understand why the police take so long with their enquiries, Mr Marklin. There's so much information to sift, so many interviews to conduct, and so many paths of enquiry to follow. The modern use of computers is beginning to speed it all up, I'm glad to say. But still . . . .'

I cut in, '. . . You still need mini computers – private eyes, rather than public ones?'

He grinned, and held out his hand. I shook it with my one good one. God knows why.

'I take it,' I said slowly, 'you won't be tackling Treasure about the toys right now?'

'I'd rather not, Mr Marklin. I would prefer to have a complete dossier than half or a quarter of one.'

'And he's a powerful man?'

He ignored the sally, but I persevered. My dander was rising again.

'How long will it bloody take you to connect Treasure with the bomb on our boat?'

'What bomb, Mr Marklin? Old boats have a tendency to catch fire, you know. Rotten electrics can spark an explosion. There only has to be a slight leak of fuel . . . .'

'And you can catch VD from loo seats, and the kiss of life is how you get Aids, and don't we all believe in virgin births in Bognor . . .' I was starting to get very, very tired.

'I know how you feel, believe me.' He got up and looked down at me, in an avuncular fashion. 'We'll examine every piece of the wreckage of the boat. And I'm sending some divers down to scour the seabed in the vicinity. We've already interviewed a lot of people at Mudeford who may have seen something.'

'Do you want yet another description of Ken Gates? I'm sure Treasure would not soil his own hands in wiring up a device to an oily engine.'

'We know Mr Gates, don't you worry.'

'Don't I worry? You must be kidding. He could kill me in hospital. That's always happening on those TV series. "Excuse me, Nurse, you're wanted down in surgery." Crash, bang, wallop, you're dead. And from a disease you didn't have when you were admitted. It's called murder and it's incurable, I'm told by usually reliable sources.'

He took my hand. 'We are aware of that, and have taken precautions. You should get back to bed, you know, and try to get a good night's sleep. It's very late.'

I sniggered, and withdrew my hand. He made for the door, then looked round.

'Mr Marklin, I want you to remember this. What you do is your own affair, you know. We'll get there all on our own, in our own way, and in our police time-scale. There's no doubt about it. You've got your toys back – and I'm privately very delighted about that, as a policeman, and as a toy collector – and you can live your life in peace now, and leave all risks to professional public servants, who are trained and paid to take them.'

I smiled for the first time. 'Talking of payment, Inspector Trevor Blake, you owe me approximately a million pounds for what I've done for you already.'

He opened the door, and beckoned to a nurse.

'I know,' he said quietly, and waved his hand in a farewell salute.

Twelve

Arabella picked us up just before twelve the next day. Our leaving the hospital did not exactly have the blessing of the medical staff, who wanted to detain us at least for a further twenty-four hours. However, I wanted to get home for a host of reasons, most of which were Arabella. Gus wanted to get back to see about the insurance on his boat, and see if it contained a clause covering 'detonations caused by hairy-handed, ambidextrous, millionaire landowners', as he almost put it. (I substituted the word 'ambidextrous' for Gus's more earthy alternative.) So we discharged ourselves after Blondie had raised our temperatures by inspecting all our bandages and plasters.

The Queen of the Mynd, bless her, had rushed to the hospital after she had heard a belated report of our little drama from her car radio, and our reunion in the ward had to be seen to be believed. I think they began considering getting a surgeon in to separate us. Gus was the soul of discretion; he turned the other bandage, and left us to it.

I worried about Arabella on the way home. Firstly, she was in a rather strange mood – her greeting of me in the hospital had been intense to the point of desperation. And, on a lighter note, she must have looked like a chauffeur to The Invisible Man, with Gus sitting there swathed from head to foot. And I wasn't much better – a kind of mobile (just) advertisement for the Band-Aid company. I even thought of selling space on my plaster.

An emaciated Bing greeted us on arrival with a fine selection of Siamese cat calls, the volume of which was turned down with a tin of Whiskas opened by my lady rescuer. (You try opening a tin with only one arm.) Gus suggested he'd better get off home, and I said he mustn't, he must stay to lunch, which he did. It was the first time I had ever tasted Arabella's cooking. Let me tell you, that girl makes a mean stuffed savoury pancake, and her pommes lyonnaise were as mouth watering as the rest of her. As

Gus pointed out, 'They beat potatoes right into the ground.'

Curiously, none of us drank very much at lunch – we didn't quite finish the second bottle of white wine. I think we were all beginning to feel the second shock wave from our brush with death. And I, for one, could not get Treasure out of my mind for more than a few minutes at a time, which did not help matters.

Soon after we had washed up and packed all the dishes away, Gus fell asleep in his chair and began making noises like a stag at rutting time. Arabella took me by the hand and led me quietly upstairs – but not for what you think. She wanted to talk. She made me rest back on the bed, while she sat on the edge and held my good hand. I felt a hundred and eight years old, and told her so. She kissed me softly between two of the plasters and said she didn't mind the age gap.

I said, 'Does that mean . . . ?'

She smiled and nodded. 'No, I'm never going to see him again, Mr Peter Marklin. Not now.'

I squeezed her hand. 'Thank God my darling, thank God.'

Neither of us said anything for a bit, and then she said, 'What are you going to do now? You must, must let the police handle it from here.'

So I told her all about my session with Trevor Blake the previous evening. She became quite upset.

'Look, you idiot, he's getting you to do his dirty work, the way Treasure gets Ken Gates to do his. And what's worse, you don't get any reward for what you do – unless you consider all the excitement of two near assassinations some kind of reward. And I don't think you're a down-the-line masochist – or are you? Certainly I'm not, and I can't watch it . . . .'

She got up and walked over to the window. Then she turned and looked at me with the wonderful intensity of her dark eyes.

'Did you tell Blake about the diaries?' she asked.

'No,' I replied weakly.

'Why not? They're probably the key to all of it. Once he has found the diaries . . . .'

'He'll never find them.'

She came back to the bed and looked down at me.

'Why bloody not?'

'He won't know where to look, for one thing,' I propped myself up on my elbow, 'any more than we do. And, for another, directly old Treasure hears of a gang of police about to

130

come up to his castle door with a search warrant, he'll have the diaries spirited away with the speed of light. Don't forget Blake has intimated pretty clearly that Treasure has friends in the local force.'

'But not in Scotland Yard?'

'I hope not, otherwise I'll never make an honest buck again, even if I survive long enough for money to matter.'

She sat down by me again, and my hand had a visit from a friend. 'It's pretty terrifying, isn't it?'

'What is?' I asked, but really knew the answer.

'To think that the whole country, the whole world even, must be full of people like Treasure who get away with, yes, murder even, and no one can touch them, because there isn't any proof.'

'And there isn't going to be any proof, unless . . . .'

She looked at me hard, then turned away.

'You're an idiot, a stark, staring, raving idiot,' she almost spat out, and it wasn't hard to detect that note of desperation had returned in full measure.

She left soon after, to help her cousin get the nursery produce and bedding plants ready to take to Weymouth the next day. Her mood suddenly switched to one of too careless humour. She stood at my shop door, wearing a ridiculous peaked hat I had never seen before, and gave a General MacArthur salute, swearing, 'I will return.' With her in charge of a US army, the Japanese would have capitulated the day after Pearl Harbor.

While missing her like mad, I was glad of a little time on my own. (Gus was still pushing zzs in the sitting-room.) I went into the shop, and opened up for business – a move I regretted in seconds, as my first customer was a local reporter, complete with camera. I gave him just the bare bones of the story, and was careful not even to hint at the likely cause of the explosion. I give him full marks for ferreting, but very few for tact, as he tried to get me to pose for a photograph with my sweater pulled up and my shirt undone to show some of my plasters. I told him firmly, in the end, that I was not that kind of fellow. He blinked, and went away frowning. No wonder reporters are often lousy at writing – they obviously have never read anything.

He was followed by some of my mates from the pub, who blew in to say get well soon, and Mrs Blunt came in, all of a dither, wondering where Gus had gone. I told her he was in the land of nod, and she said not to waken him, but she'd have a hot high tea waiting for him when he and his bandages got back home. What a nice lady; she didn't breathe a word about the four thousand separate pieces of wet wood that now constituted her daughter-in-law's dining-room furniture.

Nobody came to buy a toy, even though, wounded as I was, I had shown willing. But Gerald Rankin phoned to say he'd tracked down a fabulous collection of tinplate boats and ships in Inverness. As he was too busy to go up there for a few days, would I like to vet them for him, all expenses paid? I was amazed he hung on long enough for me to finish laughing. I know I was rude, but I couldn't help it. History has a way of repeating itself. I wouldn't repeat my mistake. I politely declined and wished him luck. I felt a four-letter word for having *ever* suspected him.

I was still smiling when he came in – an old man, quite bald, with a stoop that would not have disgraced Quasimodo. He walked slowly over to the counter, and stretching himself up slightly straighter, deposited a package in front of me. It was wrapped with the highest grade brown paper, and fastened very neatly with fine red string. He looked up at me. 'You do *buy* toys as well as sell them, don't you?' His voice was cultured and much firmer than his appearance had suggested.

'Sometimes, if they are unusual, or in very fine condition.' I replied gently. I was intrigued to see what he had brought in for my appraisal, but he took his time, carefully undoing the string, and folding back the paper. At last, it was revealed, and it was worth every second of the wait.

'I'm sorry to bother you after your nasty accident, but I wonder if that is of any use to you, sir?'

Before me was an immaculate tinplate limousine, about forty-five centimetres long, finished mainly in dark blue, but with red outlining to the doors, windows and waistline, and incredibly fine gold pin-striping on all the major body panels. There were two beautifully cast carriage lamps each side of the bevelled glass windscreen, and an intricately detailed luggage rack on the roof. Inside, the seats were bright red. Date around 1910 or so, and the maker, I reckoned, was either Carette or Bing. I looked at him enquiringly.

'Yes, you may pick it up, sir.'

I did so, and my eyes quickly noted the inimitable GNB trademark of Gebrüder Bing of Bavaria. My cat should have been there to share my excitement.

'It's quite beautiful,' I said after a while.

'Yes, it is, isn't it?' he replied, and smiled softly.

I looked at it again in detail. 'I've never seen . . .' I began, but he interrupted.

'I know what you're going to say, sir. It's not quite like the usual, standard Bing limousine of the period, is it? The colours aren't quite right, and the lamps are bigger than usual.'

'But it doesn't look repainted,' I remarked.

'It hasn't been. Let me explain. Before the First World War, my father worked for the Bing concern. This model was, if you like, the prototype of the later limousine. It has many little differences from the normal production run cars: lamps, size of doors, colours, and one very intriguing little item. May I?'

He held out his hands for the car. I carefully placed it in them. Holding the car with his left hand, he opened the small side door on its hinges with his right. Then he popped his forefinger and thumb inside, and I could see he was releasing something. Then he handed the toy back to me.

'There, Mr Marklin. A wonderful extra for any boy.'

I looked inside the door, and could see that now the rear seat cushion had been raised to reveal a secret compartment that ran the width of the car. And inside that compartment was a tiny tinplate box.

'Take it out, Mr Marklin.'

I obeyed, and I could see it had a hinged lid. I looked up and he nodded. I raised the lid, and inside was what looked like gemstones of some kind, their every facet glinting and flashing in my eyes.

'Only coloured glass, you understand, Mr Marklin. But what could they not be in the eyes and imagination of a young boy? A king's ransom, perhaps. The ill gotten gains of the rascally Raffles. A massive, political bribe to stop some mid-European conflict. There's no end to what those glinting jewels could mean, do you not think?'

I was too impressed to say anything very sensible, so I just let my eyes and face express my agreement.

'What a shame, Mr Marklin, that Bing did not have the imagination to put it into regular production. Only this one was ever made, and it has been in my family ever since 1909.'

I suddenly felt very sad. 'You know, you're right. I couldn't put a price on it. And if I did, I don't think I could afford it. You should put it up for auction, you know, in London – Sotheby's, Phillips, somewhere like that, not bring it to the Toy Emporium, Studland.' I smiled apologetically.

'Mr Marklin, that's very sweet of you to be so honest. But I would never go through all the palaver of taking it to London and all that – I really wouldn't. I would like it to have a good home. Would you not like it for your own collection – not to sell in the shop?'

'There's nothing I would like more,' I replied, 'but I really cannot afford such a thing right now. In a few years' time, maybe, but not now.'

'I'm so pleased – about your wanting it, that is. And I'm sure Miss Trench will be equally happy.'

I looked at my visitor with new and surprised eyes.

'Oh, don't be alarmed, Mr Marklin. I buy my plants and vegetables and things from Miss Trench's cousin, Lady Philippa Stewart-Hargreaves, over Owermoigne way, and she told me that Arabella – I think that's your friend's name – knew a man who was very interested in toys, and might like the Bing limousine. So I showed it to her only an hour ago now, and she said, would I bring it over to you as a favour. So here I am.'

'Yes, Arabella was quite correct. I think it is very wonderful.'

He smiled at me, and held out his right hand.

'Well, that's it then, Mr Marklin. I leave it in your loving care.' He shook my good hand and made to leave the shop.

I came out from behind the counter, and ran across to him. 'Look, you can't leave it here. It could be worth anything from two to five thousand pounds. Even more, maybe.'

He laughed quietly. 'Oh, Mr Marklin, didn't I tell you? How stupid of me. Miss Trench gave me a very handsome cheque for it there and then, so all you need to worry about is getting it insured. Good day, sir, and keep dreaming. It's the nearest we ever get to being in heaven in our lifetime, isn't it?'

And with that, he left my shop. I watched him slowly climb into the driving seat of a 1947 Lanchester Ten, that was in as immaculate condition as the miniature Bing limousine, and drive quietly away.

I had to pinch myself to make certain I had not dreamt what

had just transpired within my Toy Emporium. For not only had I just acquired the gift of a most fabulous antique toy, but also, perhaps, the key to a treasure of a quite different metal.

I woke up the recumbent bandages, and saw them home to his cottage down the sea lane. We must have looked more than ridiculous, as was confirmed by the very odd glances and whispered comments from passing holiday-makers. I couldn't resist in the end, and I said in a loud voice as we passed a young couple with a pram. 'You know, Gus, that's the last time you get me on the Studland ferry.' They looked thunderstruck, and I guessed that it would be some months before that little family ever used it again.

However, it did give me time to try out my little scheme on Gus. He was as committal as ever. He didn't say a thing, bless him. I then came to the crunch point for both of us.

'But you realize, Gus, what this means? *You'll* have to drive.'

He looked surprised, then remembered as he looked down at my fat white plaster.

'And that's more of a sacrifice for me than for you,' I went on, 'as we'll have to go in your car.'

Gus almost broke out in a smile.

'S'all right. Goes like a ...' He hesitated, and I knew he was about to say 'bomb', but thought better of it. '... bird, it does, now I got those new plugs.'

The only bird I could think of that fitted the Popular was a half-dead vulture, but I let it pass.

He stopped at his gate, and turned to me. I could see Mrs Blunt peering at us through the curtains. (Crafty old devil – she must have a key. She didn't look as if she had a credit card.)

'When do you want to go?' he asked.

'Don't know yet. Next time he takes Derek out. Hope it's soon.'

Gus nodded.

'Anyway,' I said, 'I hope there's no trouble with your boat insurance people.'

'Don't suppose there will be,' he said. 'I haven't paid a premium for nearly five years.'

'But Gus ...' I began, but suddenly caught the glint in his eye. The bastard, he'd got me going again.

The rest of the day was, despite the many and varied plasters, kind of nice. I phoned Deborah, and she promised to ring back soonest with the information I needed. I then sat down for the evening, and found I could read Woody Allen again – that has to mean something, if only that the telly was saving me electricity and intellectual frustration. And then the high point of the late hours, Arabella performed her MacArthur return. We went through a nursery (green) type *badinage*, like, did she enjoy pricking out? and if she's got green fingers, would she please keep them off me until she'd washed, and give my regards to her Aunty Rhinum, and the like and then I went and got the Bing limousine.

'My sweet, darling, precious Arabella,' I said, embracing her (I'd put the car down first), 'a million thanks for this extravagant gift, but really, I can't accept it, you know.'

I could tell from her expression, she had already worked out an answer to my anticipated reaction.

'Then I'll give it to another toy fanatic. There are a few about, you know.' She winked at me.

'But . . .' I began, but she sealed my lips (or, to be more accurate, opened them) with a kiss.

'No "buts",' she whispered in my plastered ear.

'I'm not reduced to bread and water by my extravagance, you know. My cousin has the title and little money; my side of the family has the money, and no titles.' I knew I was beaten.

'Who wants titles?' I muttered between slips of the tongue (hers), and we must draw a veil over the next hour or so. Suffice it to say, Woody Allen didn't get a look in.

We came downstairs again feeling peckish and Miss Often and I did a culinary double act. She did the cooking; I did the eating. But I did the washing up single-handed, so to speak, and got detergent up my plaster. She said it would keep my skin nice and soft, and we sang a chorus of 'Plasters that do dishes can be soft as your face'. I had not felt so happy for ages.

But soon after that, Arabella asked the inevitable question – what was I going to do next about Treasure? I parried it as much as I could, but she was not convinced.

'Look', she said, with great concern, 'there's precious little you can achieve with one arm and twenty-nine plasters. For goodness' sake, leave it alone – at least for a bit. Until you're stronger. By then the police may have . . .'

'Sure,' I said, rather cruelly. (I didn't mean to be.) 'By then money will grow on trees, the communists will love the capi-talists, a Briton will win every final at Wimbledon. . . .'

She got up abruptly. 'And I won't be here any more.'

I deserved that.

'Darling, do believe me.' I took her hand and urged her gently back onto the settee. 'There's just one more thing I have to do. And I promise you it does not get me into any danger – or any more danger than I'm already in.'

'Promise?'

'Promise,' but she did not look totally convinced.

'Won't you tell me?'

'If I do, you might want to come. And I don't want that. It's just the fabulous toy you gave me has given me an idea where the diaries might be hidden.'

She thought for a minute. 'Secret compartments?'

I nodded.

'Oh leave it to the police, why don't you?' she cried.

'Gus is coming with me,' I said quickly.

'Gus was with you when you were blown sky high,' she ve-hemently pointed out.

'But we helped each other to shore,' I weakly rejoined.

'And this is positively the last action you'll take on your own?'

'Positively, absolutely, utterly and without question.'

'How many more does that mean there will be?' she remarked dryly, then added, 'I seem to bring tragedy around with me, don't I?'

Her last remark, I could see, was more to herself than to me. She got up as if to go, but then sank back again onto the settee. Then she looked at me with deadly seriousness.

'Maybe my enemies are right: I am Belladonna, poisonous to all who wish to partake of me. . . .'

I hadn't seen her like this since the night she told me some-thing of her life, and why she had begun her association with Treasure, and what he meant to her.

I took her by the shoulders. 'Look, my darling Often, what the hell are you talking about? This whole gruesome, tragic busi-ness wasn't sparked off by you. . . .'

She pulled away. 'Maybe this one wasn't.'

I was starting to get alarmed.

'There was another one?'

She hesitated, then quite suddenly, collapsed into my arms,

and began shaking with her crying. 'Just you be careful, Peter, that's all,' she managed to stammer out between sobs.

'Just be bloody, bloody, bloody careful – for my sake.'

I would have had to have been as thick as Ken Gates to have probed any further right then, so I didn't. We just sat quietly together, and listened to the odd owl hoot on its way to a midnight snack. Eventually, we went up to bed, and snuggled very close all night to keep out the bogie men.

Next morning, Arabella left early to help her cousin at the nursery, and neither of us mentioned her rather alarming comments of the evening before. But I couldn't get them out of my mind. But soon after she had gone, I had an idea. I rang the *Daily Telegraph* Information Service and asked for all the gen they had on Trenton Public School. I did the same with *The Times*, and my old mate at the *Western Gazette*. The first thing I found out was the colour of the school tie – diagonal bars of black, maroon and yellow divided by a thin line of white. I remembered that plaster boy in his infinite youth, alone with his childish playthings atop a barn, and the colour of the tie against the grey of his shirt.

The second piece of information that intrigued me was that it was regarded as one of the more modern of public schools – and that even its buildings were not that hallowed, most of them being of post-war construction, due to a hit and run Dornier flattening most of the old in 1944. I worked out Treasure would have been about fourteen at the time, and must remember the bombing vividly – unless he had been the bomb equivalent of shell shocked. I counted myself lucky that none of my own schooling had been as terrifying as an air raid, although, I suppose, many would claim the Headmaster came close to it at times. Photographs of the school and stats of the bomb damage were promised by both *The Times* and *Telegraph* by return of post in exchange for a small fee. I sent off two cheques right away.

Then Deborah rang to say that Derek was going out to lunch with Treasure that very day, and would be eating at the Wharfside Restaurant in Poole. I knew the place vaguely, from my old advertising days – more expense account than hard-earned money eating, but quite good for all that. Being situated right on the water-front at Poole, it did not have a car-park of its own, which suited me admirably if Treasure drove himself. The only problem now was which car he would take. I prayed he would feel very important that day. I immediately ran over to Gus's place (I tell a lie; it was more of a shambling trot), and he was in the shed where I keep my old Daimler.

'Come to work on it, at last, have you?' he asked, rather grumpily, and prodded at a rusting rear wheel spat. 'You laugh at my old car, but what about this?' A few flakes of reddened metal confettied to the dirt floor.

'I don't use this every day, Gus,' I said a little irritably, knowing he was right. I just had to get round to it one day. I really loved that old car, and did not want to see it die. 'But that's not why I came. We're off to see the wizard, the wonderful wizard of Lulworth.'

'When?' he asked.

'An hour and a half.'

'In Lulworth?'

'No, Poole. Have to be there early to see where he parks. But you'll have to keep some distance behind him, Gus, otherwise he'll see us. We're not exactly inconspicuous.' I laughed as I said this, for while I was getting used to having an Egyptian mummy as a close friend, not everybody had had the opportunity so to do.

'I'll bring my sets of keys and all that.'

'You do that, Gus.'

His uncle had died some years previously, and had bequeathed to Gus quite a few of the tools of his trade as a professional garage owner over Sidmouth way. These include four plywood boards full of duplicate ignition and door keys hanging on hooks. I reckon Gus could open up half the cars in the country if he had enough time, for he always keeps a handy little file in his pocket, and what didn't quite fit, soon does, in his hands.

So, two hours later, we were parked just up from the glossy premises of Willard, Jenks and Pursar, from where we could just see their car-park, and any car that might pull up outside their glass front entrance. I advised Gus to lower himself down in his seat, just in case. He did so, without a word of a grumble, and promptly fell asleep. Some SAS operative he was turning out to be. However, he was to be, quite literally, the key to any success we might have.

At 12.47 p.m. our prayers were answered. Treasure had felt almighty enough to need a Silver Cloud image, and had not come in the Land-Rover. The flying lady on the bonnet shone in the noon day sun as Derek skipped and jumped gaily into the car almost as soon as it had drawn to a stop. I prodded Gus in an amidships bandage, and he was starting the car before I had withdrawn my elbow. Amazing man. We kept well behind that silver boot, but close enough to have it nearly always in our sights. And it was not long before we were entering Poole, and making for the water-front. I wondered where Treasure would choose to park, and hoped it would not be too overlooked by office buildings or the like. At least the car could never be seen from the Wharfside Restaurant, unless it was floating in the harbour. As it would happen, where he chose was neither great for us, nor particularly disastrous. It seemed to be a private car-park, belonging to one of the large blocks that have sprung up in Poole in recent years. There was no attendant that we could see, and the car-park was obviously on the services side of the block, for there were precious few windows, but lots of pipes, lift-shafts, ventilators and the like.

We parked further up the street and waited. In two minutes Treasure emerged with Derek. They marched off seawards, and were soon out of sight. Gus carried out the nearest approximation to a U-turn that he could muster (it was nearer to a 'z' than a 'u'), and in a moment we pulled up alongside the Rolls, the comparison being, definitely, odious.

I got out and told Gus to stay put until I had checked out fully whether there was an attendant. I strolled nonchalantly around for a minute or two, but was not accosted. I signalled to Gus, and he emerged from his Ford sarcophagus, and went over to the Rolls. I stayed where I was, by the entrance, in case Treasure came back, or worse, I saw any sign of the law. But bless him, Gus had learned a trick or two from his old garage-owning uncle, and soon I heard the clunk of the Rolls door opening. He walked quickly over and got in behind the large black wheel. I went round to the passenger side, and he leaned across and let me in.

'Well, done, Gus,' I breathed. 'Now what about the ignition?' I pointed at the lock, then saw Gus had already inserted a key. I just hoped he could handle such a big car.

'Bet it works,' said Gus proudly.

He turned it and pressed the starter.

'It works,' I emitted with amazement. He clumsily waggled the gear lever into 'drive', and we were off, in wall-to-wall leather and walnut, for a nice little run into the country.

140

'We've got half an hour or so,' I said, as poor old Gus tried to get used to the huge size of the car.

'A lifetime,' he smiled beside me. And he looked the proudest set of bandages I'd seen for a long while.

We made for a deserted track that Gus knew, over towards Wareham St Martin, where he swore no one would be able to see us. I was terrified we would get stopped on the way by some uniformed officer on the look-out for a stolen Silver Cloud, or just curious about the bizarre sight of two obvious hospital cases in such a grand vehicle; but we led charmed lives, and pulled into the field without a moment's trouble. Gus had been right – there wasn't even as much as a cow to be curious about our goings-on. It had all been so easy – it almost seemed a crime.

I told Gus I would search the inside of the car, if he would tackle the boot lid with his cracksman capabilities. He mumbled something and disappeared around the back. I dealt with the front first: glove locker, map pockets, under the dash, and under the seats. There seemed nothing unusual there. I then got in the back, and checked the picnic tables, cocktail cabinet, pockets, and went on to remove the rear seat cushions, as if I were still examining the Bing limousine. But no, there was no coffer of jewels to be found here. And no diaries either.

It was then I heard the distant sound of rending metal, and looked through the rear window to see Gus standing triumphantly with a bloody great tyre lever in his hands. Slowly the rear window lifted up with the rest of the boot lid, and I could both see and speak to Gus with ease.

'What the hell are you doing, Gus? Why didn't you use the keys?'

'I did. They didn't seem to work. Must be the special conversion has a special locking system.'

'Well, it's plain it doesn't any longer,' I grimaced, but it was pointless to waste time remonstrating at this late stage, so I got out and joined him round the back.

As you might imagine, the finish inside the boot was as immaculate and luxurious as the rest of the interior, and I had to get the tyre lever away from Gus to keep it that way. He seemed to find its use much more stimulating than a Wilmot-Breeden car key, or even a credit card.

We found the gun compartment immediately – and number fifty-six in Gus's collection of keys flicked it open. But the velvet-lined interior was quite empty – not even a cartridge case to bear witness to its proper (or improper) purpose. Atop the spare wheel well was a splendid, inbuilt picnic set with matching electric kettle and flasks. I leaned forward and unclipped the fastenings of the rear seat-back, and it folded forward onto the seat cushion with silken ease, opening up a huge area of luggage space akin to that of an estate car. You could have got a stag in there.

I could see no other compartment at all. Mr Harold Radford's special conversion did not seem to have accommodated diaries. I looked at Gus. He looked at me. And then down at the tyre lever in my hand.

'No Gus, I'm not going to smash the car to pieces to find the diaries. Besides, Treasure doesn't do that every day when he's in a writing mood, you have to agree.'

We took a last look around the boot, then refixed the rear seat and slammed the boot lid really hard to get it to stay down. Somehow or other, the broken lock seemed to hold, but for how long, we could not be sure. And neither of us could bring ourselves to speak of our mammoth disappointment at not finding a trace of the diaries.

'I'm going to sit in the back,' I declared. 'I've always wanted to be chauffeured round in one of these.'

Gus didn't argue, and I felt it might actually help our credibility on the journey back to Poole. Wounded, rich landowner with bandaged chauffeur, both injured at shoot, don't you know – Carruthers' gun went off accidentally. Silly bugger, should have known better. Never invite him again – drum him out of the club and all that.

Well, we were half way back to Poole when I found it accidentally – a little chrome button behind the centre armrest in the rear seat. I pressed it, and the deep, thick cushion of the left-hand seat-back split in two, and one half folded forward to reveal the other section – a hollow, red leather-lined area full to the brim with diaries of every size and colour. Gus almost ran into the kerb when he saw through the rear-view mirror what I had found. He pulled to a stop immediately, but I shouted for him to go on and I would gather up the diaries whilst he drove. Gus restarted, but found it even more difficult than usual to keep his attention on the road, so excited were we both with the discovery. At last we had traced the treasure chest of our arch adversary, as you might say, and I could not wait to see what evidence it might contain.

Before we had arrived back at Poole, I had discovered that by pressing the button twice, the right-hand seat-back copied the left, and a further selection of diaries came to hand. Directly Gus had laboriously parked the Rolls and relocked it, he helped me transfer the find into the rear of the Ford Popular, and we rattled off. But this time we took the long overland route back to Studland, for neither of us had any desire to be accosted by Mr Treasure whilst waiting for the undoubted extra convenience of the ferry.

Thirteen

Taking the long way home may have been our saving, or our undoing – it's difficult to tell. But it gave time for the ogre of Doom Abbey to react after, no doubt, finding his boot lid somewhat resculptured by dear old Gus's efforts to open it, for when we jerked to a halt outside ye old Toy Emporium, we knew we'd had uninvited guests around. The door was open and the glass cracked. Our normal customers usually wait until I unlock the door and am open for business.

My first instinct was to high-tail it away again, as fast as Gus could drive. But before I could indicate my intentions, Gus began sounding the car horn, beep, beep, beep, beep, beep!

'What the hell are you doing that for, Gus?' I yelled.

'Let 'em know we're back.'

I almost hit him with my plaster.

'You . . .' (I couldn't think of a word extreme enough, and while I was hunting for one, the sense of what Gus was doing suddenly hit me. I changed my tack a little.) '. . . genius,' I said, and forced a smile.

He bowed his bandages. 'Now everybody's looking at us, even if they are inside, they daren't attack us, would they?'

I looked out of the car window. Quite a crowd was already collecting, mainly of small boys on the glad way home from school.

'What the matter, mister?' one set of freckles shouted, 'Got your plasters stuck on the button?' He looked around for applause from his friends, rather like a guest on the Bob Monkhouse show. My eyes were riveted on my cracked front door, but nothing came out, not even Bing. And that feline thought gave me bravery I thought had been lost at Thermopylae. I leapt out of the car, and rushed into my shop, ignoring Gus's shouts not to be such a bloody fool.

But I found no one when I got inside – except Bing, who was fast asleep on the settee. So much for the concept of owning a watch-cat. What I did find was not very amusing. Chaos. Everything that could be opened, was – and a lot that couldn't as well. Everything that could be overturned had been, and that included my glass cabinets and their precious inmates, which were scattered all over the counters and floor. I couldn't begin to reckon how much stock had been damaged, the confusion was so total. The subtle signature of Ken Gates was not hard to define. I suddenly felt a hand on my shoulder. I whipped round, and raised my good arm.

'Don't hit me. I didn't do it.' It was only Gus, who had crept in quietly without my hearing him. How he did it through all that broken glass, I'll never know. His great feet certainly did not look like a ballet dancer's, even swathed in mutton cloth.

'Gus, what are we going to do?' I said weakly.

'Board the door up, and get out of here quick. Then we'll think.' And he moved with the speed of light into the kitchen and almost instantly was back with a hammer, nails and the length of wood I kept for Bing to scratch his claws on.

At least by the time he'd finished, we had the shop secured against, well, anyone under twelve years old or so, until we'd had breathing space to inform the police, and Trevor Blake in particular. Once back in the car, Gus turned to me and grinned.

'I did the door. Now you do the next move.'

'Westwards,' I said, with surprising decision.

He laboriously turned the car round and headed towards Swanage and Corfe.

'Which one?' he asked at the fork off to Swanage.

I pointed right. But we weren't going to Corfe, of course. We were heading for a certain nursery in Owermoigne.

Now I don't know whether you've ever called on anyone for the first time, covered in bandages and plasters, and asked if you could have sanctuary because the baddies were after you. Well it causes the reaction to be a little circumspect, however hospitable and generous natured your host may be in different circumstances. I'm sure it was only the mention of Arabella's wonderful name that prevented her cousin having a seizure or screaming for help. Even then, she looked more than somewhat dubious. Put yourself in her trembling shoes.

'I'm afraid Arabella has taken a load of bedding plants to Moreton Station to put on the train. But she won't be long. You'd better come in, Mr . . . er . . .'

'Marklin. Peter Marklin.' I came to her aid. 'And Gus Tribble.'

'Philippa Stewart-Hargreaves,' she smiled graciously, and stood aside to let us in. She didn't mention being a ladyship. In a way, she didn't need to – there was a quiet confidence about her that said it all. She was around thirty-five, a brunette, a damned sight more attractive than most ladyships I'd never met. Browner too.

She led us into a smallish living-room that was nothing like I'd been expecting. Mind you, nor was the house; it was modern for a start – very modern, but 'compact', as the estate agents term the not so big. The most striking feature was its vast expanse of sloping roof that shone with what I took to be solar panels. Inside, everything seemed to be white and cool except for the sweep of the timber frames that were left natural wood. You could imagine an Ingmar Bergman heroine being sensually enigmatic in it, if not downright incomprehensible. Meanwhile, I was just a bag of nerves.

Lady Philippa sat down on an oatmeal-coloured settee that was in its natural Habitat, and indicated two more chairs for Gus and myself. I sat down, but Gus suddenly turned and walked out.

'Your friend?' Our hostess looked at me anxiously, and crossed her long slim legs.

'I'm sorry,' I stammered. 'He's quite right. We've left some vital evidence in the car, and he's gone to get it. I'd better go and give him a hand, if you'll excuse me.'

She smiled and I left. But her elegant bare legs had reminded me of Arabella, and I prayed she hadn't taken it into her head to drive straight from Moreton to the 'Toy Emporium', for I had a feeling there was a really nasty chance she'd never get there.

'When are you going to ring the police?' Gus asked, as we carried the diaries inside. 'I thought you would be getting on with that while I was fetching these.'

'I've had second thoughts,' I said, puffing with the effort of keeping hold of the stack of diaries under my good arm.

'Ha'penny for them,' Gus muttered, somewhat disgusted.

'I want to read the diaries first. If I ring Blake now, he'll take them all away, and if there's nothing incriminating in them, Treasure's got us over a barrel for pinching them. Whereas if we skim through the relevant ones quickly, and there's nothing horrid, we can plonk them back on Treasure's doorstep with an abject apology.'

Gus paused at the front door, before going back in. 'Well, it'll have to be quick, old dear. And, come to think of it, if there's nothing incriminating in them, why did he have your house done over looking for them?'

'Easy. First, anyone can see Treasure's got a short fuse when his back is put up. Second, diaries are about the most private of all private possessions, aren't they? However innocent, no one would want the whole world reading all about one's most intimate thoughts and actions, least of all someone with the tendencies of Mr Treasure.'

Gus sniffed and went inside. I followed, and saw his point. Maybe I just didn't want Blake getting all the kudos while I did all the flaming work.

I looked at my Seiko, and Lady Philippa smiled sympathetically.

'She'll be back soon. I expect she waited for the train to come in. It's sometimes late.'

I prayed she was right. Three minutes later I heard a crunch on the gravel outside, and rushed to the huge windows. But it was only an ancient black Wolseley, driven by a white-haired lady of at least three times the car's venerable age.

'That's Mrs Duck. She's come for her cabbage plants, I expect,' my hostess remarked softly. 'I wonder if you could move your car to let her get through up to the glasshouses.'

The car! I'd forgotten it was a dead give-away as to where we were. But Gus had seen the look in my eye and was already making for the door.

'I'll find a field to stick it in,' he mumbled, 'behind an 'edge.' And he was gone.

I watched Mrs Duck get her cabbage plants from Philippa up amongst the six or so long glasshouses that lay some 150 yards from the house itself. It was a kind of idyllic country scene: the

147

old family car, the old lady, the local nurseries, the cool lady owner, the sunshine on the fields. Its contrast with my own predicament became almost too painful to bear. I turned away, and to fill the time, began rummaging through the piles of assorted sized volumes that were now stacked on the sitting-room floor. Some were as big as pretentious office diaries, others – the minority – only of the Lett's School-boy variety.

I didn't bother thumbing through every volume; in general, Treasure's private life was his own affair and should remain that way. I knew the dates I was interested in: the time of my Channel crossing earlier in the month, and March 1981, when his wife disappeared off to Lausanne, or God knows where. So that's where I started, and it didn't take long to find them. By this time Gus was back and he joined me, kneeling on the floor, puffing from his exertions in, no doubt, running back from where he had concealed his motor.

'Come on, Peter, get it over with. We're sitting ducks while we've still got these bloody books.'

I didn't need urging. I speed-read like there was no tomorrow (which was likely at the present rate), and soon found all the evidence I needed for Treasure's part in the theft of Monsieur Vincent's toys in the diary for the current year. It was all noted down in precise detail, and detail not just of the facts, but of each and every emotion that those facts excited.

It was that latter quality that made the reading so disturbing, for it was like looking through a window into the deep recesses of Treasure's soul. I could hardly keep the diary steady in my hand as I absorbed its content. Apparently, he had heard of Vincent's collection months before from a friend of his, who lived in the south of France. Treasure had approached Vincent to try and buy the toys, but the Frenchman had refused to sell to him. Some time later, he had heard from a business associate that Chalmers had an option on them and had commissioned me to appraise and purchase them. From pub gossip (poor old Gus, I never told him this bit) he had learnt the date of my trip and what route I was taking, and he had sent Ken Gates in the Land-Rover to wait at Calais for the return of my Beetle convertible. Gates had effected the switch on the crossing, in cahoots with one of the seamen on the car deck. (I wondered if it had been the spotty one.) The Land-Rover had been waved through Customs without being inspected, as greasy palms had been greased yet again. And that was that. No mention of any shadowing on the *autoroute*, and therefore, no Quinky. So, in all probability, she was entirely innocent of anything but lusting after yours truly, or she had been an emissary of Vivian Stone's. After all, he had a red Ferrari, though what he might have gained by such an action, I couldn't imagine. So I put Quinky in the steering wheel seduction category, and wished her better luck next time.

I was about to delve into the diary for 1981, when I heard Mrs Duck reversing down the drive, her rear axle growling with the effort. Then the crunching of the gravel seemed to grow louder again, and I raced again to the window. But it was no Golf convertible, just a rusting Morris 1100, that was on its last MOT, driven by a middle-aged man with a flat cap, and a Hogarth nose from filling up at pubs. I saw Philippa greet him graciously, and they both disappeared into one of the wooden sheds next to the glasshouses and emerged a moment later with a Rotavator, which the man began inspecting. Then, after getting a tool box from his car, he began what I took to be repairs. Another peaceful, pastoral scene, and the agonizing unquiet of no Arabella. I decided to ask Lady Philippa if I could ring Trevor Blake the instant she returned, and bugger the kudos.

Meanwhile, while Gus caught up on the current diary, I began the disturbing contents of the 1981 edition, to keep my mind in some sort of occupation other than going mad. And I have to confess, I skip-read a bit more than just the entry for 24 March. I had to. For I just could not believe anyone could love a woman as much as Randolph Treasure had loved Veronica Charlotte Telling. He had forgiven her the most wild and wilful infidelities, and had indulged, it would seem, her every twisted whim. And his agonizing over her repeated threats over the weeks, to join her Swiss lover, was exquisite in its intensity. On 24 March, she had carried out her threat, and flown to Lausanne to join a Boris Kaufman, taking with her five of Treasure's most loved possessions from his house to sell to 'punish him for loving her overmuch and keeping her in a possessive prison,' as she put it. These consisted of a Giacometti figurine, a Fabergé dog, and a small Russian icon. But even more significant, in the light of what was to follow, were two of his prized tinplate toys, a Distler thirties limousine, and another but larger limousine made by Tipp and Company. One of these was to bring her to her

149

death as chronicled in the entry for the evening of that day, 24 March.

I was infinitely thankful when Mrs Fitzpayne had gone for the day. Now I did not need to keep up any appearances. I could succumb to what I was. A never-ending scream, trapped in my black hole of pain. I lay on my bed, our bed no longer. And the ceiling seemed to descend on me, slowly and inexorably, like in some medieval torture chamber, and I heard her laugh ring through the room, the house, the night. I shouted, 'My darling, where are you now? Speak. Speak, before I'm crushed forever.' I don't know how long I lay there. Time had ceased to move forward at all as I relived every second of my life with her, and lingered over every silky inch of her beautiful body.

Then, suddenly, she was standing in front of me, shouting. I thought it was my imagination for a moment, but then she came and stood over the bed, and I saw what she had in her hand – the event I had so dreaded from the moment I had known she had taken that Tipp limousine. She had found it – as I felt she must. It could not be seen from the outside. It was only if you opened a door. I imagined her lover opening that door and seeing the edge of the leather shining under the tin-plate seat. And both of them exulting over what they discovered in that, my most secret of diaries. And she shouted that it was worth all the trouble of flying back that night just to see the horror on my face. And she danced around my bed, waving my little book, and raving about what she said it would mean for her and all her lovers – 'luxury for life, as we bleed you dry'.

She made for the door, saying that she would expect £10,000 by that weekend, and I felt myself rising from the bed and moving towards her. She never expected it, you see, not from me. Not from her abject slave . . .

I won't continue with the quote. You can imagine for yourself most of the rest. He strangled her because of her blackmail, and because he loved her too much to lose her to anyone else. And later the next day, he plunged her body into a shallow acid bath, which belonged to an antiques restorer friend of his, who was away in Germany delivering some furniture

150

and who used the bath for stripping wood. The remains, minus the dental parts of the skull, he carried in a polythene sack in the boot of his Silver Cloud and buried at night in the field on the outskirts of Swanage. What happened later, you know.

Whilst I had been reading the diary, Gus had evidently been reading my face. For when I put the volume down, he said very gently, 'Won't ask too much about it. Don't want to know, really. Just the one thing – did he kill his wife?'

I nodded

'So she didn't go to Lausanne, then?'

'Yes, she did. But she came back that night, because she had found a diary of his, that she thought she could use for a little blackmail – keep her and her dubious playboys in funds for life. And I guess that particular playboy was too scared to follow up her disappearance in case their attempt at blackmail had gone wrong. He's probably shacked up with some other prize lady by now, a thousand miles from Switzerland.'

'And Treasure killed her to stop the blackmail?'

'No, for love.'

Gus didn't ask any more. He didn't need to, for as far as he was concerned, that was the end of the Treasure story. But it was not for me. I wondered what that very special diary contained in its pages – what Veronica had assessed as being worth quite a tidy fortune. I had a feeling that search as I might, I would not discover it amongst the multi-coloured volumes scattered around in front of me, even if I'd had the time right then, which I certainly didn't. I looked out of the window again, and could just see Lady Philippa leaving the Hogarth nose to get on with his work, and walking back to the house. It was then I had an idea.

I began sorting the diaries into order, spreading them out on the floor.

'What the hell are you doing now?' Gus exploded. 'We ought to be going to the police right now – we've found everything we wanted.'

'Not quite everything,' I replied, too nervous and hurried to explain further. I gave him a pile of diaries. 'Help me put them out in order of years.' He looked at me as if I'd gone round the twist, but co-operated all the same. Good old Gus. In no time, we had the floor covered with diaries, beginning in the top left-hand

151

corner with 1940, a Lett's Boy Scout's Diary still with its original pencil down its spine, and ending in the bottom right with the current one, a large, leather-bound 'Chairman of the Board' variety. It was plain as a pikestaff now, the one we still had to look for, the one that had written the death warrant for Veronica Charlotte Telling.

'We haven't got 1944,' Gus offered.

'Exactly,' I accepted, as I remembered what had happened at Trenton School that very same year. At that moment, Lady Philippa added her grace to the diary-littered room.

'Arabella must have called off somewhere else, I expect,' she said, but there was little conviction in her voice. 'Could she have gone over to your place in Studland ?'

'She could. But I would have expected a phone call by now . . . .'

But I didn't have time to complete the sentence, for the gravel spoke again, and in a crunchier, racier voice. This time, Lady Philippa was nearest the window. 'It's a Land-Rover. Don't recognize the driver, but he seems to be in quite an amazing hurry.'

But by then, Gus and I were shoving the diaries out of sight under the oatmeal settee and the two armchairs.

'It's *him*,' I breathed to our now thoroughly bemused and slightly alarmed hostess. I shot a glance through the window. I was right ; the thick figure of Ken Gates was already almost at the front door. Lady Philippa reacted with the swiftness of someone from the French Resistance. Arabella must have told her about some of the recent dramas. I liked this Trench-Stewart-Hargreaves family.

'Go out the back way,' she whispered urgently. 'He won't be able to see you go. Hide in one of the glasshouses. I'll keep him busy. Promise.'

'But you might be in danger too. . . .'

'Rubbish,' she countered, and pushed me towards the kitchen. 'Treasure and my father knew each other quite well years ago. He has no reason to harm me. I'll say I've never met you.'

I was loath to leave her to the tender mercies of the concrete Mussolini, but another shove, and we were at the back door, as we heard Gates thumping his call-sign on the front. We made for the nearest glasshouse, so that we could hear if the instincts of a born bully began taking over. In which case, as seemingly born losers, we would have to go back in to see if our luck had changed.

Fourteen

There's nothing that quite has the smell of a tomato plant – especially when your nose is only a quarter of an inch away. I've gone off tomatoes for life. Gus and I were lying face down on the moist peat and God knows what else that made up the plants' soil in the glasshouse, so that we couldn't be seen from the over-windowed house. And the heat was over-powering, if you weren't alive with trusses of fruit.

We said nothing to each other at first, straining for a scream or thumps, or the sound of something breaking. But all was quiet. Very quiet. So we began airing our thoughts in whispers.

'I hope Arabella doesn't come back now,' I ventured, 'but where the blazes is she? Gates, thank God, hasn't got her.'

'Yet,' added Gus, then realized I needed optimism not realism right then. 'She'll have gone to your place, right enough,' he added.

'And find it smashed up. And then what? Go to Treasure and remonstrate?'

Gus removed a miniature truss from his nostrils. 'She's a sensible soul; won't do anything rash.'

I knew what he was thinking, blast him. 'Like you' he meant. I wondered if she had gone straight on to the police. I sort of hoped she had. But then again, I felt she wouldn't, not until she'd checked with us on what had been happening. But then that only applied if she thought we were still safe and sound somewhere. I was going steadily and inexorably out of my mind with worry. And I realized how much I needed her, how much I bloody loved her, but all she was getting out of my love was danger. Her enigmatic words suddenly came back to me – all about her really being Belladonna and poisonous to those with whom she came in contact. What the hell had she been talking about? It was I who was deadly, not her.

I could feel the damp of the earth adding to the sweat on my

154

shirt. I shifted position slightly, and then heard a diesel engine start up, and a shrapnel crack of gravel hitting wheel-arches. I looked up cautiously, and was just in time to see Gates doing a Le Mans reverse down the drive. And, thank goodness, he was still alone.

We waited until the diesel knock had faded towards the Dorchester road, then scurried like rabbits back to the house. Praise be, Lady Philippa was not only safe but smiling.

'Accepted it like a lamb,' she said proudly, 'but he left a message in case you came here.'

I asked her what it was. She blushed a little, so I helped her.

'I bet it was something like, "Censored well tell that censored censored Marklin that Mr Treasure wants his censored diaries back censored censored fast or he's as good as censored done for."'

She laughed. 'I think your censored's are three or four short. But, yes, you've got the gist.'

'Did he ask about Arabella?'

'Yes. Wanted to know where she was. I said I didn't know; I wasn't my cousin's keeper. I then told him rather sharply to get off my property, or I'd call the police.'

'And he went?'

'He censored went.' I hugged her. I couldn't help it. She was her cousin's cousin, if ever I heard one. And she hugged back, out of relief, I guess, that Gates had gone. Gus looked very left out, and pointed to the phone.

We separated, and I asked, 'May I use the phone? It's high time I informed the Law.'

'Past time,' muttered Gus. But as she nodded and I went to pick up the receiver, the telephone beat me to it and rang of its own accord. Lady Philippa answered it, then put her hand over the receiver. 'It's for you,' she whispered, and her eyes told me who it was. She resumed, 'He's not here, I'm afraid. Could I ask who's . . . ?'

I suddenly took the receiver from her unwilling hands.

'He is here. What do you want, Treasure? Your henchman has just gone.'

His timbre almost made my ear vibrate. 'Mr Marklin, I'm so glad to track you down at last. I just have a feeling it's time you paid me another of your little visits, don't you? Didn't Mr Gates tell you?'

'Why is that, Mr Treasure?' I said, mentioning his name, not for politeness, but to confirm my friends' worst fears. They gathered around the phone like lemmings. 'And no, your henchman didn't find me in.'

'Mr Marklin, don't play the innocent with me. You have property of mine that your very British sense of fair play will not allow you to keep, I'm sure.'

'I was just about to see that they were returned, when you rang,' I tried as an answer.

'How very thoughtful of you, Mr Marklin. I suggest you get in that ridiculous car of yours and come right over. Delay could be rather hazardous to health, if you don't.'

'Don't threaten me, Mr Treasure. I have rather more reason to ...' He did not let me finish.

'... Threaten me? Oh dear, Mr Marklin, you don't think I would be so foolish as to ring without having made provision for that, do you?' His voice conveyed no sense of concern, but rather the confident note of a man on a winning streak. That did rather more than puzzle me – it scared me rigid.

'And I want each and every diary, Mr Marklin. Not a single one withheld, you understand?'

'I understand, Mr Treasure, but I cannot agree. You will receive every diary but one. And that one, I'm afaid, must be seen by the authorities, as it ...'

He cut in sharply, and his voice was a load of decibels louder. 'My dear sir, I did say *every* diary. Do you never listen?'

'You are in no position ...' He cut across me again.

'It's *you* who are in no position, as you put it, Mr Marklin. Because, you see, I have something of yours. Something soft and fragile, and very vulnerable.'

My God, I thought, he's already got Arabella. 'If you harm a hair on her head, Treasure, I'll ...'

'You'll what, Mr Marklin? I do assure you, you're in no position to threaten anyone. And Deborah here, I'm sure, will agree, won't you Deborah?'

I was thunderstruck. It wasn't Arabella. It was more devious than that; he'd got my ex-wife. I heard a squeal in the background, and I shouted down the mouthpiece, 'You murderous bastard. If you've got Deborah, and you hurt her in any way, I'll ...'

'What, Mr Marklin? This is so boring – we've just been

156

through all that. There's little you can do, but exactly what I say. And I mean *exactly*, Mr Marklin . . .'

'Let me speak to Deborah.' This time it was I who interrupted.

'Certainly.' I heard the receiver put down, and some scuffling sounds, and then her voice, very faint and trembly.

'Peter, he means it. For Christ's sake, do what he says. He's got a gun and . . .'

More scuffles, and a slight cry, and his odious voice resumed.

'Satisfied, Mr Marklin? I'm sure you would not want to be the cause of a fatality, just for one little diary, now would you? Your common sense must tell you how incredibly uncaring and stupid that would be . . . .'

I had almost stopped listening, because forward planning was the name of the game just then. And I knew I had only a matter of seconds to react.

'. . . You see, you and I can have a permanent truce between us, once all the diaries are returned. And I can be very useful to you, Mr Marklin, in every kind of way. Smooth your path to a considerable standard of living. All you have to do is forget. Simple, isn't it? You forget your way into security. Many men would give their eye-teeth for such an arrangement. Indeed, many men have. I could tell you stories . . .'

I interrupted again, for I was ready now. 'Okay, you win. I'll be over in half an hour or so with the diaries – all of them.'

'One rather charming lady is awaiting your arrival, Mr Marklin,' he cooed, then added. 'And, by the way, do let's make it a cosy foursome. Bring Arabella.'

'I won't do anything of . . .' And then I remembered I didn't even know where she was, just where she wasn't, thank God.

'You will, Mr Marklin.' I again heard a cry in the background.

'Okay. Okay. Leave her alone. I'll bring Arabella,' I lied quickly, and realized why he wanted her there. For then he would have the belt and braces of knowing he could train his gun on both my ex and my current passions – just in case one was not quite sufficient, or the memory too distant.

'Half an hour, Mr Marklin, no more.'

'Half an hour, Mr Treasure, I promise.' And the line went dead.

We made Lady Philippa promise, cross her heart, that she would, under no circumstances, inform the police while we were

157

gone for fear of Deborah's life, nor let Arabella know what was happening, if she returned, for fear of hers. She crossed her heart and we left, taking the diaries with us to where Gus had hidden the car behind the hedge in a field now full of cows, one of whom had left her brown signature down the boot-lid. Seemed to sum up the predicament we were in really, and also the degree to which we were both scared.

The evening was incredibly clear. I wondered whether it was great weather when Anne Boleyn lost her head, or Charles I mounted the scaffold, or when Chamberlain flew to Hitler's lair. I bet it had been; tragedy often comes, as they say, out of the blue.

'You know what to do, don't you Gus?' He turned and gave me a weak smile. 'Don't worry, I'm not the lumbering idiot I no doubt look, old dear. I remember what you said.'

I patted his big hand, as he drove jerkily on towards Lulworth. What would I do without him? Everybody should have an occasional pain in the arse as their best friend. He dropped me off, as I'd asked him, at the end of the lane leading up to Doom Abbey.

'I don't like leaving you on your own,' he muttered. 'Ain't right. And you should, at least, take in the diaries.'

I slammed my door and went round to his side. 'Look, don't argue. It's righter for you to do what I've suggested, than for both of us to walk straight into the big spider's web and give up our only bargaining point. You're our only chance, so get going.'

He accepted the inevitable, and even spun the almost bald tyres of his car in his haste to be away. My only regret was that he wasn't driving a Fomula One Lotus; I wanted him back in double, treble quick time. For stalling had never been my forte.

After he had bounced out of sight, diaries and all, I looked at my watch. Five minutes to go to the half hour since Treasure had called. I walked slowly, and to an innocent onlooker, I must have appeared as a leisurely, country-loving holiday-maker, with not a care in the world but his broken arm, how many skylarks would sing that day and how many Heinekens were on the cold shelf at the next hostelry. But in reality, if I wasn't careful, I could very soon end up on a cold shelf of quite a different complexion. And maybe I wouldn't be alone.

For once, the great door was open, like the jaws of a killer whale. I walked straight in and tried to remember everything I'd

158

seen and read about the sAs. The trouble was, I couldn't even remember what the initials stood for, let alone anything else.

He must have heard my footfalls, for his voice boomed out from down the passage on the left.

'In the library, my friends. Do come in.'

I went on down, past the window I had Barclaycarded open (now repaired, I noticed) and stopped outside the second door on the right.

'That's it. Turn the handle, Mr Marklin, it won't bite you.'

I did just that, and it didn't. But the sight of the scenario inside the room scared me witless. Treasure was standing in front of the large, stone, open fireplace, holding that (to me) famous shotgun pointed at the settee, on which bound hand and foot, sat Deborah.

'What, all alone, Mr Marklin? Or are your friends still out-side?' The gun quivered slightly in his grasp. 'I would ask them to come in, if I were you, and bring the diaries with them.'

I cleared my throat before replying – the sign of a weak man, my mother used to maintain. I never did it normally. (But I don't think not doing it necessarily makes you a strong man.)

'I'm not you, Mr Treasure, and my friends aren't outside. Nor are the diaries.' If his eyes had had their way, I'd have been shot there and then. I went on apace. 'I've come alone to arrange what you would know as a gentleman's agreement first.'

'You, a gentleman, Mr Marklin?' His mouth laughed, but his eyes were grim.

'Yes, I am, Mr Treasure. No power, no money, no old school tie, no heraldic signs, no history, no inheritance. Just what I stand up in – me. And part of that you fractured with your bloody bomb. But I reckon I'm more of a gentleman than you've ever been. For I don't murder and I don't steal and I don't kidnap. I'm incredibly boring, and, on the whole, boringly honest.'

I could see he wouldn't take too much more of this, but I had to spin it out, given the fact that a Ford Popular would never make Formula One with the best will in the world and Gus not driving.

He waved the shotgun towards me for an instant, and I closed my eyes. When I opened them again, I was, amazingly, still alive.

'No, I'm not going to kill you yet, Mr Marklin. Not until I've heard your pathetic plan – your gentleman's agreement.' The barrels indicated a chair beside the settee. 'Come and sit down where I can keep you in my sights.'

I moved across, reached out and touched Deborah's shoulder as I went past. She whimpered, and her eyes were red-rimmed and pleading.

'It'll be all right, believe me,' I whispered as I sat down, as much to convince myself as her.

'Now we're all comfortable I'll tell you, Mr Marklin, what constitutes the action of a perfect gentleman in a predicament like yours and your former wife's. You concede graciously, like a true English sportsman, and take your defeat like a man.' He chuckled. 'You must have learnt that at school, my dear fellow, didn't you?'

He couldn't have given me a better opening.

'And what did you learn at school, Mr Treasure? Especially that fateful year during the war – 1944.'

His eyes blazed immediately, and I knew I'd hit a nerve. He tried to shift position. 'Mr Marklin, I know you're playing for time for some reason. I just hope you haven't told the police, for I'm quite willing for us all to die together, if need be.'

'No, I didn't tell the police because I knew you were fanatical enough to do something like that after your little explosion at sea. But don't change the subject.' I was surprised at the firmness of my voice. 'You kept a diary for 1944, didn't you? And I don't think it was destroyed by a German bomb, because it was the cause of everything, wasn't it, Mr Treasure? And poor Veronica paid the price for finding it, didn't she? What was so terrible in its childish pages?'

'That's no concern of yours. A diary is a personal record, not a public one.'

'But you've made it a public one, haven't you? Or rather, your wife did.'

The gun shook in his hand, and Deborah, not knowing what I was about, shot me a glance to shut me up.

'So you have been doing a little reading, have you, Mr Marklin? I'm afraid it won't aid you in any way. For neither you nor your ex-wife will go free until I have the diaries. Once that happens, that one diary will be reduced to ashes. Then it will be your word against mine. And I assure you once again, my word is worth a great deal in all the places where it really matters. I wouldn't try to check it out if I were you.'

I looked at my watch. I still needed to play for time – that's all I had on my side. 'There's still 1944, Mr Treasure. Your special diary.'

The gun quivered once more. I felt like imitating it, and I think I did, more than once.

'Come on, Mr Marklin. Forget *me*. Let's talk about you and Deborah. And come to think of it, Arabella, whom you'd better get over here fast, together with the diaries. And our little code of silence for the future. There's so much for you . . . .'

'No,' I interrupted, 'let's talk about that very important year of the war. The year of D-Day and the Allied landings, the v1s and v2s. But more importantly, the year of the Dorniers.' I watched his eyes, and went on. 'The unmistakable drone of those German engines, the siren, perhaps, sounding too late for you to get to the school shelters. Do you remember, Mr Treasure . . . ?'

'Be quiet. Damn you, be quiet.' Treasure's voice showed the first sign of uncertainty, the first shaft of fear.

'No, I won't be quiet. Any more than those bombs were quiet all those years ago. Those whistling, crunching, killing, metal containers of death and destruction . . . .'

'Shut up. Shut up! Or I'll . . .' His gun really shook in his hands now, and Deborah let out a scream, a horrible scream.

'Do what he says,' she cried, 'or he'll kill us. He's mad. You're just making him worse . . . .' She broke down and sobbed into the arm of the settee.

'He won't kill us,' I said with more confidence than reality dictated. 'He's done enough killing, haven't you, Mr Treasure?'

'Be quiet. For God's sake, be quiet.' For the first time the timbre of Treasure's voice began cracking.

I went on. 'And those bombs. You'll never forget those bombs, will you?'

He did not respond in any way, almost as if he were going numb. I could not stop now. 'They rained down on everything you loved: your school, your possessions, perhaps your favourite books and toys. And, in all probability, on your favourite people. Is that right, Mr Treasure?'

Again, no response. Deborah's sobs were now like a child's at the end of a bad dream, punctuated by sharp intakes of breath.

'You saw your best friend killed, didn't you? Your very best friend.'

Treasure slowly moved the line of the shotgun to the right. It was now pointing directly at me. I wondered how much longer I would have to wait. All I could do was keep my mind on the present, and that meant Treasure's past.

'What was his name, Mr Treasure,' I continued, 'from that roll-call of boys? Was it Julian? Or Simon? Or Matthew? Anthony, perhaps? John? Michael? Peter? Paul?' At the last mentioned, Treasure shuddered, and moved towards me.

'Shut up, I told you.' I could see tears in his eyes. 'Don't you ever bring up his name again, do you hear?'

The muzzle was now uncomfortably near my vital parts. I prayed that Gus would not be much longer. For there was little joy in being shrewd in one's guesses, if, as the royal family would put it, one was dead.

'Tell me,' I said, in an altogether more gentle and sympathetic tone (and that's the prize coward in me getting the upper hand), 'why Paul meant so very much to you?'

'You're far too intelligent not to know, Mr Marklin.' A tear fell onto the waxed stock of the gun, and beaded instantly. 'I loved him. I loved him. And he loved me. Can you understand that? The intensity of it, imprisoned as we were in that boarding school during the war. The intensity of being fourteen. He was all I thought of, every minute of every day....'

I considered jumping him – but only for a split second. For he was like a wounded bull, the more dangerous and unpredictable because of the pain. And I had a bloody great plaster.

'But why did you kill your wife, whom you loved with just the same burning intensity, Mr Treasure? That I still don't understand. The confession of your love for a boyhood friend surely was not motive for *murder*?'

'That, sir,' his voice now seemed to indicate a certain degree of recovery, 'you will never understand. For you will never find the diary for 1944. Ever. Ever. Ever.'

He started to move back from me, and the gun's aim was re-adjusted to Deborah once more. 'Now I've had enough of this, Mr Marklin. I don't care about your blundering friend, Gus Tribble, but I want Arabella here now, and with each and every diary.' He accidentally banged the stock against the stone surround of the fireplace. 'And I mean now, now, now,' his voice crescendoed, 'otherwise you can kiss goodbye to your ex-wife.'

I prayed Gus had had the sense to break into my garage and steal my Beetle (a thing I hadn't, in my panic, thought to tell him) so as to be back faster than his Ford could ever manage.

'I ... er ... er.'

'You ... er ... er ... what?' he asked vehemently.

'I'll ... er ... have to make a phone call. That's the arrangement. But that's only after you have released Deborah.'

Treasure's laugh was brimful of scorn. And rightly so, I guess, but I was at my poor wits' end.

'You'll make that phone call, now, and Deborah will stay trussed like a chicken until I've got those diaries, or ....'

'Okay, okay. I'll phone.' I looked around the room, hoping not to find a phone. I found one.

'To whom, pray?' Treasure smiled.

'To ... er ... Lady Philippa Stewart-Hargreaves.' I was glad she had such a long name – it took longer to say. Our lives, I reckoned, were now hanging on how lengthy my words and sentences were.

I sat immobile, but not for long.

'Well, get on with it, Marklin. I take it Arabella's there, her little heart pounding about the fate of her new hero. Maybe she thinks by backing you, she'll somehow expiate her own guilt. First it's a daddy figure, and now a ....'

Her guilt about what, I thought, but his gun was now pointing to the phone, and I guessed I had to obey its command and not worry about enigmatic remarks.

I dialled slowly thanks to my plaster. And, heaven be praised, Philippa took ages answering it. She must have been up at the glasshouses.

'Look, don't talk too much. Just listen, Philippa. Lives depend on it.'

She is a very clever woman. She talked. I let Treasure hear the gabbling by holding the receiver towards him.

'Get on with it,' he shouted. She must have heard that, with any luck.

'Now listen, Philippa. It's just as we arranged, only he won't release Deborah ... No, not until Arabella's here with all the diaries ... Yes, all the diaries, Philippa, including the 1981 one ... Yes, the one for 1981, you know ... (She was doing awfully well) '... yes, I know her Golf has broken down, but she will have to come in yours ... It can't be helped it's an old red Peugeot 404 estate. Tell her to put her foot on the gas. ...'

'That's enough,' Treasure boomed across. 'Tell her I give her twenty minutes to get here, or she can forget her new friend and his ex-wife.'

'Did you hear that? Yes, twenty minutes. Get her here in the fastest car you can lay your hands on. With the diaries. Right. But he's got a gun, so tell her to be ultra careful when she arrives. Bye.'

I replaced the receiver and sat myself down again. I just prayed she would read between my every telephone line, or we'd soon have a shoot-out at Doom Abbey, with, afterwards, only the police to tell the tale. But, at least, I'd bought us another twenty minutes, if something didn't go wrong in the meantime. Like where the hell *was* Arabella? Now if she walked in before the twenty minutes were up . . . I felt violently sick as I realized Arabella was our Achilles heel. I prayed and prayed to whomever it was who was watching over her. 'Please, please,' I beseeched, 'don't guide her footsteps here, whatever you do.' I didn't get a reply, unless more nausea was the sign.

Treasure moved back slightly, so that he could see the Westminster chime clock on the mantelshelf. 'Eighteen minutes, Mr Marklin,' he observed grimly. I looked at Deborah. Her eyes were now closed and her head had slumped. Every now and then her body twitched within its bonds, the only sign of life.

Nobody spoke for what seemed like a lifetime, and the old 'ding, ding, ding, ding' of the Westminster chimes reminded us unnecessarily that *tempus fugit*. (I can't hear one of those clocks now without reliving part of the horror of it all.) I wondered where Gates was. I guessed Treasure had dismissed him for the night. For henchmen often aren't allowed to see the sticky black mess that is at the very bottom of their bosses' souls, only the dying vegetation at the top layers of the pit. Even Gates's ruddy features would, I reckoned, blanch at murder at first hand. After all, a bomb in a boat could kill when the bomber was miles away. Every minute now, I expected to hear the evidence of Gus's return, but there was sweet Fanny Adams. Where the hell had Gus got to? Had his old car broken down? Was it upside-down in some ditch (its favourite pastime) or had he been arrested trying to steal my car from its plywood home? I was starting to despair, because if something didn't happen soon, Lady Philippa and the Dorset constabulary would beat him to it. The siege of Doom Abbey would start and these affairs had a nasty habit of ending with stretchers and black plastic sheets, and some rather unfeminine television reporter stating that the police had done everything they could to save life. (Except save life.)

'Ten minutes, Mr Marklin. Arabella should be well over half way here by now, or . . . .'

He didn't finish his alternative. Was it a sign of weakness, or a growing realization that our deaths might now be almost inevitable? I shivered at the thought. And then, suddenly, the whole room seemed to shiver, as a bloody great explosion went off somewhere outside. As I had planned, Treasure's attention was diverted for just long enough for me to lunge forward to get his gun. Long enough to lunge forward, maybe, but not, bugger it, long enough for me to wrench the weapon from his hairy grasp with my only good hand. For he turned his attention back from the window almost instantly. And I felt his number elevens kick me explosively in the head; the shock unlocked my hold on the shotgun and I sensed myself rolling over, not quite knowing any longer where I was. I shook my head and looked up into the sideways figure eight of the ends of both barrels.

'So that's what you were waiting for, Mr Marklin, was it? A little diversion and you'd overpower me, and be the Studland wonderboy, eh?' Treasure laughed.

I painfully and slowly got back on my feet. So much for my big bang theory. But bully for Gus. He'd done his bit. I'd just failed with mine, and my plastered arm now hurt like hell.

'Must be your friend Gus. Am I right? Well, I'll make him very welcome if he cares to join us in here.'

I prayed Gus would have the nous to stay outside, once he'd seen we weren't likely to emerge safe and sound down the front steps. But you never knew with Gus.

Deborah by now was whimpering, and, with my head throbbing, I went over and sat next to her. Curiously, Treasure didn't object to my move. I put my arm around her, and we rocked gently together like babes in the wood. I looked at the clock as soon as my head was clear enough for my eyes to focus. Only three and a half minutes left. Three and a half bloody minutes, and then . . . And I heard the footsteps. I saw Treasure's finger take first pressure on the first trigger. Deborah stopped rocking. Hell, it must be Gus, the stark staring idiot. He's walking straight in, like it was Liberty Hall. And he was obviously trying to keep the noise of his footfalls down to the minimum, for they sounded quite dainty for Gus.

I wondered if my chance had come round once more, but Treasure's eyes had not moved from the settee. Once bitten.

The footsteps stopped outside the door. We saw the brass handle turn very slowly, the door open, and then he came in. And the sight took my breath away. This was no Gus. This was a young boy of fourteen or so, dressed in a sober grey suit, grey shirt and a Trenton School tie. But that wasn't the shock. It was what had happened to his head. It was covered in the red, sticky wetness of blood which seemed to ooze from the top of his skull.

There was a terrible cry. But not from me. And not from Deborah. As if paralysed, Treasure dropped the gun, and stood mouth open, staring at the grim apparition. In a second, the gun was in my hands. The young figure moved towards me, and it was then I sighed the biggest sigh in the world. And all I could think to say, poor mutt, was 'Christ, my darling, and I prayed that you would never turn up.'

Fifteen

I won't dwell on the last moments I ever spent in Doom Abbey. For the memory, in a way, hurts us both still. Suffice it to say, we quickly released Deborah, and I asked Arabella to take her outside pronto. When they had gone, I propped the gun up by the huge bookcase that filled a whole wall of the library, and went over to Treasure. He still seemed totally in a trance.

'Goodbye, Mr Treasure. I am sorry I could not keep to the arrangement you so desired. But I will destroy all the diaries if you would like me to. Including 1981. And then, I promise, no one but we four will ever know about it.'

His eyes flickered slightly, but still he did not look at me.

'Thank you, Mr Marklin. They were not my finest hours – '81 and '44. . . .' His voice was frail now and tailed away, its timbre splintered into unrecognizable pieces. But I had understood. And I hoped he knew it.

I left the gun where it was, and descended the Abbey steps for the last time. It was almost night outside now, but I could just see Gus, the two girls and Lady Philippa down the driveway by the Golf convertible and my old Beetle, and behind them, the flashing blue lights of two police cars turning off the Lulworth road into the drive. I shivered, and began running. It was then I heard the shot reverberating behind me.

We were kept at the police station until three in the morning; until, in fact, we were rescued by Inspector Blake. I was relieved to see us all perform so admirably with our cover stories, that we had rehearsed together whilst the police were examining Treasure's body in the library. It was all very simple, but the Dorset police did not seem to find it all particularly believable. (I don't blame them – they would have benefited from at least a day for creation, and a week for rehearsal. But I didn't think the boys in blue would wait that long.)

Gus, fortunately, had left the diaries at his place, so they didn't figure in our cover story. The Inspector disobeyed every rule in his Scotland Yard bible by not raising any objections to what he knew was as much of a whitewash of Treasure as a Nixon television broadcast had been of Watergate. I guessed he had got the outcome he wanted – with no nasty scandal, no nasty smell. It was poor Lady Philippa we had to make seem the biggest fool, for being so stupid as to imagine my phone call was anything but a practical joke that went horribly and ironically wrong. 'We had no idea she would call the police,' we all lied, but hated doing so. For to embarrass the living instead of shaming the dead is, I suppose a curious kind of morality.

Finally, the Dorset boys seemed, with Blake's encouragement, slightly more satisfied that our story had some basis in fact – that Treasure had been very depressed recently, and had invited us round to cheer him up.

'Why was he so depressed?' they kept asking.

'Because he kept remembering his beloved wife, and her infidelities and final departure had got to him all over again,' we sort of explained. 'That's why he must have shot himself when we all upped and left.'

Blank faces.

Needless to say, it was not only Lady Philippa's involvement of the police that took a lot of explaining away. Arabella's boy's outfit and the red paint on her hair and face was quite a poser. The best I could do was, 'She's always been a great one for dressing up and fooling about. Her hair is funny colours anyway, only tonight she deliberately overdid it to amuse Treasure. Went a bit too far . . . .'

Blanker faces.

Still, they couldn't prove otherwise, and Blake didn't wish them to. And they had no doubt got used to weird goings-on at country stately homes. I'd read in the local rag only two weeks before about a raid they had made on a weekend house party, where they'd discovered all the men dressed as nuns, the women as monks, and the coke was the real thing.

At about ten to three, when we were all getting decidedly

168

frayed at the edges, the Inspector took me aside into one of those bare, tiny rooms that are only ever found (hopefully) in police stations. Neither of us sat down.

'I'll come and see you in the morning, when you've had some sleep,' he said quietly, and put his hand on my shoulder.

'It *is* the bloody morning,' I replied irritably, 'and, secondly, what are you going to come round for?'

He just about smiled. 'Confirmation.'

'Confirmation of what?' I said, rather more sharply than I had intended, as I already knew the answer.

'Life and death, Mr Marklin. And diaries. Please don't be obstructive at this late stage. I need to know.'

I sat down. There was no more to say. I hated myself just then. And hated him, because all along he had left the responsibility to me, and not to himself or his force. And it had ended in brains splattered across a hundred and one leather-bound volumes in a lofty room in a fortified stone abbey.

It wasn't until we were nearly back at Studland that I remembered the mess I had left the previous afternoon. (I couldn't believe it was that recent. It seemed years ago.) What was left of my spirits drained completely away. But material things were hardly of importance right then, in the wee small hours. Deborah, the police had driven straight home to Bournemouth in one of their white flashing numbers. Gus said goodnight after a quick Heineken, and Arabella kissed him. He hasn't been quite the same since. Then we crawled up to bed.

Arabella and I clung to each other very tightly all the rest of the night. That's all – just clung for dear life. Neither of us slept except in snatches, and Bing, cuddled up at the foot of the bed, became very tetchy about our restless legs and feet. For there was so much we had to say to each other, we almost didn't know where to begin, let alone where or when to end.

Somewhere along the line, I asked her where she had been all day, and what made her dress up in the plaster boy's uniform. She told me, and suddenly the true tragedy of Treasure's life, and, indeed, part of her own, was revealed. I felt incredibly small and unimportant all of a sudden, for compared to hers, or Treasure's, my life, with all its ups and downs, had been very smooth sailing. And yet I knew I grumbled all the time.

Let me tell you first what she had been up to that day. She hadn't gone straight to her cousin's. She had waited around and followed us discreetly. She had seen us pinch the Rolls, had followed us again, and watched us searching it through a gap in the hedge. She saw our disappointment as we got back in the Rolls to return it to Poole, and guessed we had found nothing. She had then gone to her cousin's nursery, and begun pricking out or whatever, and had a serious think about where the diaries might actually be. She remembered my remark about the Bing toy she had given me as a present – that it had given me an idea where the diaries might be. Well, my remark and that Bing toy with the secret compartment gave her a very different idea; that the diaries weren't in a *real* car, but maybe hidden one by one (or at least the incriminating ones) in a *toy* car. Some of the models were certainly big enough.

She still had a key to Doom Abbey that Treasure had given her at the start of their relationship, so she had driven there at breakneck speed in the hope that Treasure was not yet back from lunch with Derek. He wasn't. She let herself in and went immediately to the room where his most valuable toys – outside those in the stable block – were kept. She concentrated on the hundred-odd tinplate cars, buses, trains and a few tinplate boats that were big enough to conceal a diary of any size. She found nothing until she finally, in desperation, tried the boats. One seemed unusually heavy. (From her description, it sounded like a thirties Hornby speedboat.) She probed and found a Lett's School-boy's Diary concealed under the tinplate cover where the clockwork mechanism should have been. It was the diary for 1944. She pocketed it, replaced the tin cover and ran, expecting Treasure would be back any second.

She went back to the nursery because she had promised her cousin earlier that she would take some produce to Moreton Station to catch the train. This she did, then decided to come on to me in Studland with the diary so that we could read it together. Of course, she found my place heavily modified by the actions of Ken Gates, and guessed what had happened. She thought of going to the police, but was worried it might do more harm than good until she knew more about where Gus and I had gone. In case we came back, she hung around Studland for an hour or more. Eventually she read the diary, then motored over towards Treasure's, hoping like mad she would come across us on the way. The diary's contents were, as she put it, enough to scare the living daylights out of anybody.

If Gus hadn't taken a pet short cut of his on his way to get his grenade, they'd have met on the road – head-on, I wouldn't wonder, knowing Gus's driving. But as it was, she turned up at the Abbey after I had gone in and found Deborah. She wisely stayed outside until she had sussed out the situation – which she effected by the simple means of peeping in each ground floor window until she found us.

Gus returned to Doom Abbey, and they came across each other in the grounds. Between them, they decided they needed a back-up plan in case the grenade didn't work. It was Arabella's idea – the stratagem of the plaster boy's uniform. Gus broke into the stable and got it for her. I still dread to think of the risk she took. But why the red paint? That was from the key disclosure in that 1944 diary. The relevant pages I read, with trepidation, immediately after Arabella had told me what I've just told you.

I won't distress you with all the details. They describe, with painful precision, Treasure's growing love for a boy in his class called Paul Withers – a love that, within a few weeks, had become an obsession and a physical reality, as they sneaked into each other's beds in the dormitory. But it is clear to the writer – and to the reader – that Paul is somewhat of a fickle character, and does not reciprocate the love with the same intensity. Indeed, during the night before the fatal entry, Paul announces he won't make love any more with Treasure, and, in fact, is going to see the Headmaster in the morning about Treasure's 'lewd' behaviour. The news comes as a bombshell. Let the fourteen-year-old Randolph Treasure take over from there. The entry is for 13 February 1944. It is marked with an asterisk to show where it is continued at the back of the diary, when he ran out of space.

Had no sleep. Paul did. How could he? Would he tell on me? Must stop him somehow. He wouldn't speak to me, washing and dressing. Or at breakfast. In chapel we heard planes. Then first crump of a bomb. Stained glass windows blew in. Boys scattered and ran out. Heard siren, then whistle of another bomb. I stood still. * Paul ran to door. Huge explosion,

knocked me down, covered me with dust and debris. Saw
Paul lying under part of door. He waved at me. He was terribly
cut, leg looked broken. Began moving stones and bits of beam.
Shifted door slightly. He couldn't move. Just smiled like he
had last night, when he told me he'd tell. I picked up length of
door frame, began hitting his face. I hit him, hit him and hit
him, because he seemed to keep smiling. But he won't tell anybody now. Covered him with more stones and beams, then
crawled on outside. There were bits of other boys everywhere.
Must have fainted then because . . . .

I wanted to burn the diary there and then, but Arabella rightly
pointed out that the rest were over at Gus's place, and he would
be in the land of nod by then, deservedly so. Reluctantly, I
agreed the morning would do, when we had all had a rest. I
didn't want to commit it to ashes because his secret had been so
heinous, but because I felt truly sorry for Treasure for the very
first time. And I wished to be sure the facts of his childhood obsession would die with him, for, to paraphrase the showman's
remark at the end of *King Kong*, it was love that killed the beast.
Oh Lord, would that we could all be loved as we would wish ourselves to be.

I got out of bed to hide the diary behind the cistern in the loo,
just in case Blake made too early a visit, and then we lay quiet for
a bit. Suddenly Arabella sat bolt upright.

'I can tell you now. I've been wanting to for ages,' she said
quietly, 'and you've been wanting to know, haven't you?' She
stopped and looked a little lost for words. I sat up too, and
cradled her back in my arms.

'Yes, my darling, but I knew you'd tell me when the time was
right.' She still remained silent, so after a minute, I helped her a
little.

'Something happened, didn't it? Something you felt was your
fault?'

She nodded.

'Before you met Treasure?'

She nodded again. 'That's how I met Randolph. He extricated
me from the car, you see.' A tear beaded down her cheek. Very
soon, it wasn't alone.

'You had a car accident?'

'Yes,' she whispered, then went on so quietly I had to lean forward to catch her words. 'You must have wondered why a university girl just pricked out plants for a career . . . well, I've only done that since the crash . . . Before, I was a junior reporter on a local paper, the *Shropshire Enquirer*. I loved it. Journalism was going to be my life, young life anyway. My boyfriend, Simon, had been at Bristol University with me. I loved him and he loved me. His craze was photography. So I managed to persuade my editor to take him on as a junior photographer on the paper. We often went on assignments together in my car. One day . . . (she stopped for what seemed like an eternity, then resumed) my car was in dock – gearbox trouble – and the editor let me have a staff car, an old Citroën DS, you know, the one with all the complicated hydraulics and things. Well, I wasn't used to it, you see and . . . I missed the tiny brake pedal, it was like a button, at the traffic lights in All Stretton. A long-distance holiday coach went into us broadside – Simon's side ; he was killed outright, but, by some unfair miracle, I survived with cuts and bruises though the Citroën folded around me.'

'And Treasure got you out ?'

'Yes, he was coming back from viewing some property in Shrewsbury, and was first on the scene. Luckily, no one in the coach was seriously hurt, just bruises and shock and things . . . . He took me to hospital . . . .'

'And visited you ?'

'. . . and eventually suggested I should get away from Shropshire to get over it all. My guilt, you see, was consuming me. He told me he lived in Dorset. I thought it might help if I did as he suggested and my cousin was almost on the doorstep and needed a bit of companionship right then. Her husband had been in the Navy and was one of those killed in the Falklands war. So I went to live with her.'

I wiped her eyes with the edge of the sheet. She went on. 'I needed him – clung to him like a big father who wouldn't let me get into trouble again. And it worked for months. No commital. Just coasting. Brittle but just alive. And working with plants is a wonderful therapy.'

I remembered her remark about living things. She ran her fingers through her hair, to which some traces of red still adhered, despite our effort with thinners at the police station. 'You know why I colour my hair every which way ?'

I made a mental guess, but shook my head.

'After the accident, part of my hair went white in a great streak front to back. I guess it's still that way underneath all the tints.'

I held her very tight, and hoped my warmth would get through. I adored her, and I prayed my love would be enough for her desperate need.

Neither of us spoke for quite some time, and eventually we settled down again. I could see it was beginning to get quite light outside. After what must have been about half an hour, she spoke very softly into my pillow.

'He recognized me instantly, you know.'

'How do you know?'

'I know, that's all. I could see it in his eyes.'

'Then why . . . ? He could have killed you.'

'Because he was staggered I knew about Paul . . . I think, in his way, he loved me and he'd had enough by then. Of killing, I mean. Of hiding. Of living with 1944.'

I didn't say anything more. But at least now I knew one marvellous fact. Arabella had expiated a lot of her guilt about Simon by the tremendous risk she had taken to rescue me and Deborah. (I gathered next morning, that Gus had tried to stop her, but she just wouldn't listen.) But I wondered if she had taken on a new guilt about her role in Treasure's death. About an hour's worth of worry later, she put my mind at rest on that too.

'He's at peace now. For the first time in over forty years,' she said softly.

'Yes,' I agreed quite truthfully, 'he's at peace.' And she snuggled to me, and went out like a light.

At around eleven, when the bright, late spring sun was really burning the curtains, I got up and trundled downstairs, stark naked, to make some tea and toast. I glanced at the devastation in the shop, but again my bodily needs were greater. And of course, on the doormat were the stats I'd asked for from the *Telegraph* and *The Times*. At that moment, I felt they were better never than late.

Then Gus knocked at the unbroken side-door. I quickly grabbed a raincoat off a hook in the passageway, and let him in.

He wandered through to the kitchen, his bandages now a most attractive grey colour in selected areas. He turned and looked at me.

'Taking up flashing now, are you?' he grinned as he noticed my bare legs and feet under the raincoat. 'Shouldn't if I was you. There's not much call for it round here, you know.'

I was in no mood for jokes, which I made quite plain; and I gave him a large, brown loaf, a knife to cut it with, and pointed out the pop-up toaster.

'That's all right. I've had mine,' he said.

'It's for *us*, Gus. There are more people in the world, you know.' He grinned. He'd got me going again, sod him.

We sat for a minute while the toast toasted and the tea brewed.

'Thanks Gus,' I said quietly.

'That's all right,' he said again, 'anytime. Anyway, I like putting toast in the toaster.'

'No, I mean . . .' He held out his hand, and I clasped it warmly with my good hand. There's no one like Gus.

'It wasn't me, you know. It was all Arabella's doing.'

'It was both of you,' I responded. 'Tell me, where the blazes did you get that grenade you told me about?'

'Same fellow who sold me the Colt. You know, the soldier I mentioned. Gave me two, he did.'

'What on earth for?'

'I wanted them in case Jerry invaded, and the soldiers buggered off. Gave me a sort of feeling of confidence I'd be safe then. With the gun *and* the grenades, I mean.'

Made sense, I supposed, in those difficult days of World War II.

'You should have handed them in years ago, Gus. They're so old, they're probably unstable now.'

He shrugged his shoulders and winced with the pain.

'Anyway, Gus,' I continued, 'where have you been keeping them all this time? Surely not in the house?'

His eyes brightened. 'Nope,' he announced proudly. 'I'm not as daft as I look, you know.'

The toast popped up, and he went over and put it in the toast rack.

'Thank heavens for that,' I said. 'But where *did* you store them?'

'In the shed.' He sat down again.

175

'Which shed?' I asked anxiously.

'The big one.'

I got up, and almost killed him on the spot.

'You silly sod; that's where I keep my Daimler. It could have been blown to pieces any second of any hour of any day of the two and a half years it's been there.' Gus didn't look in the least perturbed.

'Didn't though, did it?' he said smugly. 'It was just my boat that blew up. And that was no grenade.'

I took his point, and changed the subject. I'm not very bright.

'We must burn the diaries double quick after breakfast,' I said. He nodded, and offered his jersey up to my nose. I didn't twig what he was up to until that unmistakable sweet smell of bonfire smoke got through to me.

'Done mine hours ago,' he said. 'What about yours?' I went up to the loo and fetched it. 'I'll take it away and burn it for you. You've got enough clearing up here to do.' And he was right.

I dressed, having breakfasted in bed with Arabella, and had done a great deal of cleaning up before we heard Trevor Blake's white Ford pull up outside. I let him in, thankful that Gus had already left with the 1944 diary.

I felt like a drink all of a sudden, a stiff one, I mean. And to my surprise, the Inspector joined me. We sipped our Scotches in silence for a minute or two before either of us spoke.

'He killed his wife, didn't he?' he said at last.

'Yes, I read the 1981 diary. He loved her very much.'

He looked across at me. I didn't move a muscle. 'I burnt all the diaries before you came,' I lied.

'Still,' he resumed, 'so long as you and I know. That's probably sufficient, don't you think?'

He raised his glass, but I didn't follow suit.

'Tell me, Peter – may I call you Peter? – tell me, why did he kill her? Because she had run away with another man?'

'I don't think so,' I replied quietly. 'It was because she had discovered something about his youth, in one of his earliest diaries – 1944.'

'1944,' he echoed, reflectively. 'And you've read that diary too?'

'No, I haven't. The diary was missing when I found them. So

176

we'll probably never know his motives,' I lied again. I just couldn't tell him. The passions of childhood, however misguided, seemed to me intensely private.

'They were in his car, weren't they?'

I looked across at him. 'How did you know?'

'I didn't, until this morning, when I examined his Silver Cloud. The bootlid had been forced. He would not have done that himself, now would he?'

There was no answer to that. I got up from my chair and began pacing round the room. 'Look, Inspector...'

He interrupted me. 'If I'm going to call you Peter, you ought to begin calling me Trevor, you know.'

I ignored him and resumed. 'Look, Inspector, I'm sick, sick, sick of this whole affair. You just got me to do your dirty work for you. I know you never came out and actually asked me, but that's what you did, nevertheless. I carried out all those little investigations and probings that you and your boys are not legitimately allowed to do, didn't I? You not only used my mini computer, as you called it, to supplement your big ones down at headquarters, but you damn near got me killed in the process. And it's ended up with me shouldering all the guilt for Treasure's suicide, and not you. It may be all very clever on your part, Inspector, but it doesn't look that way from where I'm standing. And I'm never doing it again – not for you, not for the Chief Commissioner of Scotland Yard, not for God himself. In future, you can get your own hands dirty, or let the bloody criminals...'

'Let the bloody criminals do what, Peter?' he asked me quietly, as I ran out of steam. He got up and came over to me by the window.

'Look outside, Peter. Beautiful, isn't it? England at her best. A sleeping seaside village, little old ladies going about their shopping, children with shrimping nets trekking off down to the rock pools, nothing but the rustle of the young green leaves, the call of a gull, and an occasional car to break the peace.'

He looked around the obviously still disarranged room. 'No sound of houses being broken into.' I didn't rise to the remark. Gates had only been doing what Treasure had asked him. And now, with Treasure's demise, he had no job.

'Forget the violins,' I said quietly. 'What you're saying, is that you can't keep it that way just with a truncheon, a pointed blue helmet, a few "Hello, hello, hellos", and a million miles of bumf diarrhoeaing out of the bowels of a computer.'

He didn't need to answer, and he didn't. It was at that moment, rather than before, that my association with Inspector Trevor Blake really started, but I never came to call him Trevor. I'm afraid I joined the criminal fraternity in dubbing him 'Sexton'.

It took many more weeks for Arabella and me really to start living, and loving, normally again. By that time, Pilot Officer Redfern had received his long-overdue right of a dignified Christian burial in hallowed ground, with a band from the RAF accompanying the hymns. And we had begun a fund raising scheme for a Warmwell Battle of Britain museum. But Arabella still wouldn't move in with me completely, keeping her things at her cousin's nursery at Owermoigne. 'One day, maybe,' was all I got and, in the end, all I pressed for.

Neither of us mentioned or questioned how long our relationship might last – we just lived every second of the times we were together to the full. And that bit was, and is, magnificent. And I like to think it's a little bit of therapy from yours truly that has got Arabella, at last, talking about becoming a reporter again – maybe on our own local paper. That might, actually, make all the difference. And not just to whether she moves into the Toy Emporium or goes on living at Owermoigne. (Although that's highest on my love agenda.) But I must give her time; everybody needs time. None of us ever gets allotted enough of it, to know each other really well. That's half the trouble. Come to think – could be the whole, couldn't it?

Still, we've got a whole three weeks of each other – starting tomorrow. We're off on a holiday to the south of France. You see, I at last replied to Monsieur Vincent's letter that asked about the toys. I said they were fine, and much admired by Mr Chalmers and mentioned a nice note of thanks he'd written about them. Then added how I loved my hour or so in his charming house in St Paul de Vence. He put me to shame and replied quickly: how would I like to spend a few weeks down here over the summer and keep an old man company? He gave me his phone number, so I rang and queried whether he minded an extra guest in female form.

'On the contrary,' he said, 'it would make it like a family again.'

We so hoped it would.

So there we are. Almost full cirle. But this time, we're going in *her* car, I've booked through a different travel agent, we're on a hovercraft not a ferry and we aren't going *autoroute*. (Sorry, Quinky, I'm otherwise engaged.) We're taking our time, getting to know a bit more of France, the old roads, the by-ways, the local bistros, a little old country hotel or two, but I guess, most of all – discovering each other.